"I love the way this man writes! I adore his style. There is something about it that makes me feel as if I'm someplace I'm not supposed to be, seeing things I'm not supposed to see and that is so delicious."
REBECCA FORSTER, USA Today Bestselling Author

This book "is creative and captivating. It features bold characters, witty dialogue, exotic locations, and non-stop action. The pacing is spot-on, a solid combination of intrigue, suspense, and eroticism. A first-rate thriller, this book is damnably hard to put down. It's a tremendous read."
FOREWORD REVIEWS

"A terrifying, gripping cross between James Patterson and John Grisham. Jagger has created a truly killer thriller."
J.A. KONRATH, International Bestselling Author

"As engaging as the debut, this exciting blend of police procedural and legal thriller recalls the early works of Scott Turow and Lisa Scottoline."
LIBRARY JOURNAL

"The well-crafted storyline makes this a worthwhile read. Stuffed with gratuitous sex and over-the-top violence, this novel has a riveting plot."
KIRKUS REVIEWS

"Verdict: The pacing is relentless in this debut, a hard-boiled novel with a shocking ending. The supershort chapters will please those who enjoy a James Patterson–style page-turner"

A "clever and engrossing mystery tale involving gorgeous women, lustful men and scintillating suspense."
ForeWord Magazine

"This is one of the best thrillers I've read yet."
New Mystery Reader Magazine

"A superb thriller and an exceptional read."
Midwest Book Review

"Verdict: This fast-paced book offers fans of commercial thrillers a twisty, action-packed thrill ride."
Library Journal

"Another masterpiece of action and suspense."
New Mystery Reader Magazine

"Fast paced and well plotted . . . While comparisons will be made with Turow, Grisham and Connelly, Jagger is a new voice on the legal/thriller scene. I recommend you check out this debut book, but be warned . . . you are not going to be able to put it down."
Crimespree Magazine

"A chilling story well told. The pace never slows in this noir thriller, taking readers on a stark trail of fear."
Carolyn G. Hart, N.Y. Times and USA Today Bestselling Author

DEAD
OF NIGHT

Thriller Publishing Group, Inc.

DEAD
OF NIGHT

R.J. JAGGER

Thriller Publishing Group, Inc.

Dead Of Night

Thriller Publishing Group, Inc.
Golden, Colorado 80401

Copyright©RJ Jagger

Library of Congress Control Number: Available

ISBN 978-1-937888-81-7 (Hardcover))

10 9 8 7 6 5 4 3 2 1

Printed in the United States of America

For Eileen

ACKNOWLEDGEMENTS

Thanks to the many wonderful readers, booksellers, editors, publishers, agents, audio producers, book reviewers, authors, groups (including International Thriller Writers and Mystery Writers of America), proofreaders and other kind-hearted souls who amplified my efforts and who encouraged me with positive vibes over the years. Without you this book would have never happened.

DAY ONE

September 21
Monday

1

Day 1—September 21
Monday Night

Dressed in all things black, Nick Teffinger—the 36-year-old head of San Francisco's homicide detail—slipped into the dead of night behind Condor's house and reminded himself one last time of the seriousness of what he was about to do. In ten seconds, if he proceeded as planned, he'd be forever dirty.

He took a deep breath.

A cool, salty breeze rolled off the Pacific and wove through the San Francisco nightscape.

Rain was coming.

Condor's house was a stately Victorian perched on Nob Hill, the coordinates of choice for the affluent and relevant. City lights twinkled below and stretched all the way to the bay.

Teffinger pushed hair out of his face.

It was thick and brown and hung three inches below his shoulders. He tucked it under a black cap, put on latex gloves and stepped to the nearest window to see if it was locked.

It was.

So was the next one and the next.

Then he found the one he wanted. He lifted it up, got the screen out, then muscled his six-foot-two body through, ending up in a laundry room where he quietly listened for sounds or vibrations.

The interior was dark.

He powered up a small flashlight and headed into the guts of the structure one silent step at a time. He didn't have a gun or knife. It would be bad enough if he got caught. It would be fatal if he ended up killing Condor, even in self-defense. If a confrontation occurred, he'd beat the man with his fists just enough to make his escape. If he got shot, well, that would just be the price.

He bypassed the kitchen and living room and headed for the den.

A laptop sat on a cherry desk. Teffinger fired it up and copied the folder files onto a flash drive while he searched the drawers. Pens, pencils, notepads, a stapler—that's what was there, nothing of relevance. He powered off the computer, stuck the flash drive in his pocket and turned his attention to the matching cherry credenza.

An inbox on top held unpaid bills.

One of them was a cell phone statement.

Teffinger left it sealed, searched for the paid ones and found them in a folder inside the credenza. Unfortunately, the individual calls weren't itemized. He wrote down the account number and returned the bills to exactly where he got them.

He heard a sound and froze.

Now it wasn't there.

Silence.

That's all there was now, just silence.

He concentrated harder.

He still nothing other than the passing of air in and out of his lungs.

He turned his attention back to the credenza, searching faster now, and found an expandable file labeled *Private* in black magic marker. Inside were several manila folders with names handwritten on the tabs.

Paris Zephyr.

Jamie van de Haven.

Pamela Zoom.

Samantha Payton.

Brenda Poppenberg.

Syling Hu.

Teffinger's heart raced. Not only were these the SJK victims but they were organized in the exact order the women had been killed.

Oh yeah.

He opened the first one—Paris Zephyr—and found a plethora of newspaper articles and information printed off the Internet, both on the murder itself and on the trial of Kyle Greyson, who turned out to be not guilty.

The other files were similar.

Teffinger put everything back exactly as he found it.

This was good.

Very good.

Beyond-beautiful good.

This was worth getting dirty for.

Now, if he could just find the souvenirs, that would be the clincher.

They weren't in the credenza.

He listened for sounds, got nothing, and headed upstairs to the master bedroom.

Thunder crackled in the distance.

The storm was close.

Upstairs he found something he didn't expect, namely a telescope on a tripod, set up by the window and pointed outside. Teffinger walked over and looked through, careful to not bump it.

What he saw he could hardly believe.

2

Day 1—September 21
Monday Night

A 15-meter go-fast picked Jonk up in Hong Kong after dark Monday night and headed west into the open waters of the South China Sea, slicing effortlessly through black chop as it left the twinkling lights of sci-fi skyscrapers in its wake. Jonk sat in the back with his 29-year-old, six-foot body jarring and his shoulder-length, spa-blond hair whipping, wondering what the hell Typhoon Joe wanted.

The twin engines were deafening.

The slapping of the hull against the water was even more so.

Jonk stared ahead with an attractive face, the kind that made women stare. The only flaw to that face was his left eye, the blind one, which had a raven-black pupil, fully dilated, in contrast to his normal hazel one. A scar ran down his forehead, across that eye, and then a little farther below. As scars went it was long but wasn't deep, or jagged, or crooked, or highly-contrasting. It was more in the nature of a thin ruler line, hardly perceptible. Some people said it gave him character. He could take it or leave it. He really didn't care about it any more.

He had no idea what Typhoon Joe wanted.

It had to be big, though, to send the go-fast at night.

Big meant money.

Money.

Money.

Money.

Money meant power.

And power meant everything.

Women.

Luxury.

Stature.

Most importantly, it meant the ability to not waste precious moments of life on mundane things like reporting to some stupid nine-to-five job just to stay alive.

Screw mundane.

Mundane was overrated.

The slapping of the hull against the waves grated on his nerves. He wasn't particularly fond of water at this point in his life. Every time he'd come close to dying, it had always been in water.

That's where he lost his left eye.

In water.

The sixty-five kilometer trip to Macau—Asia's casino-infested strip of sin, gambling and decadence—took hardly any time. Fifteen minutes after being picked up by a Ferrari at the dock, Jonk was in the penthouse suite of the Cotai Storm Hotel & Casino, one of Typhoon Joe's many holdings.

"Jonk, my man," Typhoon Joe said, slapping him on the back. "Come in my friend, come in."

Typhoon Joe looked the same as always.

Fifty.

Short.

Thin.

Balding.

Intense.

"Come on, I'll beat you at pinball," Typhoon Joe said, heading for the game room. Walking past the bedroom, Jonk looked in to see if he'd see what he thought he'd see. Sure enough, there on the bed was an unconscious woman, young, spread out, wearing only white cotton panties, a bought-and-paid-for play toy.

"You still have your vices," he said.

Typhoon Joe turned and smiled.

"A man needs vices," he said. "You want to play with her?"

"Maybe next time."

"That's what you always say."

In the game room, Typhoon Joe tested the flippers, set a ball in motion and said, "You're probably wondering why you're here."

"It's crossed my mind," Jonk said.

"How many jobs have you done for me?" Typhoon Joe said. "I mean, big ones."

Jonk tilted his head.

"I don't know, six or seven, maybe."

Typhoon Joe smiled.

"Wrong," Typhoon Joe said. "You haven't done any big ones. Everything you've done so far was nothing. This is going to be your first real job."

"How real?"

"Real enough to retire on, in luxury," Typhoon Joe said. "To do it properly, I'm going to have to tell you some stuff."

"Fine."

"Private stuff," Typhoon Joe said.

"I understand."

"Stuff that doesn't go from you to anyone else, not tomorrow, not in ten years," Typhoon Joe said.

"You know I can be trusted."

"That's what we're going to find out," Typhoon Joe said. "First, I want to be sure we have an understanding that if you double-cross me, if you do anything you shouldn't, you'll die a horrible, very painful, very slow death." The smile fell off Typhoon Joe's face and he locked eyes with Jonk. "Do we both understand what I'm talking about?"

Jonk's chest tightened.

The man meant it.

No question.

He nodded.

"I'd never screw you," he said. "You know that by now."

"If that's true then I'm going to be very happy and you're going to be very rich." He turned and said, "Follow me, I want to show you something."

3

Day 1—September 21
Monday Night

The telescope in Condor's bedroom was aimed through the small window of a commercial building a good distance away. From what Teffinger could tell, the window was situated near the ceiling, too high to see through from inside the room, probably installed for venting or sunlight. There were no other windows to the room. On the back wall was a mirror that reflected into the space. In the middle of the room was an attractive woman bound in a standing, spread-eagle position. Black leather cuffs were on each of her wrists, attached to chains that stretched tightly to the ceiling.

Cuffs were also on her ankles, secured with short chains bolted to the floor.

She faced the mirror.

Her hair was short, stylish and black.

Her breasts were ample.

Her nipples were pierced, as was her navel.

A tattoo of a dragon started on her stomach, wrapped around her ass and down her right thigh, ending slightly above her knee.

She looked to be about twenty-five.

A second woman appeared and kissed the bound woman on the mouth, long and deep, then pulled back and licked her neck.

The new woman had long, thick blond hair.

Not blond-blond.

Dirty blond.

She was naked except for black high-heels that brought a definition to her calves and thighs. Her ass was taut and round. As nice as her body was, when she turned and her face appeared, Teffinger felt his world shift ever so slightly.

She had the kind of face that could own a man.

Suddenly something weird happened—she looked into the mirror and directly into his eyes. He pulled back, embarrassed, before realizing how stupid he was. She couldn't see this far with the naked eye, not to mention that he was in the dark. When he brought his eye back to the telescope, the woman had a black mask on.

Then something grabbed his attention, namely a small tattoo just above the woman's private area, about the size of a dollar folded in half.

What was it?

A flower?

A butterfly?

It was all black, that was about the best he could make out.

He searched for more ink and found none.

The interior of the room got slightly brighter, as if someone outside the view of the telescope had turned on a light or positioned a reflector to film whatever it was that was about to happen.

Then it began.

The blond ran her fingers slowly down her captive's arms, teasingly, then played with her nipples and stomach, working her into an ever-increasing state.

Teffinger watched her every move, mesmerized.

She dropped to her knees and tongued the bound woman between her legs.

There was no denying the pleasure was real.

She knew what she was doing.

This wasn't her first time.

Teffinger's cock tightened.

He heard a faint sound from somewhere downstairs, almost imperceptible but enough to focus on for a few heartbeats. It vanished as quickly as it came.

The blond pleasured her captive for a long time, long enough to make her twist and turn and pull at her bonds and bring her to a screaming orgasm.

Damn.

Then the blond stood up, tweaked the woman's nipples and disappeared to the side.

Teffinger looked at his watch and was shocked at the time. He needed to quit screwing around and find the souvenirs, right now, this second, then get the hell out of there before it all went south.

Thunder cracked, closer than before.

One more look, that's all he'd take, just one more.

He put his eye back to the telescope.

Good timing, too, because the blond walked back into view. Teffinger focused on her tattoo once again and was able to make it out, finally—some type of foreign writing.

What'd it say?

A light drizzle suddenly appeared, blurring the night and

bringing it in and out of focus.

Damn it.

The blond took a position behind her captive and played with her hair for a few moments. Then she reached around to the front, put her hands around the woman's throat and squeezed.

The woman didn't react.

Not at first.

Then she tried to pull away.

It did no good.

She struggled.

Violently.

Panicked.

More and more animated.

Then, without warning, the blond moved her hands down to the woman's breasts and caressed them. If it was supposed to calm the woman it failed, because she twisted and fought and didn't want to be there any more.

Then it began again.

The blond grabbed the woman's throat from behind and squeezed.

And squeezed.

And squeezed

The rain got thicker.

The view got muddier.

A minute passed.

The woman struggled violently.

Another minute passed.

And another.

Then all movement left the woman's body, her head fell to the side and she hung limp from her wrists.

Suddenly a sound came from downstairs. Teffinger pulled away from the telescope and concentrated. A door slammed and a downstairs light flicked on.

Lightning flashed, close, close enough to illuminate the room.

Thunder exploded, so loud and violent that Teffinger jumped.

4

Day 1—September 21
Monday Night

Typhoon Joe led Jonk into a large corner room with lots of glass and a stunning view of the strip's neon nightscape. Several pinball machines occupied one wall. Above them hung a Picasso. An old, rusty motor scooter sat on a pedestal against the other wall. It had electrical tape wrapped on the handlebars where the grips should be. "That's from my first job," Typhoon Joe said. "Age ten, delivering groceries. It still runs. It reminds me where I came from. It keeps me hungry."

A contemporary desk sat in the middle of the room.

On it were two laptops.

"I run most of my empire from these," Typhoon Joe said, sitting down. "This one isn't connected to the Internet and never will be. Better security that way."

He stuck in a flash drive, pulled up a photograph of an ancient Egyptian mask and swung the screen around so Jonk could see it better.

"Do you know what this is?" Typhoon Joe asked.

"No."

He didn't.

"Let me tell you a little story," Typhoon Joe said. "Five years ago, a tomb was discovered in the Valley of the Kings. It was the tomb of a pharaoh from the Eighteenth Dynasty, around 1375 BC, during the period of Egyptian history known as the New Kingdom. Unfortunately, the tomb had been looted early on, probably within the first six months, and almost everything that had any intrinsic value back in that period of time was taken. Three years ago a Paris woman by the name Prarie Lafayette—who was the niece of a famous archeologist named Remy Lafayette—and an Egyptian archeologist named Alexandra Reed, found the looted contents of that tomb in a high cave located west of the Valley of the Kings. Are you following me so far?"

"Roughly," Jonk said. "Where's the Valley of the Kings?"

"You never heard of the Valley of the Kings?"

"I've heard of it," Jonk said. "I just don't know where it's at."

"It's in Egypt."

"Okay."

"Near Luxor, on the west side of the Nile."

"Okay."

"This is all just background, you don't need to memorize it," Typhoon Joe said. "Anyway, one of the jars in the cave turned out to be filled with documents, apparently authored by some rich guy who masterminded the robbery in the first place. In those notes, he talks about a pharaoh who ruled about 1500 B.C. He was an incredibly important person in his time and ruled for more than twenty years, meaning he had accumulated a considerable wealth. His tomb has never been found, to this day. The notes talk about his tomb. They describe it as being located in an area south of the Valley of the Queens. That's an area no one had really explored. This was the first known hint as to where he might have been buried."

"I didn't know you were into this kind of stuff," Jonk said.

"I wasn't always," Typhoon Joe said.

"It's interesting."

Typhoon Joe smiled.

"Interesting is one word for it," he said. "Lucrative is another. Dangerous is yet another. The Egyptian government engaged the services of the two women who found the first tomb—Prarie Lafayette and Alexandra Reed—to find this new one. They assembled a small team. One of the members of the team was a Cairo man named Amaury, who was Prarie's boyfriend at the time, but more importantly was a black market trader. They searched for two years, found nothing and called it off."

"So it's still out there somewhere," Jonk said.

"Yes and no."

"What's that mean?"

"About one year into the search, Amaury figured out where the tomb was or, to phrase it more properly, came up with a solid theory where to dig. He didn't tell anyone, not even his girlfriend Prarie. Instead, he spent another year out there in the desert sun, looking in all the wrong places and pretending he was giving them his best."

"He's more of a snake than I am," Jonk said.

Typhoon Joe tilted his head.

"He's your equal, no more or less," he said.

Jonk laughed.

"In any event," Typhoon Joe said, "after the search ended, Amaury bided his time for six months to be absolutely sure the area was dead. Then he went back, this time with his new girlfriend. His theory turned out to be correct. They found the tomb."

"Wow."

Right.

Wow.

Wow indeed.

"It was probably the most significant archeological find in the last thousand years," Jonk said. "Do you know how tombs were constructed back in that day?"

No.

Not even close.

"They were divided into a number of separate and distinct chambers. The chambers were separated by solid walls, called blockings. Amaury got lucky and hit the main chamber, the one with the mummified remains of the pharaoh, on the first dig. What he found was quite extraordinary. The most significant piece was this gilded cartonnage mask right here," Typhoon Joe said, tapping the laptop. "Do you know how mummification works?"

No.

Not a clue.

"I know how women work, that's it," Jonk said.

Typhoon Joe smiled.

"Then you've cracked the secret code," he said. "Mummification entails a number of wrappings held together with resin. For important mummifications, jewels would be embedded in the resin. In this case there were lots of jewels. Amaury pried every one of them out with a knife. For all practical purposes, the processes destroyed the remains. From a historical purpose, that was too bad. But that's what happened."

Jonk pushed hair out of his face.

"What does this have to do with me?"

"Hold on, we're getting there," Typhoon Joe said. "The other thing of interest about tombs, in case you care, is that they usually contained an inventory list that was scribed at the time of the burial. The inventory list for this particular tomb was located in the main chamber. It indicates that there are seven chambers in all and describes what is in each one. Like I said before, this guy had accumulated a considerable wealth. Although the treasures in the main chamber were almost beyond imagination, according to the inventory list, the other chambers were just as rich."

"Rich, like what?"

"Rich like jewels and gems," Typhoon Joe said, "but even more importantly, jars and jars filled with gold coins. The main chamber of this tomb, in and of itself, had 2,232 gold coins. Each one is inscribed with the markings of the time. Each one, today, is worth a fortune." Typhoon Joe pulled up a photograph on the laptop. "This is what they look like."

Jonk studied the picture and said, "Cool."

Right.

Cool.

"Amaury and his girlfriend emptied the first chamber and then reburied it," Typhoon Joe said. "They didn't want to press their luck by going into the other chambers at that time. They wanted to get at least part of the treasure secure rather than risk being spotted and potentially loosing it all."

Jonk nodded.

Good thinking.

That's what he would have done.

"I had purchased a number of black-market pieces from

Amaury over the years," Typhoon Joe said. "Amaury's first phone call, when he got back to Cairo, was to me. He told me what he had. I purchased the entire lot, every single item. That was a good deal for Amaury, because if he had to sell things piecemeal, the word would eventually get out and the Egyptian government would start hunting for him. It was a good deal for me, because first of all, I got everything for a fraction of what it's worth, but more importantly because the whole is worth more than the sum of its parts."

"Lucky you," Jonk said.

"Lucky me for a while," Typhoon Joe said. "I didn't guard it like I should have. Someone stole it right out from under my nose, not everything, not the jars or senet games or the bigger pieces, but the mask, the coins, the gems and a handful of small statues. Part of what I want is to get it back. The other part of what I want should be obvious."

"That's where I come in," Jonk said.

Typhoon Joe nodded.

Right.

"That's where you come in. Both parts. Your cut is 20 percent of what you recover, paid in kind, meaning for every ten coins you recover, you keep two. We'll have to come up with a monetary figure for your 20 percent of the mask, and we'll figure out a fair way to split up the gems and minerals."

Jonk considered it.

"This is bigger than I thought."

Typhoon Joe nodded.

"It's big enough that when you find them, a thought is going to enter your head. Do you know what that thought is?"

Jonk shook his head.

"No."

"Yes you do," Typhoon Joe said. "The thought is going to be, *I SHOULD JUST KEEP EVERYTHING FOR MYSELF. I'LL MAKE UP A STORY. I'LL TELL TYPHOON JOE I COULDN'T FIND THEM. I'LL HIDE THEM, SOMEWHERE SAFE. I'LL SIT ON THEM FOR A YEAR OR TWO OR FIVE, WHATEVER IT TAKES. TYPHOON JOE WILL FORGET ABOUT ME. THEN I'LL SELL THEM ON THE BLACK MARKET.*"

Jonk smiled.

"That's quite a scenario," he said.

Typhoon Joe frowned.

"It's just a realistic prediction of human nature," he said. "Let me emphasize, when that thought enters your head, resist it. Resist it with everything you have. The reason is this. If you don't, I'll hunt you to the ends of the earth. There won't be a rock or tree or wall anywhere on the planet that you can hide behind. I'll find you, count on it, count on it with every breath in your lungs. It may not be right away, it may even be years, but I'll find you eventually. And when I do, the pain will start. It will be a horrible, slow pain, and there won't be a thing in the world you can do or say to stop it once it starts. Are we clear?"

Jonk's chest tightened.

Then he forced his face into a smile and slapped Typhoon Joe on the back.

"Lose the drama," he said. "No one's going to screw you. I'm going to keep you in the loop. I just want to be clear that there are no guarantees, other than you'll get my best efforts. I may be able to recover them, I may not. Either way, I don't want to worry about you thinking I've screwed you just because everything doesn't magically fall back into your lap."

"If you're honest, I'll know," Typhoon Joe said. "If you're not, I'll know that too."

"Deal," Jonk said.

They shook hands.

DAY TWO

September 22
Tuesday

5

Day 2—September 22
Tuesday Morning

Song Lee had a one-room law office on Waverly Place, which was an alley in Chinatown between Grant Avenue and Stockton Street, sometimes referred to as the Street of Painted Balconies. Being on the second floor and with only a small sign at street level, hardly anyone knew about the office unless they were Chinese, so it was strange when a well-dressed Caucasian woman walked in early Tuesday morning. She was about thirty, curvy, five-seven and pretty, even with the serious expression etched on her face.

"Are you Song Lee, the attorney?"

"Yes."

Song knew the reason for the question, namely she was wearing red tennis shoes with a faded black T-shirt tucked into gray khakis. It didn't help that she was only five-two and wore black glasses, which made her look younger than her actual age, twenty-eight. Her hair was long, thick and shinny black, currently pulled back into an uneventful ponytail. She looked more like someone off the Berkeley campus than a lawyer.

"My name's Shaden Jade," the woman said. "I was wondering if I could talk to you about something."

The words were cracked with stress.

Song leaned forward and said, "Are you okay?"

"I'm not sure yet."

"What's the problem?"

"This is confidential, right? Our conversation?"

Yes.

Totally.

"This is an attorney-client communication, a hundred percent confidential even if you don't retain me."

The woman sat down in one of the two beat-up chairs in front of the desk, paused, then looked Song directly in the eyes and said, "I'd like to hire you to find out something for me."

"Find out what?"

"Find out whether I killed someone."

Song tilted her head.

"This is a joke, right? Moon Lee put you up to this."

Shaden said nothing.

Instead, she pulled a white envelope out of her purse and pushed it across the desk. "That's a cash retainer," she said. "Fifty thousand dollars. There's more if you need it. Money isn't the issue."

Song left the money where it was.

"What's this about?"

"I need to warn you in advance that this could be dangerous," Shaden said.

"How so?"

"Look," Shaden said, "I'm going to say something and I don't want you to take it the wrong way. It's pretty obvious that you could use the money. Before I tell you what this is about, though, I want you to promise me something."

Promise something?

What?

"Promise me that if you do decide to take the case, you'll do it because it fits you on a personal level, because you really want to help me deep down, not because of the money."

Song stood up, walked to the window and looked down.

Chinatown was already in full motion, even here in the alley.

She turned, locked eyes with Shaden and said, "Who'd you kill?"

Shaden exhaled.

"I'm not sure that I did," she said. "That's what I want you to find out."

"Okay, let me rephrase it," Song said. "Who is it that you think you may have killed? What's the person's name?"

"She's a woman but I don't know her name."

"Is she someone you know?"

"No, she's a stranger."

"How'd you kill her, if you did?"

"With a gun."

"With a gun?"

"Right, with a gun," Shaden said. "It's probably best if we back up and start at the beginning."

6

Day 2—September 22
Tuesday Morning

Teffinger woke Tuesday before daybreak and climbed out of the cabin of his Island Packet 35 sailboat to find a thick fog shrouding the Pier 39 Marina.

He hated fog.

San Francisco was fine as cities go but someone should have designed it without the fog. A twist to the right on the temperature dial wouldn't have hurt anything either.

Say ten degrees.

He pulled his hair into a ponytail as he walked down E-Dock, then broke into a jog out of the marina, past the Aquarium of the Bay, and down The Embarcadero, which already had more traffic than it should.

Cars.

Cars.

Cars.

Too many cars.

That's how Teffinger would die, he already knew it—some idiot car would run him over, probably a taxi. He picked up the pace, letting his legs stretch and his lungs burn.

Condor was the September/June killer—SJK.

Teffinger was 99 percent certain of that following last night.

The first victim, a young attractive blond named Paris Zeph-yr, was murdered on September 26th, three years ago. Some-one placed her on her stomach, tied her hands behind her back, tied her ankles together, bent her legs at the knees and then ran a rope around her neck to her feet. There was some slack in the rope but not much, meaning she had to keep her legs bent to keep from choking herself to death. Of course, the human body can't endure something like that forever. Her legs eventually convulsed and straightened, after a long desperate struggle, which of course was the fun part. The killer dumped her body near a boat repair yard on the southeast edge of the city. Before he left, he inserted a yellow rose in her mouth—all the way in, almost down her throat.

She was referred to as Paris Zephyr until June 5th, two years ago.

That's when another blond—a young woman named Jamie van de Haven—was murdered the exact same way, right down to the yellow rose.

At that time, Paris Zephyr stopped being referred to by her name and started to be called Number One. Jamie van de Ha-ven hardly got referred to by her name at all. She was called Number Two.

Number three was yet another young blond, a waitress named Pamela Zoom. She was not only killed the same way as the first two, but she was also killed exactly one year after Number One, on September 26th.

A pattern was emerging.

Number four, a blond named Samantha Payton, was killed the same way on June 5th of last year, exactly one year following Number Two.

September 26th.

June 5th.

September 26th.

June 5th.

That's when the press gave the killer a name.

SJK.

True to form, number five came on September 26th of last year, again a blond, again with a yellow rose in her mouth. Her name was Brenda Poppenberg, an Alcatraz tour guide.

Number six came right on schedule, June 5th of this year, a woman named Syling Hu. She was Chinese, the first non-Caucasian victim. Her hair was black, not blond. The killer dyed it blond for her.

She was born with black hair but died a blond.

That sent a shiver down San Francisco's spine because for the first time non-blonds weren't immune.

Number seven would come in four days.

On September 26th.

This time would be different, though.

This time Teffinger knew who he was after.

Even after taking a five-mile jog and swinging by his 2-bedroom condo on Masonic, just south of Haight, to shower and change, Teffinger still got to the office before anyone else.

He flicked on the fluorescents, kick-started the coffee and watched the pot as it filled.

He felt good.

No, not good.

Good.

The terror would soon be over.

He was filling up his first cup of caffeine when Neva Leya walked into the room wearing a sleepy face. She was twenty-seven, Latina, and a natural born hunter. Her only drawback was her chest. It was too big and too perfect.

She grabbed a disposable cup, threw him a sideways look and said, "Someone's up to no good."

"Me?"

"It's all over your face, Teffinger," she said. "What have you done this time?"

"Nothing."

"Yeah, right."

"Honest, nothing."

"Go ahead and be that way," she said. "The chatter's getting intense on SJK, in case you haven't noticed. It was on all the radio stations this morning. People are saying the city should close on the 26th and everyone should stay inside. I think they're right so that's what I'm going to do that day."

Teffinger smiled.

Neva added, "I think he's going to cheat this year. I think he's going to do it before the 26th."

Teffinger tilted his head.

"No way, June 5th and September 26th are his days. He's not going to deviate."

Neva considered it.

"He's going to do it earlier and the yellow rose is going to change to a red one."

"What makes you say that?"

She lowered his voice.

"To shake it up."

"I don't think so. He'll do it exactly when he's supposed to. Otherwise, it will look he's afraid of the heat that will be on him that day. He'll look like a coward. The 26th is it. Get ready for it."

7

Day 2—September 22
Tuesday Morning

J onk's redeye touched down on a foggy SFO runway just as the sun crested the earth. He'd never been to San Francisco but didn't expect much, not compared to Hong Kong. He took a taxi to the Hilton in the financial district, checked in and took a shower. He was toweling off, walking out of the bathroom, when he saw something he didn't expect: a black woman, standing by the window with her back to him, looking down on the city.

She wore white shorts that showcased a taut ass and sprinter's thighs. Her skin was mocha, not much darker than his. Her hair was straight, light brown and thick.

She turned.

Her face was nice.

Her eyes were even nicer.

Green.

Hypnotic.

"I'm Tag," she said.

Jonk ran his one good eye down her body. Her top didn't quite reach her shorts, exposing a sexy little bellybutton.

"You don't look like what I expected," he said.

"Either do you," she said. "I pictured someone with more clothes."

Jonk swung the towel around his waist, headed for the bathroom and said over his shoulder, "How'd you get in?"

"I have my ways."

"I'll bet you do." He stuck his head out and said, "What's Tag stand for?"

"It stands for Tag."

"It's not short for something?"

"No."

Tag.

Just Tag.

Nice.

"I don't like the fog," he said. "We don't get much of it in Hong Kong and now I'm glad."

"Yeah, I know."

"You've been to Hong Kong?"

"Typhoon Joe flies me there on occasion."

"So you've met him, personally?"

Yes.

She had.

"What do you think of him?" Jonk asked.

"I think he has a lot of money."

Jonk smiled.

"That's a polite way to put it. The money is his curse. He's not strong enough to control it. It takes him to strange places. It twists him."

"There are worse twists."

"Like what?"

"Like the ones that come from having no money," she said.

"The secret is to not have too much or too little," he said.

"Somewhere in the twenty to thirty million range is just about right."

"That's your goal? Twenty or thirty million?"

"I have lots of goals," he said. "Money's only one of them. Tell me why I'm in San Francisco."

"Typhoon Joe didn't tell you?"

"No. All he told me was to check into the Hilton and some-one named Tag would contact me."

She shook her head.

"That's so like him," she said. A pause, then, "What happened to your eye?"

"Why? You don't like it?"

She walked over, put a finger lightly on his forehead and slowly moved it down over his scar. Jonk closed his eyes as it passed over his left one, then opened them.

"I like it just fine," Tag said. "I'm just curious. What happened?"

8

Day 2—September 22
Tuesday Morning

S ong poured Shaden a cup of coffee and intentionally avoided looking at the envelope in the middle of her desk. "All right," Shaden said. "Where do I begin? First of all, I'm an attorney with the New York branch of Rapport, Wolfe & Lake. We have offices all over the world. Have you ever heard of us?"

Yes.

Of course.

Everyone in the legal profession had.

"Remember, what I'm about to tell you is confidential," Shaden said. "Anyway, one of the partners in the New York office is a man named Lloyd Taylor. He sent me here to the San Francisco branch to infiltrate it."

"Infiltrate it?"

"Right. There's a partner here in the San Francisco office by the name of Dirk Rekker. My job was to find out if he's dirty."

"Dirty how?"

"Taylor wasn't really sure," Shaden said. "In fact, there might not be a consistent pattern. Taylor said he'd been getting feelers—albeit dim and vague—to suggest that Rekker might be using private investigators to get dirt on people such as witnesses, judges and parties, to get them to do what he wanted in high-stakes cases. Taylor's concern was that Rekker was not only engaging in behind-the-scenes blackmail, but was actually laying bait to get dirt when the dirt wasn't already there."

"Laying bait? What does that mean?"

"It means hiring a woman to lure a man into an affair," Shaden said. "Things like that. Anyway, I came to San Francisco. The story was that I was interested in relocating to the west coast and would spend a week or two at the San Francisco office to see if I fit in. This particular branch has 117 attorneys, roughly half the size of New York."

Song nodded.

"Okay."

"I don't understand why Taylor didn't just go to the police," she said.

"He couldn't."

"Why not?"

"Because if he was right and Rekker was dirty, the entire firm would be liable for his actions, including the New York branch," Shaden said. "Those liabilities could be staggering— crippling, even. They wouldn't be covered by insurance. More importantly, though, if it became public, the firm's reputation would be forever polluted. Taylor needed to get rid of any dirt that might exist while simultaneously keeping the whole thing hidden from the world. He couldn't work with anyone in the San Francisco office, because he didn't know if anyone else was involved. If there was corruption, he didn't know how far it went. So he came up with the plan to send me."

Okay.

"So what happened?"

"It didn't go well, as you can tell by the fact that I'm sitting in your office."

Song smiled.

"I gathered that much," she said. "You want some more coffee?"

She did.

She did indeed.

"Before you tell me the rest of the story, there's one thing that's been bothering me," Song said. "Why me?"

"You mean, why am I talking to you as opposed to some other lawyer?"

Right.

That.

"Primarily because Rapport, Wolfe & Lake has something going on with almost every other firm in town," Shaden said. "I needed someone off the radar screen. I ran a conflicts check. You were clean. That's not the main reason though. The main reason is that I heard you charge only $95 an hour."

"So it's about the money?"

"No," Shaden said. "I'm going to pay you $350 an hour, same as I make, if you take the case. The $95 an hour tells me you're not in the practice of law for the money, like the other 99 percent of us. You're in it to help people. That's what I need, someone who's interested in helping me."

Song tapped her fingers.

"I've only been practicing law for four years," she said. "Most of my cases have settled. I've only had three cases that have actually gone to trial, two to the court and one to a jury. None of them went particularly well. Most of the Rules of Evidence still baffle me. I can't even spell hearsay, much less know it when I see it."

Shaden squeezed Song's hand.

"Enough."

"It's only fair that you get full disclosure," Song said. "With a few exceptions, almost every one of my cases from the day I hung my shingle has been small. Small monetary stakes. Small issues. Small bills. I'm the queen of dog bites, minor car accidents, rent disputes, leases, divorce, bankruptcy, contract disputes and twenty or thirty similar molehills. Most of my clients are Chinese, Thai or Korean. I still owe over $40,000 in student loans. Do you know where I live?"

Shaden took a sip of coffee and shook her head.

"In a two-bedroom apartment right above this office," she said. "I don't have a car."

She paused.

"Are you done?" Shaden asked.

Song thought about it.

Then she nodded.

"Okay, then let me get back to my story," Shaden said.

9

Day 2—September 22
Tuesday Morning

The blond from the dungeon last night turned out to be someone named Chase St. John, who was an attorney in Rapport, Wolfe & Lake. Teffinger knew that because he was hiding in the rainy shadows last night when she came out of the building. He got her license plate number as she squealed into the night.

Now, this morning, his watch said 7:32 a.m.

He took a position in the lobby of the Transamerica Pyramid and sipped coffee from a large, disposable cup.

She didn't show up for a full hour.

More than a hour, actually—8:43 a.m.

At first, Teffinger wasn't sure it was her. Gone were the slow, sensuous movements of last night, now replaced with the purposeful, brisk walk of an attorney about to embark on a full day of work. The long, flowing locks of last night were pulled back tight. She wore a crisp white blouse and an expensive, gray pinstriped skirt with a matching jacket. Down below were nylons and black leather shoes with a two-inch heel.

Teffinger headed over.

Just as they were about to pass, he stepped in front of her and said, "You're a lucky woman."

She looked up.

Their eyes locked.

Teffinger's blood raced.

She said nothing and looked as if she was about to step around him. Instead she tilted her head and said, "How am I lucky, exactly?"

"You're lucky because you don't have coffee all over your blouse," he said.

"Coffee?"

"In my younger days, when I saw someone I wanted to meet, I'd spill something on them," he said. "I don't do that any more."

"So now you have a new approach and this is it."

He nodded and took a sip of caffeine.

"I know, it's lame," he said. "But here's the thing. I saw you walking across the lobby. Has that ever happened to you? You see someone on the street, a perfect stranger, and you just can't let them slip away? Something just comes over you and you don't care if you have to do something stupid if it means getting to meet them?"

She ran her eyes down his body.

Quickly.

Almost imperceptibly.

"Are you an athlete?"

He shrugged.

"I can walk on my hands."

"Show me."

He smiled.

"Here?"

"Yes."

He took a long slurp of coffee.

"I will if you will," he said.

She laughed.

"That probably wouldn't be too appropriate, me wearing a skirt and all," she said.

"I won't look."

She tilted her head.

"Does this work on other women?"

He held his hands out in confusion.

"I don't know," he said. "To tell you the truth, I've never done anything like this before."

"What about all those other strangers, the ones you couldn't let slip away?"

"They slipped away."

"So why is this time different?"

"I don't know," he said. "That's what I'm trying to find out."

She walked away.

Two steps later she turned and said, "I've never seen anyone with one blue eye and one green eye before."

"I didn't think you noticed."

"Apparently I did."

10

Day 2—September 22
Tuesday Morning

Jonk tried to not stare at Tag's legs as she drove, but they were so damn perfect that it was a battle. The fog was lifting and the temperature was rising. They were headed south, to the hideaway of a black-market trader named Black Bart, who wasn't expecting them.

Anything but, in fact.

Tag explained as they drove.

"Bart put out some feelers on Sunday—two days ago—to the effect that he had an ancient Egyptian coin for sale for $5,000. Amaury, back in Cairo, had his ear to the ground for that kind of thing and got wind of it. By the description, it sounded an awful lot like one of the coins from the tomb he looted. He called Typhoon Joe to find out if he was putting the coins up for sale. If so, he wanted to warn Typhoon Joe that he was significantly under-pricing them."

"Black Bart," Typhoon Joe said. "Wasn't there a pirate by that name?"

Tag nodded.

"Believe it or not, a lot of these underground traders use

pirate names," she said. "But that's not important. What's important is that Typhoon Joe now had the first solid lead to his treasure since he'd been robbed. He wanted Amaury to go to San Francisco and find out who Bart was working for, but Amaury was leaving the next morning to go back to the tomb and break into another chamber."

"More money for him there," Jonk said, "no matter how much Typhoon Joe paid him."

Right.

Exactly.

"That's when Typhoon Joe called me and gave me the assignment to dig into it," Tag said. "I'm not just a pair of legs. I'm also a P.I., in case you didn't know."

"No, I didn't."

"No reason you would," she said. "Anyway, Black Bart's real name is Brian Zoog. He rents a house on Foote Avenue on the south edge of the city. That's where we're headed."

"Have you gone in yet?" he asked.

No.

Negative.

"That's why you're here," she said. "The last time I talked to Typhoon Joe, he made something very clear."

Jonk raised an eyebrow.

"What?"

"That Black Bart was expendable."

Jonk frowned.

"Everyone's expendable as far as Typhoon Joe is concerned," he said. "That includes you and me."

Black Bart's house couldn't have been exposed to more eyes if that was the goal. Immediately to the west was the BART line and the Southern Freeway. Immediately to the east was a busy street. His house was stuck in a throwaway wedge of land between it all.

"That's his place," Tag said as they swung by.

The windows were closed and the shades were drawn. There were no discernable signs of life but that didn't mean he wasn't home.

Jonk opened the car door.

"Wait here."

"Where you going?"

"In."

"I'm coming with you."

"No."

"Why not?"

"Because you're not."

She stepped out, shut the door and said, "Let's go."

11

Day 2—September 22
Tuesday Morning

A knock came at Song's door and a woman stepped through a heartbeat later with an empty coffee cup in one hand and a cigarette in the other. She was about thirty and wore a long-sleeve T with nothing underneath, at least as far as a bra went. Whether she had panties on was anyone's guess. Judging by her hair, she just woke up. She was Chinese but not pure, more like someone with Portuguese or Spanish in her background, a combination that worked whatever it was. She cast a startled face at Shaden, said something apologetic in Chinese and backed out.

Song laughed.

"Sorry about that," she said.

"Someone you know, I assume."

Right.

Fenfang.

Song's roommate, to be precise.

She filled a disposable cup with coffee, said "Give me ten seconds—the only coffee maker we have is the one here in the office," and headed upstairs. Twenty seconds later she returned empty handed. "She wanted me to apologize for barging in."

"No need."

"She was really embarrassed."

"Tell her she's very pretty."

"Will do."

Shaden looked at her watch.

It was getting late.

"Let me finish, then I have to run," she said. "Rekker heads up the firm's criminal defense division. One of the law clerks who works on that end of the floor is a young woman named Rayla White. She caught me snooping around in Rekker's office. I thought she was going to rat me out but it turns out that she's not a big fan of Rekker. In fact, she's always had a bad feeling about him and it's been getting worse over the last year."

Interesting.

"Rayla helped me get into Rekker's office on a few occasions, standing guard and having an excuse for me to be in there if I needed it," Shaden said. "In the end, we found nothing."

"Really?"

"Yes, but that's not the end of the story," Shaden said. "We decided to search his house."

"That's pretty gutsy."

Right.

It was.

"Did you clear it with your contact back in New York?"

"You mean Lloyd Taylor?"

Right.

Him.

"No," Shaden said. "Anyway, Rekker lives in a contemporary mansion halfway up a hill in Sausalito. The partners were having some kind of meeting Sunday night, meaning he'd be out. Me and Rayla parked a half mile away, walked to his house and hung out in the shadows until he left. We waited for ten minutes and then walked around to the back. It was dark out. We found an unlocked window, went in and turned on our flashlights."

Okay.

"We split up," she said. "I headed for the den and Rayla headed up a winding staircase to the upper level. Two minutes later I heard some kind of commotion. I came out of the den to see what was going on. Rayla was bounding down the stairs at full speed. The flashlight was jarring all over the place. She was moving so fast that she couldn't even begin to keep it pointed. Then a gun fired. It came from behind her. I actually saw the flash. Rayla screamed. At first, I thought she was hit, but she kept going."

"Wow."

Right.

Wow.

"The gun fired again, then again," Shaden said. "Rayla was running through the main part of the house. There wasn't much light in the house, but there was some, and by this time I could tell that the person with the gun was a woman. When the gun fired again, I lunged at her and we both fell to the floor. She never saw me coming. We ended up in a struggle. During that struggle the gun went off. The woman screamed in pain and doubled over, holding her stomach. I stood up, totally out of my mind, and backed away. She gurgled for a few moments, then nothing—no sound, no movement, no nothing. We just left her where she was and got the hell out of there."

Song frowned.

"Did you call an ambulance or anything?"

Shaden diverted her eyes.

Then she said, "She was dead."

"Did you check her pulse?"

Shaden shook her head.

"I didn't need to," she said. "I could tell she was dead by the sounds she made."

Okay.

"Are you ready for the last part?" Shaden asked.

Yes.

She was.

"Okay, here it comes. But brace yourself, because this is where it gets weird. Me and Rayla figured that the best thing to do would just be to report to work Monday morning as if nothing happened. We were wearing gloves when we broke in—did I mention that already?—so we weren't worried about leaving fingerprints. Also, the house was dark, both inside and out back. I don't know if there were any surveillance cameras anywhere, but even if there were, there would be a good chance that they never got a good look at us. Anyway, like I said, we decided to just go to work as usual and see what happened."

"I understand."

"Here's the weird part," Shaden said. "Rekker also reported to work as if nothing happened. He was his normal self all day yesterday. He didn't say a peep to anyone about coming back home Sunday night and finding his girlfriend or whatever she was dead in his house. Also, as far as I can tell, he never reported the body to the police."

"He didn't?"

"No. Negative."

"Why not?"

"That's the question," Shaden said. "I've been thinking about it non-stop and have come up with a theory. Do you want to hear it?"

12

Day 2—September 22
Tuesday Morning

Teffinger drove down Market with "Born to Run" on the radio, loud, the way it was supposed to be, singing along when the chorus came up. Chase St. John might be a killer, she might not. Either way, Teffinger couldn't undo what had already happened when he looked into her eyes this morning. He was on a trip, like it or not. About the best he could do at this point was hold on.

So far, no body had shown up.

So far, no call came into 911 from some freaked-out passerby who was heading to work this morning just like he'd done a thousand times before and expected to see just about anything except a dead tattooed woman stuffed under a car.

No body.

No body.

No body.

That was good.

Maybe what Teffinger saw last night hadn't been a killing at all. Maybe it was nothing more than a fake snuff, designed to trick the camera. Too bad, in hindsight, that Condor came home at exactly the wrong time. Teffinger had no idea if the victim was still hanging limp when someone took her down or whether she simply raised her head, smiled and said, "How'd I do?"

On the other hand, he never saw a camera.

It could have just been a private session.

Either way, what was Chase doing there?

She was a lawyer.

More precisely, she was a lawyer in a very reputable, conservative law firm that had a reputation to maintain.

Chase.

Chase.

Chase.

Who was she?

He wasn't sure how to handle Condor now that he knew he was SJK. He didn't want to wait until the night in question and try to nab him in the act, although it might come to that. The last thing he could afford to do was screw the case up a second time.

In fairness, Teffinger wasn't the one who screwed it up the first time.

Those honors went to Detective Frank Finger, who got obsessed with finding the murderer of Paris Zephyr, back in the days when Paris Zephyr was still Paris Zephyr instead of Number One.

What Finger did was impressive, even today.

He built a very strong circumstantial case against a man named Kyle Greyson, a filthy-rich scumbag whose only contribution to society was plying women with liquor and hanging out at the most happening haunts up and down the coast.

The DA didn't care that the case was circumstantial.

He'd take what he could get.

He had enough, that was the main thing.

Charges were filed.

Greyson lawyered-up with a team quarterbacked by none other than Dirk Rekker, head of the criminal defense division of Rapport, Wolfe & Lake.

Both sides showed up for trial.

The slugfest started.

The DA was winning.

Then everything went to shit.

Detective Finger dealt with the courtroom stress by getting seriously drunk on the Sunday before the start of the second week of trial. He got so drunk in fact that he thought it would be a good idea to punch his bitch girlfriend Haley Key in the face after she kept telling him to put the bottle down and he kept telling her to leave him alone.

She didn't file charges.

No.

She had a better idea.

She called up Greyson's attorney—Rekker—and told him all the dirty little secrets that Finger had told her—how he'd planted evidence, falsified reports and on and on, how he had to do it because he knew Greyson was guilty but he didn't have enough real evidence to prove it in a court of law.

She testified to that effect Monday morning.

Rekker called Finger to the stand directly after his girlfriend. He didn't have time to talk to anyone. He didn't know that she'd spilled his dirty little secrets. Rekker slammed him upside the head with what he'd done.

Finger lied on the stand.

He denied doing anything improper.

He even denied punching his girlfriend.

Everyone knew he was lying but the case went forward because, in the end, it was a jury question as to whether Finger could be believed or not.

Rekker spun into top gear, scrambling for extrinsic evidence to contradict Finger and prove he was lying.

He got some of what he was looking for that evening.

More on Tuesday.

More on Wednesday.

And even more on Thursday.

That night, Thursday, he met with the DA off the record in a dive bar in Tenderloin. He showed him the evidence he'd compiled this week and would be presenting in the morning. He gave the DA another opportunity to dismiss the case.

The DA studied it.

He studied it very carefully.

Then he looked Rekker in the eyes and said, "I can't do anything without clearing it with my client, obviously, but my recommendation will be to dismiss the case. I'll let you know for certain one way or the other first thing in the morning."

In the morning, the DA did exactly that, namely dismissed the case.

Three days later word broke that a body had been found, the body of a blond named Jamie van de Haven, who was killed the same way as Paris Zephyr.

Rekker called the DA.

"I heard about this second woman whose body just got found," he said. "My question is, when was she killed?"

A pause.

"Sometime last week," he said. "Tuesday or Wednesday or Thursday, we're not exactly sure yet."

"My client was in custody all last week," Rekker said.

"I know."

"I don't mind winning the trial," Rekker said, "I'll be the first person to admit that. But I wish there hadn't been one. I wish the city would have spent it's time catching the right man instead of framing the wrong one."

A pause.

Then, "You and me both. Did I say that out loud?"

Rekker smiled.

"No. I didn't hear a thing."

Two weeks later, Rekker filed a civil suit on behalf of his client Kyle Greyson, against the City of San Francisco as well as Finger, personally.

That suit was quickly settled out of court for an undisclosed sum of money.

Finger was discharged.

So was the head of the homicide detail, Alex Pacer, a man with fifteen years tenure who either knew or should have known what Finger was doing.

That's when Teffinger got the job.

And that's why he could never let anyone find out he'd broken into Condor's house.

13

Day 2—September 22
Tuesday Morning

Black Bart's house was an old Victorian built in typical San Francisco style, meaning narrow and tall, with a garage at street level and steps leading up to the main floor. Jonk rapped on the door, got no response, then did it again, louder.

No answer.

"Looks like we're in luck."

He tried the knob, already knowing it would be locked, only to find that it actually turned. He edged the door open and stuck his face in.

"Anyone home?"

A Bob Marley song came from upstairs.

Fairly low volume.

Not jammin', the way it was supposed to be.

"Hello?"

Silence.

They stepped in and shut the door. The first floor wasn't neat—anything but, in fact. Junk was everywhere, especially empty wine bottles, years worth judging by the number. Every square inch of wall and carpet and wood reeked of marijuana. Dirty ashtrays were everywhere.

A quick search showed no Black Bart.

Jonk and Tag headed upstairs, quietly.

Jonk opened and closed his right fist in successive motions, ready for whatever was about to happen, but not too worried at this point about finding a man healthy enough to put up a good fight.

They approached the master bedroom.

Jonk expected to find his target sprawled out unconscious on the bed, the victim of too much self-abuse last night. He was half right. There was someone sprawled out on the bed all right but it wasn't Black Bart.

It was a woman.

A woman wearing jeans and a pink tank.

Passed out on top of the covers.

When Jonk and Tag stepped into the room, the woman shifted slightly but didn't raise her head or open her eyes.

He checked the master bathroom to find it empty.

Same thing with respect to all the other rooms upstairs.

No Black Bart.

Not anywhere.

The rear wall of the bedroom had sliding glass doors, open, that lead to a small deck. Jonk checked it and found no one. Then he looked down, over the edge. A man was sprawled out motionless on the concrete patio below.

He wore jeans and tennis shoes but no shirt.

A lot of blood had spilled out of his face and head.

It was brown now.

Dried.

Jonk looked closer and saw something he didn't expect.

The handle of a knife stuck out from under the man's torso, at an angle to suggest that the blade was stuck in his body, between his chest and abdomen. Closer examination showed blood in that area.

"We have company," Tag said.

Jonk turned.

What he saw he could hardly believe.

The woman on the bed wasn't sprawled out anymore. She was sitting up, staring directly at them through bloodshot eyes.

"Who are you?" she asked.

14

Day 2—September 22
Tuesday Morning

When Shaden left, Song peddled her bicycle to the bank and deposited $10,000 cash into a trust account, which drew a raised eyebrow but no direct comments from the teller. She did that three more times—not wanting to carry too much cash at one time—and then headed back to get the last installment. She wasn't sure if she'd end up drawing on the account because she wasn't sure if she could do anything for her client.

So far, she had no bright ideas.

Not a one.

Shaden's theory as to what happened, while extreme, actually made sense. She believed that Rayla White may not have really been on Shaden's side at all, but might have only been pretending to be. Rayla might have been in cahoots with Rekker the whole time. The events at Rekker's house Sunday night might have been nothing more than an elaborate charade to make Shaden believe she killed someone, at which point she would back down.

The bullets might have been fake.

That's why Rekker never reported the murder to the police, because there wasn't one.

According to Shaden, Rekker was clever enough to pull something like that off. He was aware that, legally speaking, Shaden would be liable for murder even though she was trying to keep the woman from shooting Rayla. The woman had the right to fire at intruders. She also had a right to defend herself when one of those intruders—Shaden—attacked her. Even though Shaden's motives may have been good—*i.e.* she was trying to prevent Rayla from being killed—if there was a murder during the commission of a breaking and entering, she was as guilty as if she'd planned the whole thing from the start.

Rekker knew that Shaden would either know that or be able to figure it out.

Song's job was to determine if the murder was real or a charade.

Right now, Song had no idea how to go about it.

Obviously, it would be nice to know if there were actual bullet holes in the walls or blood stains on the carpet, but there was no way to know that short of breaking in.

What to do?

When she got back to her office the door was halfway open, which was strange because she'd left it closed and locked. Stepping inside, her breath stopped.

The place was trashed.

Everything on her desk had been pushed off.

Papers were everywhere.

The last $10,000 cash of the retainer was gone.

She checked the door lock closer and found it had been jimmied with a screwdriver or something.

She headed upstairs to see if Fenfang had heard anything.

The woman wasn't there.

She went back down to the office, sat in her chair and concentrated. Fenfang didn't know about the retainer, plus she wouldn't have done something like this in a hundred years.

Song dialed Shaden's direct number at Rapport, Wolfe & Lake and said, "Are you okay?"

Yes.

Fine.

"Why wouldn't I be?"

"My office was just ransacked and part of the retainer you gave me was stolen," Song said. "The only thing I can think of is that Rekker either followed you or had you followed this morning. He knows we met. The break-in is a warning to me to not take the case. By extension, it's also a warning to you."

Silence.

"That's it then," Shaden said. "I'm not going to put you in harm's way. You're off the case."

"No I'm not."

"Yes you are."

The line went dead.

15

Day 2—September 22
Tuesday Morning

Teffinger had a '58 Chevy Impala called Bertha that he bought when he was eighteen from a guy down the street who picked up a woman at a bar who became a girlfriend who didn't want to be seen dead in it. It had the classic lines of the era but that was the last good thing that could be said about it. The lacquer paint, initially turquoise and white, was dead, decayed and scratched beyond belief.

The body had dents.

Lots and lots of dents.

Some big, some small.

Teffinger counted thirty at one point, and that was years ago.

It was a convertible, which sounds like a good thing, but wasn't. The top didn't come down, never had in fact. What it did do was leak. The most prominent place was right over the driver's seat, directly into the crotch area. The seats were vinyl—the original vinyl, hard and brittle, now covered by a red flannel blanket.

The heater didn't work.

Sometimes the left taillight worked, sometimes it didn't.

The wipers worked, but only on low.

The rear bumper dipped slightly to the right.

The radio was a pushbutton with a gritty patina and hardly any bass. A pair of dice hung from the rearview mirror. They were supposed to bring good luck. As far asl Teffinger could tell, they must be broke.

His plan was to fix it up and, deep down, that was still the plan. Unfortunately, that plan was still in the planning stage.

It was the absolute worst car to own in San Francisco.

It was too big.

Too clumsy.

Too slow.

Too hard to turn.

Impossible to parallel park.

At this point, however, Teffinger was stuck. He'd owned it for fifteen years. It was now an old, comfortable pair of shoes. He wasn't supposed to drive it when he was on duty, that was the official rule, but he and the chief came to an understanding—Teffinger would break that rule so long as he kept a handheld radio with him, and the chief would look the other way, at least until and unless he got too much flak.

Right now, Teffinger steered Bertha into an alley, came to a stop and killed the engine, which died with a cough of blue smoke.

Teffinger stepped out.

The morning fog was gone.

The air was heating up.

Nice.

He jumped up, caught the bottom of a dirty black fire escape and pulled himself up. Then he climbed up to the top floor, where the dungeon show came from last night.

The exit door for that level was locked.

He continued to the roof where he found an unlocked access door that led into an interior stairway. No sounds came from below.

He took the stairs down to a hallway that fed the upper level.

Every door was locked.

Shit.

He headed back up towards the roof and was halfway out the access door when he realized he had come too far to not get what he came for.

He headed back down.

The interior door was wooden.

He rammed it with his shoulder until the jam busted, then stepped into the room where Chase St. John may or may not have killed someone last night.

16

Day 2—September 22
Tuesday Morning

J onk didn't like to kill people and so far he'd been able to get through his life without having to do it. While the woman on the bed posed a risk in that she might describe him to the police who in turn might hunt him as a suspect in the murder of Black Bart, he already knew he'd have to handle the situation in a way other than murder.

He walked over to the bed, sat down and took the woman's hand in his.

She didn't resist.

The fear on her face softened although the confusion remained.

"What's your name?" he asked.

"Winter."

"Winter? Like in snow and cold?"

She nodded.

"I like it," Jonk said. "The front door was open. We came here looking for Brian Zoog."

The woman wrinkled her forehead.

"Zoogie," she said.

"Okay, Zoogie."

"Zoogie," she called. No answer. "He should be here."

"Do you remember anything from last night?"

She ran her fingers through her hair.

No.

"My head hurts," she said. "I need aspirin."

"In a minute," Jonk said. "Are you Zoogie's girlfriend?"

"Sometimes," she said.

"Sometimes?"

"When he's nice, I'm his girlfriend," she said. "But that's not all the time."

Understood.

"There's probably no easy way to tell you this so I'm going to just get to the point. Someone killed Zoogie last night. It looks like they stabbed him and then pushed him off the deck. He landed on the patio. That's where he is right now."

"You're messing with me."

Jonk said nothing.

"Was someone with you two last night?"

She pushed off the bed, walked to the deck and looked down.

"We're not the ones who did it," Jonk said.

Winter didn't believe him.

It was on her face.

In her eyes.

On her trembling lips.

She looked around, frantic, found no escape and was two heartbeats away from jumping over the railing when Jonk grabbed her around the waist, swung her off her feet and tossed her on the bed.

He sat down next to her and got his voice as calm as he

could. "The blood's brown. He's been dead for some time. If we were the ones who did it, why would we still be hanging around?"

She didn't know.

She didn't care.

"I want to leave."

"That's fine," Jonk said. "You can leave in just a minute. First tell us where he keeps the stuff he sells on the black market."

"I don't know what you're talking about."

"He had a coin for sale."

"I don't know anything about a coin."

"We don't want it," Jonk said. "We're not going to take it, if that's what you're worried about. All we want to know is where he got it."

"I already told you—"

Jonk scrunched his face.

"He's dead because of that coin. Whoever killed him was after that coin. Would you like to help us figure out who that was?"

She looked at him.

Hard.

Defiantly.

"You killed him," she said. "So fuck you!"

She jumped off the bed before Jonk even knew what she was doing, pushed Tag in the chest so hard that she fell on her ass, then bounded down the stairs two at a time.

Halfway down her foot missed.

She fell.

Violently.

Too fast to even scream.

17

Day 2—September 22
Tuesday Morning

Song peddled her bicycle to the Hall of Justice on Bryant Street to file a formal report on the break-in, and ended up speaking to a detective named Margaret Pinch, a terrible looking woman with too much sugar in her smile. She was careful to not mention the name of any of her clients or the source of the missing cash, all of which she was bound to maintain as confidential under the attorney-client privilege. Nor did she mention her suspicion that the incident was possibly a warning in connection with a recent case—Shaden's case, to be exact— because she wasn't at liberty to even acknowledge such a case to a third party, much less discuss it.

Pinch took the information without emotion, clearly unimpressed.

She would drop by later today or tomorrow to have a look around, if Song wanted. Given the tone of her voice, Song didn't think it would be necessary, and thanked her for her time.

From there she peddled to the Transamerica Pyramid, dialed

Shaden and said, "I'm down here on the street outside your building. We need to talk."

A pause.

"There's nothing to talk about. You're off the case."

"I can't be."

"Why not?"

"Because ten thousand dollars of that retainer is gone," she said. "I don't have the money to pay you back. I have to work it off."

"Forget the money."

"But—"

"Consider it payment for the meeting and all the brain damage," Shaden said. "We're even."

"So you're giving up?"

"You mean on the investigation?"

Right.

That.

"No, I'm not giving up," Shaden said. "I'm just not going to put you in harm's way."

"If you get someone else, they're going to be in the same position. Whoever you get, Rekker will figure it out sooner or later. All you're doing is buying time."

"I'm going to get a male."

"What's that supposed to mean?"

A pause.

Then, "It means you seem like a nice person and a good attorney, but let's face it, you're a little on the delicate side."

The delicate side?

Song spotted an empty Coke can and kicked it.

Hard.

She mostly missed.

It only went a couple of feet.

She got her voice as calm as she could and said, "I'll be paying that ten thousand back to you, every single penny, I'm just going to need a little time to do it. You can stop by whenever you want and I'll give you a check for the other forty. Good luck with your new attorney."

Then she hung up.

18

Day 2—September 22
Tuesday Morning

Teffinger was a little astonished that he had negotiated his whole career without even a single thought of getting dirty and now here he was, in the middle of a second illegal entry in as many days, this time in broad daylight no less, with his personal car parked outside where anyone with two eyes, or even one for that matter, could see it and jot down the license plate number, not that they needed to because everyone in town knew it was his.

Not good.

Not good at all.

Downright, totally, one hundred percent not good.

He needed to chill out with an Anchor Steam or two or three and reflect on his sanity or lack thereof. That would be a good project for tonight.

The dungeon didn't look like a dungeon.

There were no devious contraptions.

There were no whips or cuffs or chains or ball gags hanging from racks. It was basically just a shell with industrial green walls and a wooden floor, empty except for a padlocked metal storage bin in the corner. On closer inspection, Teffinger spotted eyehooks bolted into the exposed, tress ceiling.

The chains and vibrators and other assorted goodies were probably in the storage cabinet. He took a closer look. The padlock was a tough one, casehardened. Even bolt cutters might not do the trick.

He suddenly realized he was stupid last night.

He was so excited when he spotted Chase and jotted down the license plate number of her car, he left right afterwards. What he should have done was hang around and see if a body got carried out and stuck in a car trunk.

It was so obvious, in hindsight.

Suddenly his phone rang.

It was the last person he expected.

Chase St. John.

"I'm going to let you take me out tonight," she said. "Plan whatever you want, just be sure I've never done it before. I'll be at your boat at eight."

"How do you know about my boat?"

She tapped a finger on the phone.

"See you then."

The line went dead.

He grinned an evil grin.

Yeah, baby.

Oh yeah.

Suddenly he realized something.

Something bad.

At this very moment, Condor might be looking through the telescope directly at him.

His phone rang again, this time it was Neva.

"Where are you?"

"Somewhere, why?"

"Don't tell me you forgot."

He tossed hair out of his face.

Forgot?

Forgot what?

Then it came to him.

He looked at his watch.

Shit!

"I'm on my way," he said. The surroundings made him pull up an image of Chase strangling the tattooed woman. "Hey, wait a minute, are you still there?" She was. "Have any dead bodies been called in today?"

No.

Why?

"Are you expecting one?" she asked.

"No, just curious. On my way."

"We'll save you some coffee."

"Save me all of it."

19

Day 2—September 22
Tuesday Morning

Winter crashed at the bottom of the stairs at a terrible angle that slapped her head against the wall. She moaned for a second, then curled into a ball and didn't move. Jonk got to her in a heartbeat. Her forehead was already swelling up and lots of blood was coming from it.

"Call 911!"

Tag pulled her phone out, then hesitated.

"They'll trace the number to my phone," she said.

Damn it.

That was true.

Jonk had seen a land line somewhere in the house but couldn't remember where. Then it came to him. "There's a phone on the kitchen counter."

Tag ran that way.

Jonk put pressure on Winter's head with his hand to control the bleeding. Suddenly Tag appeared next to him and said, "I called. They're on their way."

Jonk's chest tightened.

"Look around and see if you can find a laptop," he said.

Tag scouted the first floor, animated, frantic, then said, "Nothing down here!" as she ran past Jonk to the upper level. Jonk patted Winter's pocket, detected something hard and found what he hoped to find, her cell phone.

He shoved it into his pocket.

Blood was still pouring out of her head

Blood.

Blood.

Blood.

So much blood.

Tag bounded down the stairs with a laptop in hand.

"Got it!"

"Wait for me out back."

Jonk kept pressure on Winter's head until the ambulance screeched to a halt in front of the house. Then he ran out the back door so fast that he tripped over Zoogie's body.

"Come on!" Tag said.

Jonk got up and almost ran, but something in the deep recesses of his mind made him stick his hand into Zoogie's jean pockets first. He grabbed what was there—a wallet and a cell phone—and took off.

They ran into a grove of trees at the end of the street.

A BART train shot past close, no more than thirty or forty feet.

Faces in the windows stared at them.

They saw two frantic people running: a Chinese guy and a black woman with nice legs, carrying a laptop.

One of them, the guy, had blood all over his hands.

He was clutching something.

Possibly a wallet.

"Fifteen people are calling the police right now," he said.

"I already know that," Tag said.

20

Day 2—September 22
Tuesday Morning

From the Transamerica Pyramid, Song peddled back to her office with her head down. She had always had a fear, deep down, that she wasn't destined to be a lawyer of importance. Now here she was with her first big case, fired within hours.

She didn't own a car.

She was twenty-eight.

Single.

Sometimes when she drank wine at night, she wondered if she'd screwed up her life. She wondered if she had made bad decisions and squandered opportunities. She wondered if she should just pack a suitcase, change her name and get on a bus to New York.

Start fresh.

London.

That's what she'd change her name to, if she did it.

London Lee.

A person could get ahead in the world with a name like London. With Song, not so much.

She was a lawyer of little consequence. She had hoped that it was because she was still new to the profession. It took time to build a practice and a reputation, especially solo. But now, after getting fired by Shaden right out of the gate, she had no option but to take a good hard look at herself and face the realization that she might still be small because that's all she would ever be.

She'd never land the big case.

She'd never hold a news conference.

She'd never walk down the courthouse steps arm-in-arm with a exuberant client while reporters shoved microphones in her face and asked how in the hell she did it.

Small.

Small.

Small.

That's what she was.

Or, to put it even more accurately, delicate.

She hadn't been in her office for more than two minutes when Fenfang busted through the door with a cigarette in her mouth, studied her for a heartbeat and said, "What the hell happened to you?"

"I got robbed."

"I already know that," Fenfang said. "I'm talking about your face."

"Why? What's wrong with my face."

Fenfang blew smoke.

"There's no life in it."

"Yeah, well, that's what happens when you're delicate."

Fenfang tilted her head.

Then she grabbed Song's hand, sat her down on the couch and put her arm around her shoulders.

"Talk to me," she said.

Song hesitated.

Legally, she couldn't.

It was all confidential.

Then she exhaled and said, "I'm going to put you on the payroll of the law firm, starting now."

"Sure. Why?"

"Because if you're part of the firm, I'm allowed to share attorney-client information with you," she said.

Fenfang took a long drag.

"How much are you paying me?"

"A dollar an hour."

Fenfang smiled.

"That's not minimum wage, but fair enough. Now tell me what's going on."

21

Day 2—September 22
Tuesday Morning

The conference room was packed when Teffinger walked in with a cup of coffee in hand, twenty minutes late. Neva made a face, which he took as a warning that something bad was about to happen. Every homicide detective was there, plus the DA and the chief, C. C. Castenaux—Triple-C. To the chief's right was someone Teffinger hadn't expected, namely the mayor. On the chief's other side was a new person—a man about fifty, with a tough, creased sailor's face. His hair was half-gray and half-brown, swept straight back. His eyes were intense and fixed on Teffinger the way a predator stares down prey. He wore a crisp, dark-blue suit with an expensive hang.

Teffinger didn't like him.

The chief introduced him as Lance Northstone.

Teffinger recognized the name immediately.

Northstone was the head of New York's homicide department. He'd built an international reputation over the last ten years for his uncanny ability to hunt down the worst of the worst, not just here in the States but also in Europe and Asia.

"He's here as a resource," Triple-C said. "So, now that we're all here, how do we catch this son-of-a-bitch? What's the grand plan?"

Teffinger swallowed.

Every face in the room, with a few lazy exceptions, was looking for a team position, an assignment, a role in what would be one of the greatest hunts in San Francisco history. The worst thing he could do right now would be to mention Condor's name, because a group can't be controlled, even when it was a group of professionals. Everyone in the group would be on the move. The noise on the street would be deafening. Condor would pick up on it, go deeper, get smarter, maybe even change his pattern altogether by striking earlier or later.

But what was Teffinger supposed to do?

Tell the group to chill out?

To not be a detriment?'

He brought the coffee cup to his mouth and took a noisy slurp. Before the caffeine hit his stomach, he knew what to do.

He set the coffee down and said, "Obviously I've been thinking about this a lot and have a number of ideas. What I didn't know, until just now, is that we'd have someone as renowned and experienced as Lance Northstone with us. What I'd like to do, unless there's an objection, is turn the meeting over to Lance and see what his thoughts are." He looked at Northstone. "Lance, would you be willing to do that?"

No problem.

No problem at all.

The man stood up, walked to the white board, uncapped a blue erasable marker and started talking.

There.

Done.

Northstone had the group.

That freed Teffinger to hunt on his own.

He ducked out the back of the meeting ten minutes later.

The phone rang.

Being the only one there, Teffinger answered.

The voice of Barb Peterson from dispatch came through. "Teffinger, is that you?"

It was.

"You never answer the phone."

"I do when it's you."

"Are you sweet talking me? Because if you are, we can make it work."

He smiled.

"What's going on? You got some job security for me?"

She did.

She did indeed.

A man named Brian Zoog got himself stabbed in the gut with a large knife and then pushed off a second-story deck onto a concrete patio. "He tried to stop his fall with his face."

Teffinger winced.

"That's never a good idea," he said. "Is he dead?"

"Twice, apparently."

Teffinger looked at his watch.

"I better get down there and talk to him before someone shoots him too," he said. "You got an address?"

She did.

Foote Avenue.

He made a pit stop at the men's room before heading out. The DA, Paul Lancaster, was walking towards the sink as he zipped up.

"I still want a search warrant for Condor's house," Teffinger said.

"You got something new to justify it?"

"No."

"Well, all I can say is that the Fourth Amendment hasn't changed all that much since the last time we talked. It still doesn't run on gut feelings."

Teffinger frowned.

"We got that witness," he said.

"She's not a witness," Lancaster said. "She's someone who didn't identify Condor at the lineup. In fact, she said he wasn't the guy she saw."

"By that time she was too scared," Teffinger said. "Condor was the guy she saw that night. I was looking at her face when he was marched in. It was him."

"Maybe you're right," Lancaster said. "Either way, she said what she said, that it wasn't him. To be honest, even if she had identified him, that still wouldn't be enough for a warrant. All she did was see him on the street, in the vicinity at the time of the crime. She didn't actually see him do anything. There were other men in the area too."

Teffinger stepped to the urinal and unzipped.

"What if I get her to tell the truth and admit that she lied at the lineup?"

Lancaster turned.

"You haven't heard?"

No.

Heard what?

"She was in that twin-prop airplane that went down off-shore last week."

"She's dead?"

Yes.

"Don't you watch the news?"

"Apparently not."

He was walking to Bertha when his cell rang and Neva's voice came through. "For what it's worth, Triple-C is a total prick for not telling you about Northstone before the meeting. It was wrong of him to spring it on you that way. Totally wrong."

"He's just covering his bases."

"That wasn't covering bases, that was an ambush. Why the hell did you just hand the guy the reins? That's what I don't get. You're not quitting, are you?"

No.

No.

No.

"Listen, do me a favor. Make sure you don't get so entrenched that you can't free up if I need you," he said.

"Why? What's going on?"

"I'm not sure yet."

22

Day 2—September 22
Tuesday Morning

Jonk and Tag swung around to pick up her car, then parked four blocks down from Tag's apartment and walked the rest of the way. She grabbed a key out of the kitchen drawer and led Jonk to the unit directly above hers, where they watched the street from behind closed blinds. "A friend of mine lives here," she said. "I'm watching her plants."

Jonk looked at the plants.

The tips were brown.

The leaves sagged.

"I hope you never have to watch me," he said.

"Not funny," she said. "Who killed Zoogie?"

"That's the big question, isn't it?" Jonk said. "It's possible that Typhoon Joe sent another recovery team besides us."

"You think?"

He shrugged.

"You know Typhoon Joe, always minimizing the risk," he said. "It could also be the Egyptian government—they keep their ear to the ground as to what's going on in the black market. They have special people they can call in to do recoveries.

They don't ask a lot of questions as to how things get done, so long as they do. Or it could be something as simple as another black-market trader. Someone who knew or suspected that Zoogie got fed by a bigger source."

Tag peeked out the window, saw nothing of interest, then pulled two diet Cokes out of the fridge and handed one to Jonk.

He popped the top and took a long swallow.

Very good.

Ice cold.

"Maybe it wasn't even related to the coin," Tag said.

Jonk nodded.

"There's always that, too. But backing up for a minute and assuming it's because of the coin, the question is whether he gave up his source or not. I think he did, otherwise the guy would have done exactly what we did, namely take his cell phone and laptop. That's why he didn't interrogate the girl. He already had what he wanted."

"I can't believe she slept through the whole thing."

Jonk grunted.

"That's drugs for you."

"If you're right that he gave up his source, then someone's ahead of us."

"Way ahead," Jonk said. "What we need to do now is fire up the cell phones and see who they've been talking to."

Tag put her hand on Jonk's.

He looked into her eyes.

There was something there he hadn't seen before.

Something deep.

Something real.

"That was pretty nice what you did with that woman, keeping the pressure on her bleeding until the very last second," she said. "If she lives, it's because of you."

"Us," he said. "You hung around to the last second too, if my memory serves me."

She smiled.

"Okay, us, but 95 percent you."

Jonk fired up Zoogie's cell phone. "This is risky, because when it's on the cops can get a GPS. If my guess is right, though, they're still working the scene. I'm going to read off phone numbers. You program them into your phone."

"Go."

23

Day 2—September 22
Tuesday Afternoon

Song called her malpractice insurer to see if, by chance, the theft of the $10,000 retainer money was a covered loss under her policy. It wasn't. "That kind of claim might fall under your premises insurance. Check there."

Yeah, right.

As if she had any.

Suddenly music vibrated up through the floor.

Great.

Her office was above a Karaoke bar. Most of the time it was dormant and not a problem. But sometimes the owner let people come over and practice, like now, apparently. The music began to take shape and turned out to be Madonna's "Material Girl." A terrible female voice suddenly rose up over the music. It vibrated into Song's feet and straight up her spine.

Suddenly the door opened and someone barged in.

It was the last person Song expected.

Shaden Jade.

"Are you aware of what your roommate just did?"

"Fenfang?"

Right.

Fenfang.

"She called me and chewed my ass out," Shaden said. "Did you give her authority to do that?"

"No, I had no idea."

"She said she was working for you now, as part of the law firm. Is that true?"

"No."

"No?"

"No."

"Then why does she know the details of my case?"

"Wait, yes."

"Yes meaning she's part of the firm?"

"Yes."

"Does that mean you're going to take responsibility for what she did?"

Song exhaled.

"Yes," she said. "Whatever it is she said, I'm sorry. It won't happen again."

"Do you know what she told me?"

No.

She didn't.

"She said she's on the run from an abusive boyfriend," Shaden said. "She said she was at the end of her rope and ran into you at a noodle bar. She said you took her in and gave her a place to stay until she could get on her feet. Is that true?"

Yes.

It was.

"She said she'd probably be dead if it wasn't for you," Shaden said. "She said you were the best person she'd ever met in her life and that I was a total scumbag for firing you."

Song pictured it.

"I had no idea she was going to do anything like that," she said. "All I can do is apologize."

Shaden pointed to the chair in front of Song's desk.

"Can I sit down?"

Sure.

Of course.

"I've never had anyone do for me what Fenfang did for you," Shaden said. "I think I underestimated you. Don't get me wrong, when I said you were perhaps too delicate, I still think I was right to an extent. But it was wrong of me to pull the case and not at least give you a chance to prove yourself."

She exhaled.

"I guess what I'm saying is that if you're still interested in being my lawyer, you have the job."

Song chewed on it.

"Fenfang's part of the firm now," she said. "If you hire me, you're hiring her too, assuming she wants to get involved."

Shaden nodded.

"I have no problem with that," she said. "I just want to be absolutely sure she appreciates the risks." The music below got louder and even more terrible. "Is someone down there killing Madonna?"

24

Day 2—September 22
Tuesday Afternoon

Teffinger had seen worse but, still, Brian Zoog didn't die pretty. The girlfriend, Winter Smyth, slept through the whole thing. When she woke this morning, two people were in the bedroom.

One of them was a man.

A Chinese man, about thirty, with blond hair, a bad left eye and a scar.

The other one was a black woman.

Light skin.

Nice legs.

"They were after a coin," Winter said.

"What kind of coin?"

"Old, real old, that's all I know about it," Winter said. "That's what Zoogie did. He bought and sold old things. Black-market things. One of the things he had for sale was an old coin—Egyptian, I think. As soon as he put it on the market, he started getting calls like never before."

"So what happened to it?"

"Well, he had it for sale for something like $5,000," she

said. "When the calls came in, he knew it was worth more. He raised the price to $20,000. Someone was supposed to get it tomorrow—well, today now that I think of it. I forgot it's already Tuesday."

"So he still had the coin as of last night?" Teffinger said.

Winter nodded.

"Where did he keep it?"

She didn't know.

"He didn't keep his business stuff in the house," she said. "He had some other place where he kept everything."

"Where?"

"I don't know."

"Are we talking about a friend's house, or a storage unit, or another apartment, or what?"

"All I know is that he didn't want the stuff at the house, for my protection," she said.

Teffinger studied her.

"You look really familiar," he said. "Do I know you from somewhere?"

She shrugged.

"I used to dance at Cadillac Sam's, if you've ever been there."

Teffinger nodded.

"That's probably it."

"You don't recognize me with my clothes on."

Teffinger smiled.

"I know you're joking, but there's probably some truth to that."

"There definitely is," Winter said. "I see lots of guys from the club on the streets. They have no idea who I am. That's where I met Zoogie. Cadillac Sam's."

Zoogie's cell phone was nowhere to be found, so Teffinger got the process in motion to get the records from his provider.

He interviewed neighbors.

He took notes.

It was doubtful that the Chinese man and the black woman were the killers because one of them—the woman, to be precise—called 911 after Winter fell. But it sounded like they were after the same thing as the person or people who killed Zoogie, meaning it would be nice to round them up and ask a few questions.

His thoughts turned to Chase St. John.

He'd see her tonight at eight o'clock.

25

Day 2—September 22
Tuesday Afternoon

Jonk paced nervously outside a BART station two miles down the road while Tag drove past Zoogie's house every half hour to see if the cops had finished processing the scene. After two hours she called and said, "I think they left. All the cars that were in the driveway and street are gone. The front door's shut and has yellow crime-scene tape over it. I don't see anyone left."

"Okay."

"No, not okay," she said. "There's nothing about any of this that's okay. I think we should abort."

"We can't."

"Yes we can."

"It'll be fine."

"Then let's at least wait until dark."

Jonk exhaled.

"No time," he said. "Wait for me where we discussed."

"Jonk—"

"Are you going to be there?"

"Yes."

"Are you sure?"

"Yes, don't worry."

Jonk hung up, got on the BART, took it to the station just south of Zoogie's house, then walked the rest of the way on foot.

He entered the property from the back.

He had to admit, this wasn't the most insane thing he'd ever done, but it was right up there. Breaking into a crime scene was a serious offense. Doing it as soon as the cops left was a particular slap in the face.

Jonk stepped over Zoogie's blood—which was a lot more prominent now that the man's body didn't cover it—then tried the back door.

It was locked.

So were the windows.

He looked for nosy neighbors, saw none, shimmied up the post for the bedroom deck and found the sliding glass door closed but unlocked. He stepped inside cat-quiet, shut the glass behind him and stood still, listening for sounds.

He heard nothing.

Only silence.

The place was pretty much as he last saw it. In fact, it looked like the cops had taken an effort to disturb things as little as possible.

Jonk started in the bedroom.

He checked the mattress and found no trap compartments.

He tugged at the carpeting along all the edges where it met the walls and found it solidly tacked.

He checked behind the posters taped on the walls and found undisturbed plaster.

He checked the master closet and found no false ceilings.

Same for the bathroom.

He headed downstairs.

Zoogie wasn't the world's biggest or greatest black-market dealer, but he was a player nonetheless, meaning he needed at least some storage space. Not everything would be as small as a coin. In fact, artifacts of any significance ended up with custom cases for protection during shipping and storage.

Those filled up space.

It took some time, but Jonk searched every nook and cranny of the entire house, including the garage and the attic. He didn't find a single place devoted to artifact storage and, on the contrary, learned that every cubic centimeter was taken up with junk.

He did find something of interest, though, namely Zoogie's checkbook, which he shoved into his back pocket.

That reminded him to look for bank statements.

He found those in the bottom drawer of the desk on top of a pouch of pot.

He left the pot.

He took the papers.

26

Day 2—September 22
Tuesday Afternoon

Song's job, now that she had it, was to find out if Shaden actually killed a woman Sunday night or whether the whole incident at Rekker's house was a charade. She had no idea how to go about it but Fenfang did.

"I'll cozy up to him."

Song rolled her eyes.

"Stop it," she said. "We need to be serious."

"I am serious." She retreated in thought, then said, "I got it. I'll hire him as my lawyer."

"Yeah, right."

"It's either that or try to meet him by accident," she said. "The accident route would be cheaper if he fell for it, but the problem is that I might not be able to get his attention long enough to set a hook. That wouldn't be an issue if I walked into his office as a client." She took a long drag, blew smoke at Song and said, "So what do you think? Accident or client?"

"I think you're crazy."

She headed for the door and said over her shoulder, "Call Shaden and see what she thinks."

"Where you going?"

"Cigarettes," she said, crinkling an empty pack and tossing it in the trash. "Think of a good case, if we go that route. Make it something where I'm all vulnerable and innocent and at-risk and need him to protect me. You know, a damsel in distress."

"Where do you get this stuff?"

Fenfang ignored her.

Then she said, "That will be your contribution, to come up with a good fake case. Also, be sure it's something where I only have to go to his office once or twice or three times. We can't afford too big a deal, not at his rates."

The woman smiled and left.

Song went to the window and watched her walk down the alley and disappear around the corner. She had to admit, the woman had a good wiggle.

Her office was cluttered with legal files.

Sitting on this.

Leaning on that.

Every single one of them was small.

Suddenly her whole office was too small. The walls were too close, the ceiling was too low and the windows didn't have enough light. She headed outside and walked, not in any particular direction, but eventually finding herself getting closer and closer to the financial center.

This is where the power was.

The money.

The movers and shakers.

The oversized, contemporary offices.

The skyscraper views.

The fountains.

She walked all the way through the district and didn't stop

until she got to the Ferry Plaza Farmer's Market, where she strolled around in the crowds and bought a plate of sushi.

Shaden Jade was her first big case.

She wasn't going to blow it.

Fenfang's accidental meeting concept, while potentially viable, was fraught with too many problems, the biggest of which is that an opportunity might not materialize for weeks or even months. The more Song thought about it, the more she liked the client concept.

Okay.

Think.

Turn Fenfang into a damsel in distress.

Seagulls flew.

Sailboats sailed.

She hardly paid attention.

Twenty minutes later she got to her feet, surprised at what she'd come up with.

She was halfway back to the office when she turned to check for cars before crossing California. Thirty steps behind was a long-haired man with a blue bandana.

She'd seen him before, earlier today.

She remembered, partly because his face was rough and manly, but more because it was tanned, as if he wasn't from around here.

He wore dark sunglasses.

The sleeves of his T-shirt were rolled up.

Muscular arms stuck out.

Right now, his face was pointed at the ass of a woman walking in front of him. When he turned to Song and saw her looking at him, his step slowed, not much but definitely some.

Then he cut to the right and disappeared into the crowd.

27

Day 2—September 22
Tuesday Afternoon

Normally Teffinger would have jumped head first into Zoogie's murder and, to give him credit, he did get a BOLO out for the blond Chinese guy with the scar and his African American companion. His head, however, was filled with Condor.

Condor.

Condor.

Condor.

Teffinger needed to get back into the man's house and find the souvenirs. Then his certainty would go from 99 percent to a hundred. He pointed Bertha that way, just to swing by and take a look.

Traffic was snarled.

Fender-benders were everywhere.

It took him more than half an hour to get to Condor's and, when he did, he saw something he didn't expect, namely the man's six-four frame walking down the front steps. He stopped at street level and looked around as if expecting someone to pick him up.

He wasn't bad looking, better than average actually, with a hefty resemblance to the look Nicholas Cage had in Bangkok Dangerous, except Condor was stronger. Teffinger was in better shape and could take him in a bare-knuckles fistfight if it ever came to it, but it would take some time and wouldn't come easy. If Condor had a weapon, even something as simple as a baseball bat, the end result might not be good.

Teffinger's chest tightened.

He was going to drive right past the man.

There was no way to avoid it.

He stared straight out the windshield, as if oblivious to the fact that he was anywhere near the man's house. Just as he passed, Condor slapped the passenger door.

Teffinger turned.

What he saw he could hardly believe.

Condor was waving for him to stop.

The man wanted to talk.

There were no parking spots on the street.

There never were.

Teffinger pulled into a private driveway two doors down, shifted into park and waited.

Ten seconds later, Condor leaned his head in the window and said, "Teffinger, I told you before, this is not a good surveillance vehicle. What do you call this thing again?"

"Bertha."

"Right, Bertha," Condor said. "That's the good thing about the old classics, you can give them a name and no one bats an eye. Try doing that with your two-year-old Honda Accord."

"That's a valid point."

"Bertha," Condor said. "I like it. It fits."

"I'm glad you approve," Teffinger said.

"Hey, I'm actually glad I caught you driving past, because it will save me a trip down to the station," Condor said. "I need to make a report about someone breaking into my house last night."

"Really?"

Condor nodded.

"I wouldn't have even known about it except for one small thing," Condor said. "There's a sliding glass door in my bedroom that leads to an outside deck. That door was locked before I left last night. When I came home, it was unlocked, as if someone had been in the house and left that way."

Teffinger cocked his head.

"Were you drinking?"

Condor nodded.

"Maybe you're not remembering things clearly. That happens sometimes."

"Right, I agree," Condor said. "Except this time, there was something else funny. It was raining last night. The bedroom carpet was wet by the door."

"Maybe you have a leak."

Condor tilted his head.

"Maybe."

"Was anything taken?"

"Not that I know of."

Teffinger shrugged.

"I don't know what to tell you."

"It's not a big deal, I just thought I'd mention it when I saw you driving past," Condor said. "Maybe you could clarify something for me. If someone breaks into my house, I have the right to shoot them, don't I?"

Teffinger flicked hair out of his face.

"You do, but only if a reasonable man would view the situation as a threat to their life. So if they're running away, you can't shoot them. If they're coming at you, or even just standing there and not backing down, you can."

"So I need to be careful to not shoot them in the back."

Teffinger nodded.

"Right. Shoot them in the chest. Or better yet, the face."

"Why the face?"

"Because they don't wear bulletproof vests over the face."

Condor smiled and said, "Thanks. I knew you'd be able to help."

The man walked away.

Teffinger tapped his fingers on the steering wheel.

Then he opened the door and stepped out. "Hey, Condor, wait a minute."

The man stopped and turned.

Teffinger walked over to him.

"SJK will be coming around pretty soon."

"That's true."

"Maybe you should come down to the station that night, just hang around in sight, that way we can cross you off the list once and for all."

Condor smiled.

"I'd like to, but I already have plans," he said. "Thanks for the invite, though."

28

Day 2—September 22
Tuesday Afternoon

Jonk dyed his hair black and wondered if it would be best to split with Tag at this point. Separately, they'd be almost invisible. Together, not even close. On the other hand, she knew the geography and had nice eyes.

"Got something," she shouted.

"What?"

"Something good."

"Like what?"

"Like something you need to see."

He headed for the bedroom and found her on the mattress wearing only a pair of white cotton panties and a lacy white bra. Zoogie's monthly bank statements were on the sheets to her side. She was on her stomach, propped on her elbows, studying Zoogie's checkbook.

Her ass stuck up.

"It looks like someone got comfortable," he said.

She sat up and said, "Focus, Cowboy. Look right here."

He looked.

She was pointing to a line entry where Zoogie wrote a check

to MCM in the amount of $113.32.

"He writes the same check every month," Tag said. "It's the only monthly check that isn't a phone bill or water bill or something explainable. This has to be for rental space."

Jonk nodded, impressed.

"MCM; what's it stand for?"

She flipped back even further and found an entry in the same amount, $113.32, for Marina. "It's either Marina CM or MC Marina."

"Google 'em," Jonk said.

She did, then smiled.

"Mission Creek Marina," she said. "It's on the bay side of the city, just south of South Beach Harbor."

She wiggled into jeans.

"Pure poetry," Jonk said.

As Tag drove and an old Van Morrison song, "Brown Eyed Girl," spilled out of the radio, Jonk worked the Internet with his handheld, checking out what might be available to rent at the Mission Creek Marina. "You can't get a slip for $113 a month, not even close," he said. "They're a lot more. This has to be for dry dock."

"You mean like a boatyard?"

"Right," he said. "The rates vary depending on the length of the boat but the fee's going to be right around what he's paying, give or take. The question is, how do we find out which one's his?"

Tag tilted her head.

"Easy, we ask."

"We ask?"

Right.

"And by we, I mean me," she said. "You stay in the car."

There was no separate office for the marina. Everything from slips to boat rentals to gas to hot dogs was run out of one main building. Four or five employees bustled behind the counter. Tag waited until one got free, a tall skinny girl with a nametag that said Carly, and asked, "Do you know Zoogie?"

Yes.

She did.

"His boat's for sale and I'm here to look at it," Tag said. "Can you tell me where it is?"

"Dry dock."

"Right, I know, I just don't know where in dry dock."

Carly looked it up.

"One oh one."

"One oh one?"

"Right, the spaces are numbered. His is one oh one."

Tag smiled and headed for the door.

"Thanks."

Over her shoulder she heard, "Do you want the code to the gate or do you already have it?"

She stepped back and said, "I have it, but you may as well give it to me again, just to be on the safe side."

Dry dock was just south of the loading ramp, enclosed in a chain-link fence, home to hundreds of boats on trailers. Most were sailboats, midsized, twenty to thirty feet, but there were plenty of larger vessels too, including several on stands that looked like they'd been there since the dawn of time. Tag pulled up to the key box and brought the car to a stop.

She couldn't reach the pad from her window and Jonk opened the door to get out.

Just as he did, a loud chain rattled and the gate pulled to

the right.

A black van was on the other side, waiting to come out.

Behind the wheel was a woman.

Her head was bandaged.

She looked familiar.

Tag was punching the radio buttons, stopped on an old Rihanna song, "SOS," and cranked it up.

The gate opened far enough for a car to pass.

The van sped out.

"Shit!" Jonk said.

"What's wrong?"

"That was Zoogie's girlfriend, the one from his house last night—"

Go!

Go!

Go!

29

Day 2—September 22
Tuesday Afternoon

Song turned abruptly several times on the walk back to her office and never saw the blue bandana again, but it didn't matter because she could still feel him. A private investigator, or muscleman, or hitman, or whatever he was didn't come free. Rekker was shelling out money. That meant Shaden posed a very real threat to him—so much so that he was not only tailing Shaden but her lawyer as well—which in turn meant he was dirty.

How dirty was the question.

And in what way, that was the other question.

Maybe the incident at Rekker's house Sunday night was an actual killing, but Rekker couldn't report it because the gun the woman had in her hand was dirty—previously used in another crime, or unregistered, or something like that.

Maybe the woman herself was dirty.

Maybe she was a fugitive being harbored by Rekker, or something like that.

Something was going on.

Something big.

That much was clear.

Back at the law office, the door wouldn't open, which made sense because Song was using a four-year-old key in a three-hour-old lock. She eventually got inside to find everything as she'd left it.

Good.

She locked up and headed upstairs.

Fenfang was in the bathroom, blow-drying her hair that was now blond instead of black. She saw Song's reflection, grinned and said, "Pretty sexy, huh?"

Actually it was.

"I talked to Shaden about the fake-case idea," Song said. "She thinks it's brilliant and has told me to go forward and spare no expenses. There's a new problem, though. I went for a walk and was pretty sure someone was tailing me, a guy with a blue bandana."

"Why?"

"I don't know exactly, I only know it's not necessarily a good thing."

Fenfang smiled.

"Not necessarily a good thing. I love the way you talk sometimes."

Song ignored it.

"The problem is, I don't know how much surveillance they've done without us even knowing it," she said. "You might already be on their radar screen."

Fenfang shrugged.

"Doubtful."

"Why?"

"Because we haven't been outside together."

Song chewed on it.

Maybe she was right.

Maybe she wasn't.

"If we go forward, we're going to need to get you out of my apartment and set you up somewhere," she said. "You'll need a cell phone, a name, a wardrobe, spending money, the works."

"Rain," Fenfang said.

Song heard the word, but it didn't make sense.

"Come again?"

"Rain," she said. "That's what I want my new name to be."

"First or last?"

"First."

"It sounds too hippie."

"I don't care, it's my name and that's what I want."

Song considered it.

"What do you want for a last name?"

"I don't care, it just has to go with Rain."

"How about Cloud?"

Fenfang punched her on the arm.

"Not funny."

"It goes."

"Yeah, too good," Fenfang said.

"Okay, then, Shower."

"What'd you do, take an evil pill this morning?" A pause, then, "Did you come up with a fake case yet?"

"Actually I did."

"Let's hear it."

"Soon," she said. "First let me finish working out the details."

30

Day 2—September 22
Tuesday Afternoon

Teffinger just got Bertha back into traffic when his phone rang and the voice of the chief, Triple-C, came through. "We need to talk." Twenty minutes later, in the chief's office, the man lit a cigarette next to the windows, took a long drag, blew the smoke outside and got right to the point. "I never took you for a quitter."

Teffinger tossed hair out of his face.

"What are you talking about?"

"You know what the hell I'm talking about," Triple-C said. "We can't have you dropping out of this SJK mess just because of some bruised ego. Yeah, we brought Northstone in. And, yeah, we should have told you about it beforehand. But you need to stay on the team, whether you like him or not."

"I don't have a problem with him."

"Bullshit," Triple-C said. "You dropped out. You handed the reins to him and dropped out. You didn't even stay for the whole meeting."

"I went to the restroom," Teffinger said. "A homicide call came in. I was the only one there. I took it."

Triple-C frowned.

"Play games if you want, but what I need is for you to be on the team," he said. "I'm not going to belabor it. Make up your mind whether you want to be around here for the long term or not."

A knock came at the door.

Lance Northstone walked in, looking intense. He saw Teffinger and said, "Sorry. Am I interrupting something?"

Triple-C shook his head.

"No. Come in."

Northstone sank into a chair and said, "We know he's going to put a yellow rose in her mouth. Maybe he clips them from somewhere or maybe he buys them from a florist. We can't track clippings but we can track purchases."

Triple-C nodded.

"Okay."

"What I propose is that we cut off every yellow rose growing anywhere in the city to make sure he has to buy it," Northstone said. "We'll get in touch with all the florists in the city except a half dozen and get them to not stock yellow roses. That will force him to go to one of our finite sources—again, five or six stores. For those stores, we'll set up surveillance and monitor every purchase."

The chief cast an eye on Teffinger for his reaction.

"There are a lot of roses in Golden Gate Park," he said.

Northstone showed no expression.

"Then we'll need a lot of clippers," he said.

Ten minutes later, Teffinger spotted Neva at the coffee pot and headed over. "What was the big meeting with the chief all about?"

Teffinger frowned.

"He's totally stressed. I got the feeling he thinks his job is on the line," he said. "He's ready to follow this Northstone guy wherever he leads him. Now they're on a gardening adventure."

She wrinkled her forehead, confused.

"Come on, I need you," Teffinger said.

"Why? What's up?"

Teffinger took a long noisy slurp of coffee and lowered his voice.

"Pull the file on Pamela Zoom," he said.

The third victim.

The waitress.

"Why?" Neva asked.

"I just bumped into Condor."

"Condor?"

Right.

Condor.

"That witness said he wasn't the one she saw," Neva said.

"Yeah, yeah, I know all that," Teffinger said. "Here's the thing. The third victim, Pamela Zoom, the waitress, was wearing small loop earrings during her shift the night she disappeared. They weren't there when she was found. Do you remember?"

No.

She didn't.

"They had a real small diameter," Teffinger said. "Half an inch, maybe less."

Okay.

"So?"

"So, Condor was wearing an earring exactly like that when I saw him not more than a hour ago."

Neva frowned.

"That's a generic thing," she said. "You can walk down Market Street and find ten more in as many minutes, both guys and girls."

Teffinger didn't care.

"It's so perfect," he said, "wearing a souvenir out in public. That's exactly the kind of guy we're dealing with. Here's what we're going to do. We're going to go through all the files and refresh our memories as to every souvenir that got taken. Then you're going to follow him. You're going to mark down every place he goes. We're going to get every security tape we can and see what else we can find him wearing—rings or chains or whatever. With any luck, he switches to something new every day."

"You're not serious," she said.

He was.

Dead.

"This is just between you and me," he said. "I don't want anyone else to know about it."

She almost asked why.

But said, "Okay."

31

Day 2—September 22
Tuesday Afternoon

By the time Tag got her Accord turned around from dry dock, the black van was a long ways down the road, swaying dangerously as it disappeared around a curve. "We're losing her," Jonk said.

"I know that."

"Go."

"I already am."

Jonk pushed Tag's right knee towards the floorboard, forcing her foot all the way down on the pedal. The car sped up, not a lot, but perceptible, then swung around the curve.

The van came back into sight.

So did something they didn't expect, namely another car, a white sedan with dark tinted windows, right on the van's bumper.

What the hell?

"I can't drive this fast," Tag said.

"Yes you can. Don't slow down."

"We're going to crash."

"No we're not. Just keep going."

They were heading south, paralleling the cold choppy waters of the bay to their left. It wasn't clear if the sedan was chasing the van or was just a tailgater.

Then it rammed forward.

The back end of the van swayed momentarily then straightened out.

"Who is it?" Tag said.

"The guy who killed Zoogie."

Tag's foot eased up.

Jonk pushed her leg down.

"Don't lose them."

The sedan rammed the van again.

The swaying in the van's backside got more and more pronounced.

"She's going to crash," Tag said.

"I see that."

The sedan rammed forward again. The van veered to the left and crossed the center line, out of control, then overcompensated to the right and flipped. It rolled once, landed back on the wheels, rolled to the left and then disappeared over an embankment.

"Shit!"

The white sedan crossed the centerline and screeched to a stop at the edge of the embankment. The driver looked down, briefly, then floored it, throwing gravel from the front wheels. It was already around a twist in the road by the time Tag got there and slammed the Accord to a stop.

Jonk got out and ran to the edge .

The water was a good ways off, fifty yards minimum, down a precipitously steep cliff. The roof of the van was visible in the water, twenty meters off shore. The air inside was keeping it afloat, but not for long. Not much of it was showing, and even that disappeared when a wave rolled over it.

Jonk headed down.

It was steep, a lot steeper than he thought.

He got ten yards, then the inevitable happened.

His foot twisted.

He lost his balance.

Rather than tumble, he kicked off with his other leg, trying to get enough air to carry him past the jagged rocks below and into the water.

Halfway down he saw he wasn't going to make it.

32

Day 2—September 22
Tuesday Afternoon

L ate Tuesday afternoon, Song walked through Chinatown and looked in store windows, ostensibly shop-
ping, but using reflections and mirrors to see if Mr.
Blue Bandana was in tow. She didn't really expect to see him
and wasn't prepared for it when it actually did happen.

There he was.

Across the street.

Three stores down.

Her instinct was to run, just get the hell out of there at
full trot, so fast that he couldn't dare follow without becoming
obvious. She took two brisk steps and stopped. Then she did
something she didn't expect.

Something un-delicate.

She looked directly at him and headed that way, already pic-
turing the conversation. *Get the hell off my tail or I'll haul you and
your little boss Rekker into court for a restraining order.* Five steps
later, the man turned and walked briskly around the corner. By
the time Song got there, he was gone.

Her heart pounded.

Her hands shook.

She held one in the other to steady them. Then she turned back, abruptly, needing more than anything to get out of there. Wheels suddenly squealed and a vehicle slid into a panic stop just short of running her over. It came so close that it actually touched her stomach.

She was in the street.

It was her fault.

The driver was wide-eyed, even more startled than she was.

The vehicle was a taxi.

No one was in the back seat.

Song slapped her hand on the hood, got into the back and said, "Drive!" The man turned and stared at her for a second, then took off.

At first, she made him head down Jackson Street out of the area. Then she made him go back and zigzag through Chinatown. What she hoped and feared would happen actually did—she spotted the blue bandana.

"Pull up next to that guy and stop!"

The driver said, "In English, lady."

She repeated it.

In English this time.

The car slid to a stop.

She threw a twenty into the front seat and stepped out.

33

Day 2—September 22
Tuesday Afternoon

Late Tuesday afternoon Bertha decided to break down.
In true diva style, she didn't do it on a side street. Oh
no, not Bertha. She broke down on Market Street. Not
on the side, either, but directly on the cable car tracks. As if
on some type of conspiratorial cue, a trolley clanked down
the street almost immediately, jam-packed with passengers to
the point of hanging off the back. It was all the startled driver
could do to release the car from the cable and get the peo-
ple-moving beast to a stop before rearranging Bertha's posterior forever.

Traffic backed up.

Horns honked.

No one was amused.

Five guys came over and helped Teffinger push Bertha up
the street into the first available parking spot, which was a lot
farther than any of them wanted it to be.

Teffinger offered money.

They refused.

He was glad.

He was popping the hood when his phone rang and the voice of Neva came through.

"Bad news," she said.

"Hold on."

Teffinger got the hood all the way open and said, "Go ahead," as he looked around. The fan belt was in place, frayed, but still alive and living where it was supposed to.

"Condor made me," she said.

Teffinger leaned against Bertha's front fender.

"Tell me you didn't say what you just said," he said.

"I don't know how, I was way back," Neva said.

"How do you know he made you?"

"Because he looked directly at me and did one of those things with his fingers," she said.

Huh?

What things?

"You know, where you take your index finger and middle finger and point them at your eyes, then you turn them around and point them at someone else. It means *I see you* or *I'm watching you*. That's what he did to me."

Teffinger exhaled.

"Bertha just had a nervous breakdown," he said.

"Another one? You need to retire that girl. Honest, Teffinger, I was being careful with Condor."

"I know you were."

A pause.

Then she said, "Now what?"

"Now we go to Plan B."

"What's Plan B?"

"I don't know," he said. "I didn't even know we needed it until ten seconds ago."

"I'm sorry."

"It's not your fault," he said. "Forget it."

Thirty seconds after he hung up, Teffinger figured out the cause of Bertha's indigestion, namely the negative battery terminal was all crusted over.

He cleaned it up.

Bertha thanked him by firing.

"Good thing you're so cute," he said.

Two blocks down the road he called Neva and said, "Meet me at the boat."

"Why?"

"Because I just figured out Plan B."

34

Day 2—September 22
Tuesday Afternoon

The swell rose up just as Jonk landed, giving him two feet of water over the jags of the rocks, not enough to keep him from making contact but enough to keep him from hitting full force. His head went under. The water was cold and immediately filled his eyes and nose and ears. A sharp pain fired from his left shoulder and shot straight to his brain. He swam to the van, frantic.

It was lower than before.

Only one corner of the top broke the surface.

He took a deep breath and dived down to the driver's door. Visibility was next to nothing. He felt around for the doorknob, found it and swung the door open.

"Help me!"

Bubbles shot to the surface.

Just like that, the air from inside was gone.

The van was already sinking, fast.

Jonk grabbed the woman, pulled her out, tucked her in one arm and swam for the surface. The woman kicked and fought but he didn't let go.

Hold on!

Hold on!

Hold on!

When they broke the surface the woman screamed, "I can't swim! Don't let me die!"

"Relax your body!"

She didn't.

Not even close.

Instead she tried to climb up him. He was the only solid thing there, the only thing she could get on to get her head out of the water.

Jonk couldn't get her into position.

"Calm down!"

She didn't.

Anything but.

Her fingernails gouged into Jonk's skin.

He had no choice but to punch her in the face.

As soon as he did, the fight went out of her body. When it did, Jonk was able to lock an arm around her and get her to shore.

They collapsed on the rocks just out of reach of the water, too exhausted to go another step, and didn't move for a long time, ten or fifteen minutes at least. Then Jonk got some wind back in his lungs, pulled the woman—Winter—to her feet and said, "Let's go."

She cast an eye on the embankment.

"It's too steep."

Jonk agreed.

They walked down the shore, eventually found an easier way up, then doubled back in the direction of Tag's car. It came into sight around a curve, still three or four hundred yards away. Jonk hoped that Tag would spot them and double back but that didn't happen because that's the way his life worked.

They had to walk all the way to the car, every single step.

When they got there, Tag was gone.

The keys were in the ignition.

Her purse was in the console between the seats.

But she was gone.

Jonk shouted, "Tag!"

No answer.

"Tag!"

Nothing.

"Where are you!"

Silence.

He ran to the embankment and looked down.

No Tag.

He looked up the road.

No Tag.

Same thing the other direction.

The white sedan must have swung back and taken her.

His brain spun and he slammed his hand on the trunk of the car so violently that Winter jumped.

35

Day 2—September 22
Tuesday Afternoon

The blue-bandana man didn't see Song until she grabbed his arm from behind and spun him around. "Who the hell are you?" The shock on his face was palpable. "Why are you following me?"

His eyes darted across the street and then back at her. .

"Lower your voice. You're making a scene."

"I don't give a shit. Stay away from me. You got it?"

She expected him to back off and disappear into the crowd.

Instead, he grabbed her hand and pulled her into the nearest doorway, which turned out to be a Chinese herb shop filled with aromas that dated back to ancient times. He pulled her to the window and pointed across the street.

"See that man over there?"

She focused.

"Which one?"

"The one in the white shirt."

She saw who he was talking about, a Chinese man in his late twenties. His right arm was heavily tattooed.

"Do you know him?" the man asked.

"No. Why?"

"He's been following you."

"Why?"

The man ignored her and instead looked towards the back of the shop. The shopkeeper was an elderly Chinese woman with a shy face.

"Is there a back way out of here?"

"No English," the woman said.

Song repeated the question, in Chinese.

The woman nodded and pointed towards a smaller, adjoining room.

"Leave that way," the man told Song.

"I don't understand. What's going on?"

"Just do it."

Then he left out the front door and walked in the same direction as the man in the white shirt.

Song stood there, uncertain what to do, then left by the back door and walked to her office through the thickest crowds she could find, with one eye over her shoulder.

Maybe what just happened was real.

Or maybe the blue bandana duped her.

She couldn't know which.

One thing she did know, though. Blue bandana would be replaced with a fresh face now that he was busted.

This was all related to Shaden's case.

Something was back there in the shadows.

Something big.

Something that didn't want Song poking around.

She locked the office behind her and walked up the wooden steps to her apartment.

Fenfang wasn't there.

She poured a glass of white wine, made a half-sandwich and carried them back down to her office, together with a small bag of chips.

She was taking the first bite out of the sandwich when her phone rang.

36

Day 2—September 22
Tuesday Afternoon

Teffinger's sailboat had a name painted in red letters on the transom. The previous owner had a different name, NO VNE, which stood for No Velocity Not to Exceed. That made sense for him, being a jet pilot, but didn't for Teffinger, who could hardly even be a passenger much less a pilot. It was bad luck to change the name of a boat but he did it anyway.

Now it was Bad Add Vice.

He didn't come up with it, an old girlfriend named Chance did.

"The Bad stands for you, because you're such a bad ass," she said. "The Add Vice stands for the fact that you need someone to add vice to your life."

"Like you?"

"Precisely," she said, "like me. The whole thing together, Bad Add Vice, stands for the fact what whenever you give advice, it turns out to be bad. So it's multilayered. What do you think?"

He laughed.

And that was it.

In many ways the vessel was the nautical equivalent of Bertha, meaning good bones but bad skin. Being an older model, there was a truckload of exterior teak, too much for anyone who had a job to keep sanded and fresh. The hull was thick and built for the worst. It was also faded to a flat, industrial off-white.

The window trimmings were brass, crusted with blue.

The interior by contrast was spacious and nice, with rich wood, a complete galley, a head with shower, and most importantly a forward berth big enough for Teffinger's frame.

He was sitting on the deck, leaning against the mast and eating a bowl of cereal, when Neva showed up.

She looked at her watch and frowned. "We're in the middle of a workday, SJK is right around the corner, and here you are doing some kind of Jimmy Buffet thing. Why are we here instead of at the office?"

"Nice to see you, too," he said. "Want some cereal?"

"Cereal? They still make that stuff?"

He patted the deck next to him and she sat down.

Seagulls flew overhead.

A sea lion's bark came from down the dock.

"I have it on good authority that Condor has files of all the SJK victims in his credenza," he said.

Neva looked skeptical.

"How would you possibly know that?"

"I have my sources," he said. "Don't tell anyone, though. It's confidential information. No one's supposed to know. Can you do that for me? Keep quiet about it—"

She nodded.

"Of course."

"I'm telling you because I need you fully invested in this," he said. "I'm going to bring him down. I'd like you to help."

She retreated in thought.

"What else did the birdie tell you, besides the files?"

"Nothing."

"Did the files contain photographs or anything like that?"

"No, nothing that incriminating," Teffinger said. "They were newspaper clippings and things like that. My guess is that he collected them after the fact as sort of a little shrine to himself."

"Not necessarily."

Teffinger wrinkled his forehead.

"What do you mean?"

"Think about it," she said. "We have that witness who said she saw someone on the street near Syling Wu's house the night she got murdered."

"Exactly."

"Hear me out," she said. "She said he looked a little like Nicholas Cage from his Bangkok Dangerous movie."

"Correct."

"You had seen someone like that several times in the Nob Hill area and tracked down Condor. You brought him in for a lineup. The woman said it wasn't him."

"She was lying," Teffinger said. "She was scared and she lied. The files prove it."

"Not necessarily."

"Why not?"

"Think it through," Neva said. "Condor has money and rubs elbows with lawyers. Sooner or later, he's going to mention that he was actually pulled in for a lineup as a possible suspect in the SJK killings."

"Okay. So what?"

"The lawyer's going to give him some advice," Neva said. "Do you know what it's going to be?"

"No. Enlighten me."

"It's going to be for Condor to get information on when each of the SJK killings took place and find out which ones he has alibis for—out of town, at a function, whatever," she said. "That way, if the police ever came snooping around again, he could whip it out and cut things off at the base."

Teffinger's chest tightened.

She could be right.

The explanation was potentially real.

"You have a remarkable ability to take something that's crystal clear and make it muddy," he said. "Did anyone ever tell you that?"

"Syling Hu was the first victim who wasn't blond," he said. "All the others prior to her could have been random choices. I think she was connected to the killer."

"I thought your theory as to Syling Hu was that SJK was just screwing with the city so no one would feel safe," she said. "He was looking to make his footprint of fear bigger. He was becoming a publicity hound."

He shoved cereal in his mouth and chewed.

"That was my theory," he said. "It still is, but only 10 percent. Now I'm more of the theory that she's connected to the guy."

Neva wasn't impressed.

"We ran down every single person in her life," she said. "Everyone checked out."

Teffinger nodded.

It was true.

"I've come up with an extension of that theory," he said.

"Here it is. She was connected to the killer but she didn't know it. She was connected to him because she posed some kind of a threat to him. That's why he killed her."

"What kind of a threat?"

"I don't know," he said. "But that's what I want you to work on, with an emphasis on whether she had any information, knowledge or possessions that might have been a threat to Condor."

She frowned.

"This is thin."

"I'll take thick if you have it. Do you?"

She punched him in the arm.

"I have a thick-headed boss," she said. "Does that count?"

37

Day 2—September 22
Tuesday Evening

Minute after minute passed, then hour after hour, and still the people from the white sedan who took Tag didn't call to negotiate her release in exchange for whatever information Jonk or Winter had as to the location of the treasure. Maybe they were busy interrogating Tag to exhaustion first. Maybe they had already killed her. Jonk didn't know. All he knew is that he was going to hunt them to the ends of the earth and rip their eyes out if they hurt a single hair on her head.

That would be his life mission.

Guaranteed.

End of story.

Winter wasn't going to leave Jonk's side, not a chance, not after he snatched her from death's grip. She'd help him in any way she could. In fact, she'd already answered every question he had.

Her story was simple and believable.

She was Zoogie's partner in crime, but only to an extent.

Zoogie was the mastermind and the dealmaker.

Winter was the gopher.

She picked up items, often out of state.

She made deliveries.

Zoogie kept everything at the dry dock, in an old sailboat with a fortified interior.

Earlier today, Winter went to the boat and cleaned out everything. One of those things happened to be the ancient gold coin, which she shoved in her pocket. That was the only artifact of ancient Egyptian heritage. All the other things, while interesting and potentially worth a fair dollar, weren't of interest. Right now they were in the van at the bottom of the bay.

No doubt salvageable.

Jonk could care less.

Winter had no idea who the people in the white sedan were. All she was able to see is that there were two of them. The driver was a man. The passenger was a woman. They had dark complexions and black hair.

"Egyptian?"

"I don't know," she said. "Foreign, for sure."

The big issue of where Zoogie got the coin still remained. Winter didn't know anything about that. Zoogie didn't have a notebook or anything similar where he kept a written record of what he bought and sold.

"He kept it all in his head," Winter said.

She took the coin out of her pocket, twisted it in her fingers and took a long look at Jonk.

"Do you want this?"

He shook his head.

"No, that's yours."

She put it back in her pocket and said, "I think it's cursed." A pause, then, "You like her."

"Who?"

"Tag."

He retreated in thought.

"The first rule of my job is to not get emotionally involved with anyone," he said.

She studied him.

Then she said, "You like her. It's okay."

Winter turned out to be one of those people who was easily underestimated at first, both in looks and intellect. When Jonk first saw her, she struck him as cute. Now she was more than that. Now her smile was slightly crooked, her teeth were whiter and her voice sounded like a song. She wasn't just a pothead, either. Maybe at night, but not in the day. Her stomach was taut and peeked out every time she raised an arm and her shirt rode up. In another time and place, Jonk would have been interested. He got the feeling she might have been, too.

Right now, however, he could only think of Tag.

They ate supper at Cha Cha Cha on Haight Street, a lively place that served Latin American food in a variety of small dishes.

Jonk showed her the phone numbers and contact information he'd copied from Zoogie's phone. She studied them and said, "I just thought of something."

"What?"

"Zoogie was supposed to sell the coin tonight."

Right.

Jonk remembered that.

"Maybe the buyer knows where Zoogie got it," she said. "There must have been some discussion, wouldn't you think?"

Jonk shook his head in disapproval.

"What, you think I'm wrong?" Winter asked.

"No, I think you're right," he said. "I'm just amazed that I didn't think of it myself."

"You have an excuse."

"I do?"

Yes.

He did.

"You got Tag on the brain," she said.

Jonk heard the words but hardly processed them. "Where would Zoogie meet the buyer?"

"He had a place."

Jonk stood up, pulled two twenties out of his wallet and slipped them under the water glass on the table.

"Come on."

38

Day 2—September 22
Tuesday Night

Tuesday night after dark, Song watched the alley from behind a slit in the window covering of her apartment. The headlights of a taxi pulled to the edge of the alley and stopped. She bounded down the stairs two at a time with a manila folder in hand and hopped into the back. The driver took off as soon as the door closed.

A light but steady rain fell out of a black sky.

The driver was a heavy-set man with a thick, rippled neck and a crew cut. Rapid gum chewing popped his jaw muscles.

"You're Song, right?"

Yes.

She was.

"Where are we going?" she asked.

"It's a secret," he said. "I could tell you but then I'd have to kill you."

He turned and gave her an evil look to punctuate it.

She smiled.

He zigzagged around the city with one eye in the rearview mirror to be sure they weren't being followed, then dropped

Song off half an hour later in front a powder-blue house on Balboa street, wedged in a long string of connected houses.

"This is it," he said. "Your friend already paid the fare so you're good to go."

Song stepped out, hunched against the rain and ran up the front steps.

The door opened before she knocked.

Fenfang pulled her inside, gave her a quick hug and said, "Welcome to my humble abode."

The woman was transformed.

Incredible.

Beyond incredible.

She wore makeup, not a lot, but enough to do the trick. Her hair was blond now; long, straight and thick. The jeans were gone. In their place was a sexy black dress that showcased firm arms, perfect legs and a touch of cleavage. A cigarette dangled from pink lips.

Song must have had a look on her face because Fenfang blew smoke and said, "I'll take that as approval."

Good.

Because that's what it was.

A definite approval.

"Where have you been hiding all this?"

Fenfang smiled. "Do you think he'll be interested?"

"Hell, I'm half interested myself."

Shaden walked into the room from the kitchen, handed a glass of wine to Song and looked at the manila folder in her hand. "Is that our case?"

"It is."

"Well, let's see what you came up with."

"I did the damsel in distress thing."

"Good, because we obviously have a damsel."

They ended up at the kitchen table where Song explained the fake case she'd come up with. Fenfang—actually, Rain—was driving on the south side of Hong Kong Island with her boyfriend, Kong, on a stormy Saturday night six months ago. Rain was behind the wheel and Kong was in the passenger seat. They were drunk and shouldn't have been on the road.

Rain was singing and pushing the radio buttons and having a good time when she looked up and saw she was on the wrong side of the road.

Another car was coming right at them.

The other car swerved at the last second and crashed into a telephone pole. Kong wanted to keep going but Rain turned around to see if anyone was still alive.

That was a bad move.

Another car pulled up while they were there.

The driver—a young woman—got a good look at them.

They ran to their car.

Kong had the presence of mind to get the woman's license plate number as Rain squealed out.

They spent the night in a hotel, went back to Hong Kong the next day and continued their routines as if nothing had happened.

Time passed.

The witness turned out to be a hostess girl from Hong Kong by the name of Tan Kwon. Kong got more and more worried about her randomly bumping into Rain or him on the street and calling the cops.

He started to talk about killing her. Rain wouldn't hear of it and told him to just let it be. Then things got strange. Unknown to Rain, Kong learned the identity of a man who was killing young women in Hong Kong. He anonymously black-mailed the man into killing the witness one night when he and Rain had public alibis.

Rain didn't know about it until afterwards.

When Kong told her, she left him and ran away to the United States—San Francisco, to be precise.

That was a month ago.

Three days ago, Rain got a call from Kong's phone, but the caller wasn't Kong. It was a mean-sounding man who said, "You're next."

Rain called everyone she knew to see if Kong was okay. No one had seen or heard from him for the last four days. The killer must have found out that Kong was the one who black-mailed him. He must have killed Kong.

Now he was after Rain, no doubt thinking she was in on the whole blackmail scheme with Kong.

"That's the bare bones of the story," Song said. Tapping the manila folder she added, "A lot of it dovetails with real events. That was the hard part. There really was a family run off the road on the south side of Hong Kong Island. Also, a hostess bar girl named Tan Kwan really was murdered a month ago. Finally, many other women have been murdered in Hong Kong over the past few years. It's entirely possible that some of those killings may have been done by the same person." A pause, then, "So what do you think?"

Shaden leaned back and studied the woman. "How the hell did you think this up?"

Song shook her head.

"I don't know. It just came to me."

"How much am I paying you an hour?"

"Three fifty."

"It's not enough," Shaden said. "Tell me how Rekker fits into this."

Song nodded.

Good question.

"Rain meets with Rekker for a number of reasons," Song said. "Primarily, she wants guidance as to what to do at this point. The killer might very well be headed to the United States right now, as they speak. Hell, he might have even landed and be waiting for her down the street. Should she get fake papers and try to disappear? Should she hire a bodyguard? Should she go to the police? What should she do and what are the legal ramifications of the various choices?"

Shaden chewed on it.

Then she said, "The more I think about it, the more perfect it is. Rain's not squeaky clean because she drove drunk, but that was more in the nature of bad judgment rather than evil intent. After the accident, her actions were pure. At this point she really is a damsel in distress. Rekker will want to protect her. I can already see the drool dripping off his tongue."

Song pictured it, then changed gears. "I was thinking of something on the way over. We need to stake out Rekker's house. The woman might have been a girlfriend or something like that. If we see her coming or going, that will be a pretty good indicator that she's not overly dead."

Shaden retreated in thought.

"You and me will do it," she said. "We'll need to keep Fenfang—I mean Rain, we better stay in character—as clean as possible. If Rekker spots her anywhere she shouldn't be, her cover will be blown." A beat, then, "We'll need binoculars. I'll pick some up in the morning. We'll start tomorrow night."

They looked at Fenfang.

Her face was pensive.

"Can you pull it off?" Shaden asked.

Fenfang held up her hands in surrender.

"It's more complicated than I thought," she said. "Let's go over the details again. I need to get it etched into my head better."

39

Day 2—September 22
Tuesday Night

Tuesday night Teffinger climbed out of the cabin of Bad Add Vice at exactly eight o'clock and looked down E-Dock to find Chase walking towards him, not a minute too early, not a minute too late. He hadn't talked to her since the one and only phone call this morning and had no idea what she'd be wearing. He suspected it would be something, but didn't expect this, namely a short black dress, black high heels and long, loose hair.

Lots of skin.

More than a taste of cleavage.

Her skirt shifted from side to side as her thighs pushed against it.

Nice.

Very nice.

So nice that Teffinger felt his world shift, just a tad.

Every once in a while he came across a woman he could get lost in. It didn't happen often—in fact, rarely—but Chase was one of those women. He could picture them together in bed tonight. He could also picture them going for a sail on a sunny afternoon five years from now.

Ten steps away, she smiled.

"I didn't know if you'd come," Teffinger said.

"How could I not?" she said. "You owe me a handstand, remember?"

Teffinger stepped onto the dock, got his bearings, kicked his legs up and stood on his hands. Then he walked on his arms for two slips, turned around, came back and dropped onto his feet.

Chase smiled.

"Impressive."

The sky was thick with twilight but wouldn't be dark for another half hour. Chase looked around the marina, saw no one and handed Teffinger her purse. "Hold this a second." Then she kicked her legs up and got into a handstand. Her dress dropped down, first to her stomach then all the way to the dock, over her face.

She wore a white thong.

Teffinger had never seen anything so sexy.

Ever.

That was the truth.

"I'd walk for you but I don't know where I'm going."

She was about to drop down when Teffinger said, "Stay up."

She did.

"Okay, turn right a quarter turn."

She did.

"Now walk towards the sound of my voice. Just do it one arm at a time."

She did.

Ten steps later, Teffinger grabbed her around the waist and

swung her right-side up just before she was about to go off the dock.

She tossed hair out of her face and said, "Thanks."

"It's the least I can do and that's what I always do," he said.

She smiled.

"I don't do that for everyone," she said.

"You should," he said. "The world would be a better place."

"What makes you think I care about making the world a better place?"

He tossed his hair.

"Don't you?"

"Not particularly," she said. "You do, though."

"What makes you say that?"

"You're a detective," she said. "That's what detectives do. They get rid of the bad guys. The world turns into a better place."

"How do you know I'm a detective?"

She said nothing and instead cast her eyes on the boat.

Then she slipped her high-heels off and said, "Give me the grand tour."

40

Day 2—September 22
Tuesday Night

J onk and Winter drove up Twin Peaks Boulevard, pulled
into the viewing area parking lot, killed the engine and
stepped out. A panoramic vista of San Francisco spi-
aled outward in all directions, as if they were in a plane coming in for a landing. Up an even higher hill, surrounded by thick
eucalyptus groves, sat the red and white Sutro Tower, which
carried antennas for most of the city's TV and radio stations.

Twilight was heavy.

It would be dark in another half hour.

Lots of city lights already twinkled.

Jonk looked at his watch: 7:55.

"We just made it," he said. "Five minutes."

"Right."

Jonk looked around for the buyer. He saw couples, sightse-
ers, a group of teenagers, but no one alone, no one studying
them and wondering if they were Zoogie.

"Maybe he heard the news that Zoogie's dead," Winter said.

"Let's hope not."

They leaned on the side of the car and watched the city.

At exactly eight o'clock a red Mustang pulled into the parking lot and the headlights went out a heartbeat before it came to a complete stop. The driver got out, paid no attention to the view and scouted the lot as if looking for someone.

Jonk grabbed Winter's hand, pulled her in that direction and said, "We're up."

The person was a female.

Casually dressed.

Wearing a baseball cap with her hair pulled through the back.

Late thirties.

Rough around the edges.

"Are you looking for Zoogie?" Jonk asked.

"Maybe. Are you him?"

"Sort of."

He explained what was going on, namely that Zoogie got murdered last night, Winter was Zoogie's girlfriend, Jonk was helping her find out who killed Zoogie, they suspected it had something to do with the coin.

"Did he say anything to you about where he got the coin from?"

The woman studied him.

"So there isn't going to be a deal?"

"No," Jonk said.

The woman made a face.

"Then I'm wasting my time." She opened the door, slid inside and said to Winter, "I'm sorry about your boyfriend, but I have my own fights to fight."

She pulled on the door but Winter grabbed it before it shut.

"Wait a minute," she said. "You came for the coin. I have the coin."

"You do?"

Yes, she did, and pulled it out of her pocket to prove it.

"I'll do the deal. But you need to tell me what you know. Fair enough?"

The woman hesitated.

Then she said, "Let me see the coin."

41

Day 2—September 22
Tuesday Night

S ong got home Tuesday night to an empty apartment, which shouldn't have been of significance but was. Fenfang had become a bigger part of her life than she realized and her absence was palpable.

A heavy storm beat against the windows.

Wine flowed in her veins.

This was the time to go to bed but the significance of tomorrow weighed on her.

Fenfang needed to be dead-on.

Rekker wasn't a stupid man.

If he knew Fenfang was playing him, there would be consequences.

So far, Song had been nothing less than a hundred percent honest in her life, in everything she said, in everything she did and in everything she was. Designing a fake case was the first time she'd ventured out of her comfort zone. So far it had just been a plan, something that would happen in the future, so she hadn't dwelled upon the moral implications too much. But now, with the plan set to go forward tomorrow morning, it was more than just a concept.

Was she doing something illegal without realizing it?

Or was she simply learning, finally, how to play in the big leagues?

The thought nagged at her so much that she logged on to Westlaw and researched the issue. As far as she could tell, an hour into it, a lawyer—Rekker—owed a duty of honesty to the client but the client—Fenfang—didn't have a similar duty to the lawyer. A lawyer wasn't entitled to lie to a client as that would be a breach of the attorney's fiduciary duty. If a client lied to a lawyer, however, the lawyer had no cause of action against the client. The client's primary obligation to the lawyer was to pay the bill.

So, it was legally permissible for Fenfang to approach Rekker with a fake case and, by extension, it was permissible for Song to assist Fenfang in the matter.

There was a limit, though.

Fenfang couldn't have Rekker actually file a lawsuit against a third party based on knowingly-false information. In that instance, she could potentially be held civilly liable to the third party for any damages sustained.

It wouldn't get to that point, though.

There.

Song felt better.

She brushed her teeth, stripped down to a T, turned off the lights and got into bed.

The storm beat down, wild and violent.

She flipped the pillow to the fresh side, snuggled in and closed her eyes.

She was almost asleep when she thought she heard something.

She raised her head to listen with both ears.

She heard the weather.

Nothing else.

She listened harder.

Still nothing unusual.

She laid her head back down and listened with one ear.

Then her mind wandered and sleep took her.

42

Day 2—September 22
Tuesday Night

Rain came, hard and fast. Teffinger closed the hatch all but a few inches and said, "I was afraid this was going to happen. Now I'm going to have to go to Plan B."

"What's Plan B?" Chase asked.

He shrugged.

"I don't know. I never make it until I need it."

"Okay, then, what was Plan A?"

"Plan A was to motor over to Alcatraz Island," he said. "They let me tie up there after hours, off the record, so long as no one raises a stink, which no one has yet. There's a rock cropping off the beaten path where I like to sit and drink a couple Anchor Steams and watch the city." He paused. "I don't know, maybe that was too lame anyway."

Chase shook her head.

"No, actually it sounds nice. Did you ever break in, you know, after dark?"

He smiled.

"Not since I was a kid," he said.

"You did it then?"

"I did everything then," he said. "That's one of the only drawbacks to my job. Now I have to stay clean."

"No, you just have to not get caught."

He flicked hair out of his face.

"Unfortunately, staying clean is the best way I know to not get caught."

"See, I'm just the opposite," Chase said. "I'm more of a nature to do what I want when I want, and screw the consequences. Nine times out of ten it never catches up to you."

"Yeah, it's that tenth time you have to watch for."

"Not really. You smile, apologize, beg for forgiveness and keep moving forward," she said. "Life's too short to not grab those other nine things. Don't get me wrong, I'm not talking about cheating. I've never cheated on a man, not once, ever. That's one of the places in life where I live by the rules. That and my health, I never try to cheat my health." A beat, then, "You know what I want on my tombstone when I die?"

"What?"

"I want it to say, *Not wasted.*"

"Sounds reasonable."

"We're all wolves inside," she said. "The secret is to not get caged." She studied him and added, "I'm one-eighth Cherokee." Teffinger must have had disbelief on his face because she added, "I'm serious. My great-grandmother was a full-blooded Cherokee named Bandhura, which means pretty. Her daughter—my grandmother—spoke pretty good Tsalagi, in spite of governmental policies that cropped up in the fifties and forced the removal of children from Tsalagi-speaking homes. The language got passed on to my mother who then trickled as much as she could of it down to me. I'm not fluent but I can make out what's being said, or at least I could three or four years ago. That's the last time I heard it spoken. It's almost extinct at this point. It's really sad."

Teffinger was impressed.

"You're lucky to have a heritage," he said. "My dad died when I was fifteen."

She studied him.

"You have the eyes of a wolf. Let's take a walk."

"In the rain?"

"Yeah, it'll be fun. Let's get drenched."

He considered it.

"Come on," she said. "I want you to see me ugly, with my hair flat and my makeup smudged and water dripping off my nose."

DAY THREE

September 23
Wednesday

43

Day 3—September 23
Wednesday Morning

Jonk found himself on a couch in an unfamiliar room when he woke Wednesday. The first rays of morning were just beginning to shift through bent, aluminum blinds. He sat up and stretched. A gray cat trotted over and jumped into his lap. He gave it a pat on the head and got his bearings. The room was cluttered with twice as much stuff as it needed, maybe three times.

Cheap pine tables.

Torn-shade lamps.

A jammed bookcase.

An oval throw rug with years of wear.

The place belonged to Winter's friend, Brittany Stevens, who put them up last night. That was safer than a hotel since the cops were looking for him in connection with Zoogie's murder.

He headed into the bedroom, carrying the cat.

The women were still asleep and so buried in the covers that he couldn't tell which was which. He headed over, took a closer look, figured out which one Winter was and shook her gently on the shoulder.

She opened her eyes.

He held the cat in front of her face and said in his best cat voice, "Time to wake up."

Then he headed for the shower.

Forty-five minutes later he and Winter were on the road in Brittany's car—bless her heart—with more than enough pancakes, strawberries and coffee in their guts.

Winter drove.

Jonk checked Tag's cell phone to be sure it still had power for when and if Tag's abductor's called.

It did but the battery was fading.

They bought a pair of Bushnell PermaFocus binoculars at the first open store they passed that might sell such a thing, then headed to the place where Winter's van plunged into the bay yesterday.

There was no activity on the water.

Good.

They parked a mile down the road, headed back part way on foot, took a position behind a rock outcropping and waited.

The plan was simple.

The other people, the ones from the white sedan, wouldn't know if the treasure was in the van or not. For all they knew, the whole cache could have been in Zoogie's possession and stashed at the dry dock. Winter might well have loaded every bit of it into the van. It might be sitting there in it's entirety under the water right now, this moment.

They'd have to check.

It was too realistic of a theory to not pursue.

An hour passed.

No one showed up.

"Maybe they came last night," Winter said. "Maybe they did a night dive."

"I doubt it," Jonk said.

"Why not?"

"Unless they're divers, they're going to have to hire somebody. They didn't have time to do that yesterday, not to mention they were busy with Tag. Plus this place was pretty hot yesterday. I don't know if they stuck around long enough to see what happened to you. It's possible they think they killed you. It's also possible that someone saw the whole thing and told the police about a white sedan." Jonk shook his head. "Yesterday was too risky. Today's risky too, for that matter, but they can't put it off forever. They'll scout the area, confirm the cops aren't hanging around and then go for it." A pause, then, "That's what I'd do."

They waited.

An hour passed.

Then another.

Nothing happened.

Their stomachs began to grumble.

Then Jonk's phone rang.

The caller turned out to be Typhoon Joe from Hong Kong wanting an update, which Jonk gave him.

"I'm sorry about Tag but there's bound to be collateral damage in a project like this," Typhoon Joe said. "Your job is to not get distracted."

Jonk's chest tightened.

"Meaning what?"

"Meaning keep doing what I'm paying you to do."

"What about Tag?"

"We'll come back and attend to her after the treasure's in

hand," Typhoon Joe said. "The important thing right now is to not waste a second of time, especially now that we know we have competition."

Jonk chewed on whether he should say what he was about to say, then decided to just do it. "You didn't send a second team here, by chance, did you?"

Silence.

"I did," Typhoon Joe said.

"You did?"

"Yes."

"Why?"

"That doesn't concern you," Typhoon Joe said. "They're on a separate mission."

A separate mission?

What kind of separate mission?

"They're focused on a man named Nathan Rock," Typhoon Joe said.

"Never heard of him."

"No reason you would," Typhoon Joe said.

Jonk frowned.

"What's this Rock guy have to do with this?"

"Nothing," Typhoon Joe said. "He's just a loose end I'm tying up. If it turns out he factors into the equation somehow, you'll be briefed."

"Maybe they're the ones who took Tag."

"Never."

"How do you know?"

"Because I trust them."

Jonk grunted.

"No one's trustworthy when the stakes are this high," he said. "It's very possible that they're double-crossing you and they're the ones who took Tag."

Silence.

"Call them off," Jonk added. "If they haven't mutated, they might. I can't work if everything around me is polluted."

A long beat.

Then Typhoon Joe said, "Let's get something crystal clear right now. It's my treasure at stake, not yours. I'm the one in charge of this mission, not you."

Jonk exhaled.

"I didn't come here to be working in a blind spot," he said. "Either get me fully in the loop and let me call the shots or find yourself someone else."

"Be careful what you say, my friend."

Jonk kicked a rock.

"Make up your mind and do it now," he said.

"Don't force my hand."

Jonk took a deep breath and said, "Make up your mind."

"Okay then, have it your way," Typhoon Joe said. "You're out of the deal. Get your ass back to Hong Kong."

44

Day 3—September 23
Wednesday Morning

The first thing Song did when she woke Wednesday morning was put on her glasses and peek through the corner of the blinds to see if anyone strange was lurking around in the alley. She saw no blue bandanas or strange Chinese men in white shirts.

The storm from last night was gone.

Puddles lingered but the sky was clear.

She showered, filled a bowl with cereal and milk, carried it down to her office, got the coffee pot going and reacquainted herself with the Chin file. At 7:45 she strapped her briefcase onto the back of her bike and peddled down to the San Francisco District Court for an 8:30 status conference.

She was on her way back to the office, peddling next to heavy traffic, when her phone rang. She kept one hand on the handlebars and answered with the other.

It was Fenfang.

"I have an appointment with Rekker at two o'clock this afternoon."

"Good."

"What are you doing, jogging?"

"Peddling."

"Same thing," Fenfang said. "You need to cut out all that health crap and start smoking."

She smiled.

"The apartment was strange without you there last night," she said.

"You should have stayed over."

"Next time. When did Shaden leave?"

"She didn't."

"She didn't?"

"She was too drunk to drive—not by a lot but by enough. I hid her keys. That pissed her off but too bad. The last thing she needs is to kill someone else."

"Allegedly kill someone else."

Right.

Allegedly.

Back at the law office, Song made a fresh pot of coffee and logged on to the net. Shaden had been sent to the San Francisco office to investigate whether Rekker was engaging in bribery, blackmail or other illegal activities to get an edge in high-stakes litigation.

Getting Fenfang on the inside was one way to potentially crack the question.

Realistically, though, it was a long shot.

There was another shot to take, also a long shot, but a shot nonetheless. And that was to locate all the high-stakes cases that Rekker had been involved in over the last several years, get into the guts and details of those cases, and see if anything unusual or unexpected happened.

A witness suddenly changing testimony.

Or an opposing counsel not taking a key deposition or not subpoenaing a key witness for trial.

Or a settlement of case on terms ridiculously advantageous to Rekker's client.

Something like that.

There were a lot of databases that could be tapped for information. Westlaw contained most published court opinions, both state and federal, as well as many unpublished ones. It could be searched by keyword, including an attorney's name. That would be a good starting point to identify the cases where Rekker was an attorney of record.

Then there were local court records, also accessible online by members of the bar, which showed all docket entries for a case, including motions filed by either party and orders issued by the court. Not only were those items listed, but the actual documents could be pulled up and read.

Then, of course, as a last resort, any member of the public could go to the clerk's office and ask to see the actual case files.

Song accessed Westlaw and did a search for "Rekker.".

A number of cases popped up.

She printed the page.

Then she took a sip of coffee and clicked open the first case.

45

Day 3—September 23
Wednesday Morning

Teffinger jogged before sunrise Wednesday morning, paying enough attention to traffic to not get run over but otherwise focused with all his might on Chase. Last night had been nothing like what he expected. All day long he anticipated getting her on her back, peeling her cloths off one beautiful layer at a time and slowly turning her into a heap of nothing but raw animal lust.

That didn't happen.

It could have.

He wanted it.

She wanted it.

But it didn't happen.

He didn't know why at the time but now by the light of day did, namely they were building something bigger than that.

Nice.

Exciting.

But dangerous.

If she turned out to be a killer, then what? He didn't know, but did know one thing—he needed to see her again.

Tonight.

Back at the sailboat he took a shower, ate cereal and headed to the parking lot to see if Bertha was in the mood to start. He stuck the key in, said *Come on, baby,* and turned the ignition. Bertha sputtered in protest for five seconds and then coughed blue smoke out the tailpipe as she reluctantly rumbled to life.

Teffinger patted the dashboard.

That's my girl.

He was usually the first one to work so it was a shock to find everyone already there, spread out in the conference room. All eyes were on Northstone who was standing at the front and talking animatedly. Teffinger opened the door, walked in and took a seat in the back. The chief turned briefly, threw him an evil look, then refocused on the man from New York.

Northstone didn't motion for Teffinger to join him up front.

Teffinger tried to listen but his mind kept bouncing to Chase.

Then Condor.

Then Zoogie.

Then back to Chase.

Something in his peripheral vision got his attention. He turned to find Tracy Pendergast waving at him through the window. He got up as unobtrusively as he could and headed for the door, looking back only long enough to see the chief watching him with a mean face.

Tracy Pendergast was from the missing persons unit.

Teffinger had asked her to immediately notify him of any women who were reported missing, regardless of age, hair color or ethnic background.

"You got something?" he asked.

"I got this," she said, handing him a photograph.

It was a woman.

Nice looking.

Mid-twenties.

African American.

Black hair.

"Her name's London Fogg."

"Like the raincoat?"

"Exactly like the raincoat, except two g's," Tracy said. "According to her roommate, she went missing last night. I'm sorry to pull you out of the meeting, but you wanted me to tell you about any female missing person cases right away, so that's what I'm doing."

46

Day 3—September 23
Wednesday Morning

J onk knew that if he didn't show up in Hong Kong by tomorrow at the latest, Typhoon Joe would conclude that
he was hanging around San Francisco to try to recover
the treasure for himself. Typhoon Joe would send a hitman to
be sure that didn't happen. Jonk would never see him coming.
Right now though, at this moment, he didn't care. The only
thing that mattered was Tag.

Late morning came.

Nothing happened. No dive team came around to salvage
the contents of the van.

Noon came.

Same thing.

"If I don't get food I'm going to disintegrate," Winter said.
Jonk didn't want her walking down the road alone, nor did he
want to leave his position to watch over her.

"Call for pizza," he said.

"You're kidding, right?"

No.

He wasn't.

So she called.

Half an hour later a pizza delivery guy pulled to a stop on the side of the road, not exactly where instructed but within fifty yards. Winter waved him in the rest of the way, gave him a twenty-dollar tip and carried everything midway down the bluff to the hiding spot.

Greasy.

That's what the pizza was.

Greasy and good.

They were halfway through it when a fishing boat meandered into the area and dropped anchor twenty yards from where the van went down.

Jonk pulled it in with the binoculars.

"Bingo."

"Is that them?"

He passed the binoculars and said, "You tell me."

"I'm almost positive the dark skinned guy is the one who was driving," she said. "He has that same look. I don't see the woman who was in the passenger seat."

"She's probably watching over Tag."

There were four men on the boat, total. Two of them suited up with wetsuits, tanks and fins and jumped overboard. Within the hour, they had everything salvaged out of the van.

Suddenly the Egyptian-looking man pulled a cell phone out of his pocket and dialed.

Inside Jonk's pocket, Tag's phone rang.

Jonk answered.

"You want your friend Tag back, right?"

Jonk didn't have to ask who was calling.

He was actually watching the man through the binoculars as the words came out of the phone.

"If you hurt her, you're dead," Jonk said.

"Save the drama," the man said. "We want Brian Zoog's girlfriend, Winter, the one who was driving the van. We'll make you an even trade—Tag for her."

47

Day 3—September 23
Wednesday Morning

If there was one thing Song discovered during her research, it was that almost every single case Rekker touched was high-stakes in one way or the other. She also discovered that he touched a lot of cases.

There was a lot to run down.

Too much.

The biggest case, of course, was Rekker's defense of Kyle Greyson who was charged with the murder of Paris Zephyr, the first SJK victim. That was the case where the head detective, Frank Finger, had been telling his girlfriend how he planted evidence to implicate Greyson. He got drunk and beat her up the day before he was set to testify. She retaliated by telling Rekker about the fabrications and then testifying to the fact at trial. Finger never admitted any wrongdoing but everyone knew he was lying. Based on the girlfriend's testimony, the DA dismissed the charges during trial.

Song checked the docket sheet.

The girlfriend's name was Haley Key.

Seeing it in writing jogged Song's memory.

The woman had been beat up pretty bad by Finger. When she testified, her eye was almost closed shut and the entire side of her face was black, green and purple.

Haley Key.

Haley Key.

Song's stomach churned. She looked at her watch to find the morning entirely gone, plus half the noon hour. She locked up and headed down to Utopia Café which was next to Double Dragon Massage, a place she was tempted to peek in every time she passed it.

Fenfang would be up at two.

By midafternoon, Song would know if Rekker had taken the bait.

She ate a full bowl of veggies.

Still hungry, she ordered a second.

The place buzzed.

Everyone was in motion.

She could hardly think, but that was okay because she wasn't in the mood.

Suddenly, a very strange thought entered her head. It had to do with the girlfriend, Haley Key. What if Rekker had dug up some dirt on her, something she wouldn't ever want the world to see? What if he came up with a perfect plan, namely that she tell the jury that Finger had told her he had fabricated evidence? What if everything she said was a total fabrication? What if Finger never beat her up at all? What if those injuries were inflicted by Rekker himself, with her consent, as part and parcel of the scheme?

Rekker would have known that his client, Kyle Greyson, was innocent. He would have known that from their private conversations and from looking into the man's eyes.

He would have also known, however, that Greyson might nevertheless go down.

He'd want to protect him any way he could.

Even if it meant putting pressure on a witness to lie.

The ends would justify the means.

Song finished her noodles and headed back to the law office with a pounding heart.

She needed to dig into Haley Key's past.

She needed to find the same dirt that Rekker had found.

Once she did that, she'd confront the woman head on.

48

Day 3—September 23
Wednesday Morning

Londong Fogg turned out to be a high-priced escort, very high-priced in fact, upwards of $4,000 a session. For that the client got four hours of company in either a private or public venue, ten minutes of oral gratification and a missionary-style ending. The price went up from there, depending on the particularities of the client's palette. London's roommate—a stunning blond by the name of Savannah Anderson—knew and knew full well because she was equally employed, right down to the same prices.

"Me and London have an understanding," she told Teffinger. "We either come home at the end of the night or we call to say we won't. Last night, she didn't do either."

Teffinger probed her.

She told him London wasn't the kind to forget or get too wrapped up in something to space it out.

She didn't do drugs, well, nothing heavy, and never with clients.

"Her phone is shut off. I can't even leave her a message. That's totally unlike her. She never shuts it off."

"So, who are you two employed by, exactly?"

Savannah hesitated, deciding.

"It's a group called Passionate Interludes," she said. "They set up the sessions and keep half the money. The woman gets the other half. They're supposed to screen the guys but they don't. They only care if the credit card clears." She exhaled and said, "Here's the problem. Last night wasn't a company session. All the girls set up sessions on the side, you know, to keep all the money. This was one of those. It was supposed to go from eight to midnight. London never told me the guy's name. He almost positively would have been someone she met through the company, someone from that group."

"Do you know where she was supposed to meet him?"

No.

She didn't.

"All I can tell you is that she left in her car at around 7:30," she said.

Teffinger's cell phone rang and Neva's number popped up as incoming. He stepped into the hall and answered.

"Where the hell are you?"

He told her.

"So your theory is what? That SJK is going to abduct someone in advance and hold her until the due date?"

"Right."

"He's never done that before," she said.

"He's never had this kind of pressure before either," Teffinger said.

"Do you want some advice?"

"No."

"Good, because here it is," she said. "Get back up here to the meeting before the chief fires your ass. He doesn't see the humor in you being AWOL all the time."

He looked at his watch.

The morning was already moving on.

"I have a better idea," he said. "Come down here and sit in on the rest of this interview. Then I'm going to want you to cross-reference this London Fogg woman to all the SJK victims."

"You're not serious."

Wrong.

He was.

Dead.

He printed a photograph of Condor's driver's license from his office computer, went back to the interview and handed it to Savannah. "Have you ever seen this guy before?"

She studied it.

"He looks a little like Nicholas Cage."

Right.

He knew that.

"From that movie, Bangkok Dangerous," she added. "Where his hair was longer."

"Did London ever mention him or anyone like him?"

She searched her memory.

"Not that I remember."

"Would she have mentioned it, if she knew him?"

"Probably not, unless there was a reason."

Teffinger paced.

Then he grabbed Savannah's hand and pulled her up. "Come on, we're going to take a little field trip."

49

Day 3—September 23
Wednesday Morning

When the Egyptian man offered to trade Tag for Winter, Jonk's first thought was to do it—be careful, be sure it went down the way it was supposed to, but do it. For a split second, he even pictured being in bed with Tag this very evening, screwing like there was no tomorrow. But when he looked at Winter and saw the trust and innocence in her eyes, he knew he couldn't.

"Yes or no?" the Egyptian man said. "You have five seconds to decide."

Jonk hardened his face.

Then said, "Yeah, sure, fine. When and where?"

"I'll call you in an hour."

The phone went dead.

Jonk took one last look at the man through the binoculars, then dropped to the ground.

"What's going on?" Winter asked.

"They want to trade Tag for you," he said.

"Why?"

"Because they didn't find the treasure in the van," he said. "They want to interrogate you to see if you know where it is."

She processed the words and then sank to the ground next to him.

"I don't care if they interrogate me if that's what it takes to get Tag back," she said.

"That's a nice gesture."

"It's not just a gesture. I'm serious," she said. "I don't know anything. Sooner or later they'll figure that out."

Jonk threw her a quick glance.

"And then what?"

"Then they know I'm no use to them."

"And then what?"

She shrugged.

"And then they let me go, I guess."

"You guess wrong," he said. "Then they kill you."

"You don't know that."

Jonk grunted. "Zoogie's the proof," he said.

She picked up a rock and threw it.

"So what do we do?"

"We only have one choice," Jonk said. "We play along like there's going to be an exchange and hope to hell we figure out a way to get Tag loose." He studied her and added, "Are you up for doing that? For playing along?"

She nodded.

"Of course. You two saved my life. This is called payback."

"It will be dangerous, make no mistake," he said.

"I already know that. I don't care."

Jonk looked at his watch and stood up.

"They're going to call in fifty-five minutes," he said. "Do you know anywhere we can get a gun in that time?"

"No."

"How about Zoogie? Did he have one?"

"No. That wasn't his style."

50

Day 3—September 23
Wednesday Afternoon

The Internet never heard of Haley Key outside of her trial testimony, which brought Song's quest for dirt to a very sharp and very premature halt. She took her glasses off, leaned back in her chair and spun around with her eyes closed.

Now what?

If the dirt was there, who would know about it?

The ex-boyfriend might.

Detective Finger himself.

Ex-detective, actually.

If he knew about it, though, he could have whipped it out at trial. He could have testified that Haley Key was making the whole story up, possibly to hide her own dirt. He could have then told the jury what that dirt was. At the very least, that would have put her credibility in issue and taken some of the heat off him.

He didn't do that, though.

That meant he didn't know about it.

It was secret dirt that even he didn't know about.

Song spun around again.

Wait a minute, there was another possible explanation too. Maybe he did know about it but didn't want to put her in the hot seat even to save his own posterior. Maybe he still loved her in spite of what she was doing to him. Maybe he understood that she had no choice in the matter.

So, Finger might possibly know what the dirt was.

But even if that was true, how could Song get him to tell her what it was?

She couldn't.

That's how.

She was halfway through another spin when her phone rang. She jerked the chair to a stop, put her glasses on and answered.

"Good news," Fenfang said.

"How good?"

"Well, I just got out of the meeting with Rekker," she said. "He was very cool and sophisticated and didn't say or do anything improper, but he wants in my pants like nobody's business."

"You think?"

"Oh yeah, big time."

"Did he buy the story?"

"As far as I can tell, yes, but we didn't get into it that deep," she said. "He only had a half hour for me because he was squeezing me in between other meetings. He was busy through six but said he'd fit me in after that if I wanted, given that the case was so volatile and time-sensitive. He said that's when he usually ate dinner. I could either join him if I wanted or meet with him afterwards."

"That's called the politically correct way to ask your client to dinner. What'd you say?"

"I was just as politically correct and said dinner would be fine."

Song spun the chair 360.

"That raises a point."

"What point?"

"We never talked about the boundaries," she said. "No one expects you to sleep with him or anything like that."

Fenfang laughed.

"What's so funny?" Song said.

"If I do—sleep with him, that is—that pretty much makes you a pimp. I'm going to buy you a big pink Cadillac and a leopard jacket."

51

Day 3—September 23
Wednesday Morning

George Karamaza was slight of build, slight of hair, slight of looks and over-closed his eyes when he blinked, almost in the nature of a twitch. Forty years ago, he was the kid who got beat up for his lunch money.

Teffinger didn't like him.

He didn't trust him, either.

Luckily, neither of those two things factored into the equation. Karamaza was one of the co-owners of Passionate Interludes, a man who had learned to take his love for porn and find a way to make money at it. He was only meeting with Teffinger because Savannah pressed him to.

His office was big but had no windows.

The walls were covered with smut, mostly lesbian stuff.

Young lesbians.

Borderline kiddie-porn.

A five-line phone sat on his desk, next to a credit card processor.

He studied the printout of Condor, frowned and said, "I've never seen him but that doesn't mean much. I hardly ever see anyone. If you want, I'll tack it on the wall and ask the girls about him when they come in."

"You got a pair of scissors?"

Yes.

He did.

Right there in the drawer.

Teffinger cut the printout so that only the face was left and handed it to the man. "Tack that much up. Here's the more important thing, though. I have a credit card number I want you to run through your system. Find out if it's ever been used here."

The man brightened.

"I can do that, no problem."

He ran it and smiled.

"He's a customer alright."

The corner of Teffinger's mouth turned up, ever so slightly.

Yeah, baby.

Yeah.

"Give me the date."

"Let's see … okay, June 5th," Karamaza said.

Teffinger heard the date, heard it clearly, but still couldn't believe the man actually said it.

"Did you say June 5th?"

Right.

June 5th.

As in, one, two, three, four, 5th.

The man must have read something registering in Teffinger's brain because he scrunched his face, then brightened and said, "That's when SJK struck, isn't it? June 5th."

Teffinger nodded.

"Wow, what a coincidence." He got a distant look, then refocused and said, "Stress relief. That's what you're looking at, stress relief."

"What do you mean?"

"He kills the woman earlier in the evening and gets all turned on," Karamaza said. "Then he comes down here later that night for stress relief. Let me see … yeah just what I thought. His card got run at 11:42 p.m. that night."

It made sense.

It really did.

"Who did he meet with?"

Karamaza consulted the ledger and frowned.

"Not good," he said. "Falcon, that was her call name, her real name's Kristie."

"Kristie what?"

"Kristie I-Don't Know and I never know because no one in this business has a last name," Karamaza said. "What I do know is that she stopped working for us right after that." His eyes fell on the ledger, then came back up. "June 27th was her last session."

"Where'd she go?"

Karamaza shook his head.

"They never say," he said. "They just disappear."

52

Day 3—September 23
Wednesday Afternoon

The fishing boat pulled anchor and headed north. Jonk and Winter ran to the car and drove in the same direction, using the binoculars to keep it in sight as best they could and relying on Winter's familiarity with the streets when they couldn't. That actually worked for a while, then the worst thing that could happen did.

Flashing lights appeared behind them.

Winter looked down at the speedometer—52.

She was in a 35.

"Shit!"

She said, "Oops," and smiled her best smile when a cop appeared at the window. He wasn't impressed and kept his face stone-cold to prove it. He was even less impressed when he found out the car didn't belong to her. He had to run the plates to be sure it wasn't stolen. There were computer problems on the other end. After an eternity he finished what he was being paid to do and headed back to his car. Winter crumpled the ticket, tossed it on the floor and cut back into traffic.

"They weren't swinging around to the north piers," she

said. "My best guess is they're headed to one of the marinas up around Sausalito. Should we try it?"

"Yes, go."

Ten minutes later, crossing the Golden Gate Bridge, Jonk pulled out the binoculars again and scouted the waters, training on one boat after another.

"Nothing," he said.

Winter cut in and out of traffic, not to the point of being dangerous but to the point of racking up more than a few honks and just now even drawing the finger.

"Someone just gave me the bird," she said.

Jonk wrinkled his forehead.

"The bird?"

"Yeah, you know, the bird." She gave him the finger. "The California state bird."

"Oh, that bird," he said.

Sausalito turned out to be an attractive area given to water-side roadways, marinas filled with floating houses, quaint boulevards, cliffs, beaches, lush greenery and enough seagulls to keep the sky cluttered. There were worse places in the world to be.

Ordinarily, Jonk would be captivated.

He hardly paid any attention.

His mind was getting haunted by Typhoon Joe.

"What's wrong?" Winter asked.

"I got too emotional after Typhoon Joe told me to forget about Tag," he said. "I cut myself out of the deal. What I should have done is just agreed with him and then focused on Tag anyway. He would have never known."

"Call him back and patch it up."

Jonk considered it.

"I'm not a perfect guy," he said. "I've done a lot of stuff in my life. But even with all that, Typhoon Joe disgusts me. When he called Tag collateral damage, something snapped. I'm really not interested in breathing the same air as him anymore."

"So what are you going to do?"

"Tag's top priority," he said. "But if I can get her back, then I'm going to go after the treasure."

"You mean steal it out from under Typhoon Joe?"

Jonk shrugged.

"That will be up to him."

"I don't get it."

"I think what I'm going to do is this," he said. "If Typhoon Joe doesn't send a hitman after me, I'm going to honor the deal I had with him, if I find the treasure. If he sends a hitman, though, all bets are off. I'll keep the whole thing."

"How will you know?"

"Know what? If he sends a hitman?"

Right.

That.

"If a bullet enters my brain, or tries to, that will be my first clue."

Winter looked ahead to find that the car in front of her had slowed and she was about to ride up the bumper. She slammed on the brakes, dropped a safe distance back and said, "I want in."

"No you don't. Typhoon Joe's a mean man," Jonk said.

"I don't care."

"Easy to say."

Silence.

"There's a marina coming up in a half mile that caters to fishing boats."

Jonk put his sunglasses on.

"Pull over a hundred yards before we get there."

53

Day 3—September 23
Wednesday Afternoon

With the prospect of finding dirt on Haley Key in stall mode, Song refocused on Rekker himself, who turned out to be quite the public speaker. In the past few years alone he had been a keynote speaker at several luncheons across the country and had participated in more than twenty continuing legal education seminars.

Clearly the man never slept.

One of the themes he repeatedly hammered following the Greyson trial was that criminal defense attorneys should always question whether the cops fabricated the evidence. "I know, I know, I know. It seems improbable. Hell, it seems impossible. It seems like there would be too many checks and balances in place, but the reality is that any detective who gets motivated enough to make up evidence can do it. That's the sad reality."

The Greyson trial was the poster child.

To punctuate his point, he occasionally brought Kyle Greyson himself to the seminars so the members of the bar could actually lay eyes on a real, flesh-and-blood person who almost got sucked into the vortex of a fabricated world.

Ironically, Rekker and Greyson were actually participating in a seminar in London, England in late September, almost two years ago, when Pamela Zoom—the third SJK victim—was murdered.

In the end, Rekker's speaking engagements were interesting but they were also wasting Song's life.

She turned her attention back to his cases.

There was dirt there somewhere.

She just needed to get smart enough to find it.

54

Day 3—September 23
Wednesday Afternoon

Early Wednesday afternoon, Teffinger maneuvered Bertha across the Golden Gate Bridge, which was always risky because that's where she liked to break down the most. In Sausalito, he wound his way up to the narrow lanes that fed the cobblestone driveways and gated estates of the people who had too much money. The people who weren't detectives.

Chase St. John lived in the last house on the right.

A six-foot, stone wall overgrown with vines shielded the property from view. The drive was guarded by an ornate, wrought iron gate with stone lions on each side.

Luckily, that ornate gate was already open.

Teffinger drove through and hated what he saw.

The house was contemporary with rich textures, lots of windows, an expensive entry and a gray tile roof. The circular driveway wrapped around an Italian fountain.

Bertha's brakes squeaked as she came to a stop.

Teffinger turned the engine off.

Blue smoke shot out of Bertha's tailpipe with one last gasping cough.

The radiator hissed.

Then everything got quiet.

Teffinger stepped out, shut the door and walked towards the entry. It was only ten or twelve steps away but it gave him more than enough time to absorb the reality that Chase was out of his league.

He looked back at Bertha.

She was already dripping oil.

He got his finger to the buzzer but didn't push.

It would be better to just turn around.

End it now.

Move on.

Suddenly the door opened and Chase was there before him. She wore a black tank-top that didn't go all the way down to her skirt, leaving her bellybutton showing. Her skirt was white, short, expensive and flimsy.

Below that were legs.

Below those legs were bare feet with pink toenails.

Teffinger didn't know why he was there. All he knew is that Chase called and wanted to talk to him about something as soon as possible and asked if he could meet her at her house.

She brought a small twisted cigarette to her mouth, took a long drag, held it and then blew smoke.

It wasn't a regular cigarette.

It was one of those special ones.

She handed it to him, turned and headed into the structure. "Come on in."

Teffinger closed the door.

He debated for a heartbeat and then took a long drag as he followed her through a vaulted space with middle-eastern rugs and antique busts on black contemporary stands.

"We made a mistake last night," she said.

"Like what?"

"Like not doing what we should have," she said. "All I could think about since I left was correcting that mistake." At the base of a winding staircase she stopped and turned. "Do you want to see the bedroom or the dungeon?"

Teffinger took another hit.

"You have a dungeon?"

"Doesn't everyone?"

She led him downstairs.

55

Day 3—September 23
Wednesday Afternoon

L ost Mango. That was the name of the diving boat they were looking for, a white Boston Whaler thirty feet or thereabouts with twin outboards. Jonk studied the maze of marina vessels through the PermaFocus while Winter pulled to the side of the road short of the marina. There must have been four or five hundred boats there, each hiding behind the other.

Half of them were sailboats.

The marina was a giant porcupine from the sky.

"See it?" Winter asked.

"No."

"Should we go in?"

Good question.

They'd be obvious if they walked in together. But it would be dangerous to leave Winter alone. Jonk trained the binoculars on the open water—no Lost Mango. Suddenly Winter put her hand on the top of his head and pushed down, simultaneously falling to her side.

"He's coming our way."

Jonk stayed down.

"Walking or driving?"

"Driving."

They waited while the noise of an approaching car got louder and then whooshed past. Jonk looked out the back window to see a white sedan going the other way. The driver had dark hair.

"Are you sure it's him?"

"Pretty sure."

Winter stayed as far behind as she could, trying to keep at least two cars between them. "I have to be honest, I think it's him but I'm not positive."

"If it's not, don't worry about it. We'll just come back."

They headed south, across the Golden Gate Bridge, through San Francisco and out the other side.

"We never talked about what my cut's going to be," Winter said.

"What do you think's fair?"

She shrugged.

"I don't know, 10 percent?"

"Okay," he said. "It's settled."

"Ten percent?"

"No, one-third."

"One-third?"

"You deserve it for what they did to Zoogie," Jonk said. "Make no mistake, though. If you participate, Typhoon Joe will find out. He'll hunt you for the rest of your life. He'll hunt you to the ends of the earth. You'll need to become someone else and move to another city or, better yet, another universe."

"Paris," she said.

"Whatever," he said. "I just want to be sure you know what

you're getting into."

She tilted her head.

"I can speak Spanish," she said. "Language comes easy to me. I'll bet I could learn to speak French. Have you ever been to Paris?"

"Yes, absolutely."

"Tell me about it."

"It's like every other place in the world," he said. "If you're young, good looking and have money, you own it. The only difference is that it's a better place to own than most."

"I want to see the Mona Lisa."

"You strike me more as an impressionist woman. Van Gogh and Renoir, that kind of thing."

She exhaled.

"That whole hippie thing was more Zoogie's deal than mine," she said. "I like to be comfortable, don't get me wrong, but I'd like to be classy some day."

Jonk looked at her.

"You already are."

She smiled.

"You know what I mean."

He did, he did indeed.

"I could see you at a who's-who party in a long black evening dress with your hair up and a not-too-big but not-too-small diamond necklace around your neck."

She considered it.

"I never went to college," she said. "If I ever got money, that's what I'd do. You can't be classy without being educated. Did you ever go to college?"

He had.

Hong Kong University.

He had a Bachelors degree and a Masters.

Both in mathematics.

"You're lucky," she said. "I had a sister. Her health wasn't good. That's probably the main reason I never went."

"Is she still alive?"

"Yes, but only in my memories."

The white sedan entered a rough industrial warehouse area not far from a blue-water dock. Most of the traffic had thinned away.

"Drop off," Jonk said.

Winter made the first turn she could then pulled over and stopped.

They both knew what was going on.

Tag was hidden away back in there somewhere.

"We'll give him ten or fifteen minutes to get where he's going and get inside," Jonk said. "Then we'll drive around until we spot his car."

"Okay."

They sat in silence, keeping a lookout, watching everything that moved—mostly 18-wheelers, vans and pickup trucks.

"I was wondering what happened to your eye," Winter said.

Jonk shifted his position.

"I don't like to talk about it."

"Sorry."

A minute passed and then another.

Jonk looked at his watch.

"We'll give him a few more minutes."

56

Day 3—September 23
Wednesday Afternoon

Song's bike was an 8-speed Fugi, leisure style, with a comfortable seat, sensible handlebars and a rack over the rear wheel. It had no suspension and wasn't the lightest thing on the road but it wouldn't set her back too much when it got stolen. At night she kept it in her office. In the day she chained it to a light post in the alley.

Every once in a while she'd look down and check on it.

This time when she did it, her breath stopped.

There was a man by it.

He didn't wear a blue bandana but had the same movements and posture as the man who did. He did something to the seat, looked quickly around, then disappeared down the alley at a brisk walk.

What the hell?

She waited five minutes, didn't see him again and headed down. Under the seat was some type of transmitter, about the size of a cigarette lighter. She left it in place and headed back up to the office.

What else was bugged?

Her office?

Her apartment?

Her whole life?

She turned on the radio to a Chinese station and spent the next hour silently going through her office, looking for hearing devices or transmitters or anything in a different place than where she left it.

She found nothing.

Something was there, though.

She could feel it.

Late afternoon she zigzagged around Chinatown until she was as sure as she could be that she wasn't being followed, then jumped on the back of a cable car at the last minute and disappeared down the street.

She saw no one come into view, pissed that she'd gotten away.

She got off in the financial district.

It was 4:45.

The buildings were already emptying.

People were everywhere.

The place buzzed.

She took an inconspicuous spot across the street from the Transamerica Pyramid and focused on the stream of people getting revolved out of the lobby doors.

At 5:05 the person that she hoped would emerge did.

Rayla White.

The law clerk who worked in Rekker's department. The one who befriended Shaden and came up with the idea to break into Rekker's house. The one who was present Sunday night when the mystery woman got killed.

Or didn't get killed.

The one who might be in a conspiracy with Rekker.

Song followed her to a bus stop, hung behind her as good as she could, then hopped on the same bus and shielded her face as she walked in. The woman walked all the way to the back and sat down. The only other vacant seat was the one directly in front of her.

Song took it and pointed her face forward.

The bus spit out a plume of diesel and rumbled down Market Street.

57

Day 3—September 23
Wednesday Afternoon

Chase St. John's dungeon wasn't the harsh, nasty thing that Teffinger envisioned. The lower level of the house had a walkout basement with walls of glass and a commanding view of the Pacific throwing itself onto jagged rocks at the base of a cliff. The dungeon was on that same level except through a wooden door that led to a windowless room.

Lush carpet covered the floor.

The lighting was recessed into the ceiling. Chase dimmed it until it was hardly there, then powered up an elaborate sound system built into a wall. A song dropped from rich, crystal-clear ceiling speakers.

It was edgy and erotic.

Teffinger liked it immediately.

"What is it?"

"It's called 'Touch Me I'm Going to Scream,'" Chase said. "It's by My Morning Jacket. Have you ever heard of them?"

"Not really."

She lit another joint and swayed her body seductively to the music.

The movements of her hips and arms reminded Teffinger of the snake-dancing scene by Selma Hayek in Dusk 'till Dawn. He pictured her sticking her toes between his lips and pouring beer down her leg into his mouth.

That's not what she did, though.

What she did was take a padded cuff off the wall and fasten it securely to her left wrist, not so tight as to cut off her circulation, but more than enough to be inescapable.

Another one went onto her other wrist.

Then two went onto her ankles.

"I'm not into pain," she said. "What I like is to be controlled. Put me in any position you want. Be my total and complete master."

"What are the limits?"

"None," she said. "Do whatever you want so long as it doesn't involve pain."

Teffinger looked around the room, deciding. There was a rack, an X-frame, ceiling hooks, spreader bars, gags, blindfolds, and some kind of device that reminded him of a gymnastic horse.

He stretched her out on the rack.

Tight.

Barely able to move.

"Looks like someone's stuck," he said.

"Looks that way."

She still wore her clothes.

He unbuttoned her blouse and pulled it to the side as her chest heaved up and down. Underneath was a flimsy, white bra. He pulled it up, exposing perfect tits.

He ran his fingers on her nipples in light circles, barely touching.

She closed her eyes.

"I'm not going to let you go for a long, long time."

"You're so evil."

He raised her skirt up.

She wore a thong.

White.

He bent down and kissed it, then harder, with more pressure.

Then he put a blindfold on her.

"You're in some serious trouble," he told her.

"Prove it."

58

Day 3—September 23
Wednesday Afternoon

After crisscrossing the area for some time, Jonk and Winter spotted the white sedan tucked in a narrow alley between two prefabricated metal warehouses. They almost missed it as they drove past but saw enough to tell it was a white sedan, nose in, tail out with no one inside. They turned right at the first corner and pulled over fifty yards down. Jonk stepped out, walked around to Winter's side and leaned in the window. "Drive off a mile or so and wait for my call."

"But—"

"No buts."

She gave him a look.

"If I don't call, don't come back, don't even swing back simply to drive past and see what's going on. That's the important thing. Understand?" She nodded. "If I don't call, just get somewhere safe and hole up." He slapped his hand on the roof. "Go."

She took off.

Then he was alone, walking down a cracked and potholed

asphalt street. There were no sidewalks. Weeds choked the sides of the buildings. He looked for a weapon and saw scrap remnants but nothing of substance.

Go for the man.

Forget about the woman.

Do it fast.

Do it with full force.

Don't worry about whether he dies.

He deserves to die.

He turned the corner and hugged the structures as he came up the street. The man was undoubtedly in one of the buildings on either side of the alley but there was no telling which. An 18-wheeler rumbled through an intersection a hundred yards down the road and disappeared.

Go to the car.

See if there's a building door near it.

That'll tell you which one he's in.

His veins pounded.

Flatten the front tires before you go in.

Don't give him a way to escape.

He spotted an empty beer bottle, picked it up and broke it against the ground as quietly as he could. The break was perfect. He had a full grip left at the bottleneck and sharp deadly edges at the business end.

Bottle versus face; bottle wins every time.

In ten more steps he got to the building on the left of the alley. It had a loading dock in front but the overhead door was down. He walked past it and came to a steel door. He put his hand on the knob and silently twisted.

It was locked.

He listened for sounds inside.

He heard nothing.

He continued on, got to the alley and stuck his head around the corner.

What he saw he could hardly believe.

59

Day 3—September 23
Wednesday Afternoon

Song was vague in her own mind as to exactly what she hoped to get out of following Rayla White. Initially she thought she might get some kind of vibe from the woman, something to indicate whether she was capable of conspiring with Rekker and participating in a plot to make Shaden believe she had killed someone. If that was the reason then, in hindsight, it was a stupid one. The woman wasn't giving off any vibes. She was just a woman heading home on the bus after a long day at the office.

Song stared out the window.

San Francisco rolled by.

Her heart pounded. This was a lot more exciting than sitting alone in her office behind a desk. It brought out her sharper edges and made the corner of her mouth turn up ever so slightly. Maybe tomorrow she'd follow Rekker himself just for the hell of it.

A phone rang behind her.

"Hey," a woman said, then got silent, listening. "Okay, nine o'clock at Danny Dan's. Yeah, don't worry."

Danny Dan's.

What was that?

A bar?

Six blocks later Rayla got out.

Song followed.

The movement felt good.

All her life she'd felt like a lamb.

Delicate.

Suddenly she felt like a wolf.

Not a big wolf, not the meanest wolf in the world, but a wolf nonetheless.

Cool.

Rayla went two blocks north and then walked up the steep steps of a narrow house sandwiched between more of the same. She stuck her hand in her purse, fumbled around for a long time, made a mean face and finally pulled out her keys. She stuck them in the lock, turned the knob and opened the door. She didn't step through, though. Instead she spotted something on the landing by her foot.

She picked it up and looked at it.

It was a yellow rose.

Part of Song wanted to hang around and continue the hunt. Another part of her warned that she'd already pressed her luck. She headed back towards Market Street but turned one last time to look at the house.

Was that someone behind the curtain?

Watching her?

She picked up the pace.

The wolf feeling was gone.

The lamb feeling was back.

60

Day 3—September 23
Wednesday Afternoon

Teffinger would rot in hell. There were lots of reasons that would eventually happen but the one that developed this afternoon with Chase was the worst, namely he took valuable time away from the SJK case to feed his own selfish pleasures.

Lust.

It would eventually kill him.

Then it would make him rot in hell.

It was all just a matter of time.

He left Chase's place with one thought and one thought only on his mind. He needed to find Falcon, aka Kristie, to find out what Condor said when he used her services on June 5th. He went back to Passionate Interludes with a few more questions for Karamaza.

"Falcon was sort of a loner," the man said. "I don't think she was that tight with anybody. About the closest friend she had, at least that I'm aware of, is a girl named Amanda."

Last name unknown.

Address unknown.

Cell phone no longer in service.

No photographs.

She quit Passionate Interludes more than a month ago. Karamaza had no idea where she went. She might still be in town or she might be farming carrots in Iowa.

He had no idea.

Once they're gone, they're gone.

"She was about twenty-five and had short black hair, sort of stylish," Karamaza said. "That's about all I can tell you."

Teffinger frowned.

Damn.

She'd be just as hard to find as Falcon.

Suddenly Karamaza's face brightened. "I just remembered something. She had a tattoo."

"Where?"

"It was a dragon. It started on her stomach, that's where the head was, breathing fire. Then its body wrapped around her ass and down her right thigh, with the tail ending slightly above her knee."

Teffinger pictured it.

Déjà vu.

He'd seen it.

Where?

Then, wham.

That was the tattoo on the submissive woman he saw through Condor's telescope Monday night. She was the woman Chase killed.

Outside, he slipped into Bertha and might have felt a spring pop in the seat but wasn't sure. He turned the key, said Come on, baby, and exhaled when she fired up. He rolled the window halfway down and sat there, wondering what to do. Chase knew Amanda, in the context of the dungeon scene if nothing else.

Amanda knew Falcon.

The question was whether Chase knew Falcon.

Either way, Chase was his best lead right now.

He needed to be careful, though.

He needed to figure out the best way to approach her.

Clouds were building and the wind was kicking up.

Teffinger shifted into drive and took off. Bertha responded with a wobbling and resistance that couldn't mean anything good.

He got out and checked.

The front tire was flat.

61

Day 3—September 23
Wednesday Afternoon

The white sedan was gone.

The alley was as empty as empty gets.

Jonk ran through it to the end and saw nothing in either direction. What the hell was going on? There hadn't been time to get Tag out of the building, into the car and take off, Jonk would have heard it. Was the whole thing a setup? Did the Egyptian spot them following and lure them back into this dirty little corner of the world? Was Tag actually somewhere else, a hundred miles away?

Suddenly his phone rang and Winter's panicked voice came through.

"He's chasing me!"

"Who? The sedan?"

"Yes! He's right on my ass! He's trying to make me crash!"

The grating of metal pounded into Jonk's ear.

"Winter!"

She shouted something but her voice was far away, as if the phone had dropped.

Then she screamed.

Almost immediately a loud, crashing sound came from the phone, followed by brutal silence.

The connection was gone.

Jonk ran down the street in the direction Winter had driven.

Asshole.

That's what he was.

A raging asshole for being so stupid.

First he let Tag get taken.

Now Winter.

He brought his knees up higher, sprinter style, and kept them there even when the burn turned to fire and then moved from his muscles into his brain. His lungs sucked air, deep and hot and furious.

His body wanted to shut down.

He wouldn't let it.

Screw it.

Screw everything.

He ran even faster.

62

Day 3—September 23
Wednesday Night

D anny Dan's turned out to be a dive bar in the Tenderloin district. Song stuck her head inside at 8:45,
just to kill her curiosity, and found the place to
be narrow and long with a bar down the right side, red vinyl
booths and battered wooden tables on the other, and a pool
table in the back. The clientele was an overly-loud eclectic mix
of grade-C hookers, guys looking for hookers, those already
drunk and those on their way.

The place was crowded.

It smelled like stale beer.

Two of the wobblier drunks were leftover remnants from
five o'clock, still in suits and ties. Cockeyed ties. The ugly one
with the big gut spotted her and said, "Hey baby, come over
here and give me some."

She said, "Sure, I'll be right back," and walked out.

The night was dark and windy.

She took an inconspicuous spot in the shadows across the
street and waited.

Time moved slowly.

Rayla White showed up at 8:58 wearing jeans, tennis shoes and a long-sleeve shirt—clearly not a hooker—and disappeared inside.

Two minutes later, at exactly nine, a silver BMW drove past the bar and parked down the street. A man got out and headed back on foot. He wore ordinary clothes but had a confident, important strut. He was older, late forties or early fifties, with a square jaw like a boxer's.

He wasn't Rekker.

Song memorized his face.

He disappeared inside.

Now what?

She headed over to the BMW, wrote down the license plate number, then reclaimed her spot in the shadows.

Someone walked out of the bar.

It was the ugly guy with the gut.

"China doll, where are you baby?"

Shit.

Did the jerk really think she was coming back?

He looked around.

Then the worst thing that could happen did.

He spotted her.

"There you are! Come here and give daddy a kiss."

63

Day 3—September 23
Wednesday Night

Chase was a drug. Teffinger couldn't get her out of his blood. He'd had more than his fair share of women but this was different. This was—wham!—you've been smacked in the forehead with a baseball bat, now deal with it.

She called him at 7:30 and made a suggestion.

A lewd suggestion.

A lascivious suggestion.

He listened.

Then he said, "Sounds reasonable."

"What would be a good place?" she asked.

"I'd probably go with Cadillac Sam's for something like that. You ever heard of it?"

"No."

He gave her directions.

"Nine o'clock," she said.

"Okay."

Teffinger got there a half hour early, found the place a lot more crowded than he expected, ordered an Anchor Steam and leaned against the bar. The stages were all packed. Grade B-plus strippers gyrated with every ounce of sex they had. Guys stuffed dollars into their g-strings.

Girls too, for that matter.

Zoogie's girlfriend, Winter, said she used to strip here, which is probably why the place was on Teffinger's brain. Being here ignited a recessed visual. He actually remembered Winter on the far left stage one crowded drunken night. Teffinger wandered over with too many beers in his gut and tipped her a five. She put her legs over his shoulders and rubbed her g-string in his face, actually touching.

She smelled like perfume.

Later she gave him a free table dance.

How did he forget all that until just now?

Suddenly his cell phone rang and Neva's voice came through. "Don't forget about the strategy meeting in the morning. Six sharp."

He took a long swallow of beer.

Nice.

Cold.

Damn good stuff.

Teffinger pictured Northstone at the front of the room, working the whiteboard with colored markers and making serious faces.

"We just had one this morning," he said.

"They're every morning," she said. "Don't you check your emails?"

He hadn't, not in a week.

"Of course I do."

She said, "Where are you, anyway?"

Suddenly a woman was at his side, young, blond, brushing up against him with an evil look and running her fingers through his hair, wearing next to nothing.

"Hey, cowboy," she said.

"Hey back at you," he said. Then into the phone, "I'm working on the Zoogie case."

"Can I give you some advice?"

"No."

"Good, because here it is," she said "Stop making me worry about you. I don't like it."

The line went dead.

He was downing his third Anchor Steam when someone came up from behind. He turned to find Chase, wearing a short white skirt, facing the other way and rubbing her ass against his.

"Did you bring it?" he asked.

She nodded.

"I'm already wearing it."

"You're so evil," he said.

"Thanks to you."

He kissed her.

They got drinks and took seats at the far back stage which was being worked by a stunning Asian dressed in knee-high socks, a short plaid skirt and white blouse tied above her stomach.

"Give me the controller," Teffinger said.

Chase looked around to see if anyone could see what she was about to do. A few could, if they were paying attention, but they weren't. She reached inconspicuously under her skirt, pulled out a controller attached to a thin cord, and put it in Teffinger's hand.

At the other end of that cord were vibrating eggs, strategically placed.

Teffinger flipped the switch.

Chase's face immediately changed.

He smiled.

Suddenly the dancer unbuttoned her schoolgirl blouse, pulled it to the side and ran fingers over her tiny but firm breasts. Her nipples got erect.

Teffinger laid a five in front of Chase.

The dancer got down on all fours, crawled over until her face was inches away, then stuck a tongue in Chase's mouth.

Teffinger dialed the power up on the controller.

64

Day 3—September 23
Wednesday Afternoon

J onk's muscles burned, they burned bad, so bad that they seized up and slowed him to a jog. Vomit shot up into his mouth. He swallowed it down and kept going. Fifty yards later, even deeper into the rat's nest of industrial pollution, an intersection appeared. Winter's car was smashed broadside into a cinderblock building, as if it had tried to make the turn at too great a speed.

Steam came out of the hood.

Jonk tried to run faster.

He couldn't.

Suddenly the Egyptian man came into view, walking briskly towards a white sedan twenty or thirty yards farther down, carrying a limp body in his arms.

"Hey!"

The man turned, startled, then broke into a trot and got to the sedan just as Jonk came around the corner. He pulled up the trunk, dropped the body inside and slammed the lid. Then he got in the driver's door, fired up the engine and floored it.

Jonk was right there, so close he could touch it.

He dived onto the trunk, found nothing to grab and got thrown off, smacking the side of his head on the asphalt.

"Goddamn it!"

The car sped down the street.

Shit!

Shit!

Shit!

He twisted around, frantic. There was nothing around, only Winter's car, dead on the street. Something on the ground next to it caught his eye.

It was a cell phone.

He picked it up.

It wasn't Winter's.

Hers was pink, this was black.

The Egyptian man must have dropped it.

Steam continued seeping out of Winter's hood, no doubt from a punctured radiator or hose spewing antifreeze onto the engine. The driver's side of the vehicle was smashed all the way down. The passenger door was open, left there after the man yanked Winter out. Jonk had a wild idea, catapulted himself through the door. The key was still in the ignition, in the on position. He turned it off, then back on.

The engine didn't respond.

Shit!

He got out and kicked the ground.

Wait.

The transmission was probably still in drive.

He checked, found that it was and shifted into neutral. Then he turned the ignition key again.

This time the engine fired up.

He shifted into drive and floored it.

Ten seconds later he had another wild idea. He opened the cell phone and redialed the last number that had been called. A woman answered in a middle-eastern tongue.

"English," Jonk said.

"Who is this?" she asked in English.

"Listen very carefully because if you don't do exactly what I tell you to do, the man is going to die. Do you understand?"

A pause.

Then, "Yes."

"Let Tag loose right this second, give her the cell phone and tell her to keep the connection open. Tell her to run and to let me know when she's safe. If I get the word within three minutes that she's okay, I'll let the man go. If I don't get it I'm going to kill him. This is a one-shot deal and it starts right now, so go!"

DAY FOUR

September 24
Thursday

65

Day 4—September 24
Thursday Morning

The silver BMW at Danny Dan's turned out to be registered to one Nathan Rock who was a lawyer in Rapport, Wolfe & Lake specializing in international law. What Song couldn't figure out is why he was having a clandestine meeting with the criminal department's law clerk, Rayla White, off-site last night at a dive bar. The obvious theory—that they were having sex or an affair—didn't seem to fit because Rayla left fifteen minutes after Rock showed up. Rock, on the other hand, hung around for another hour and eventually staggered out with a woman wearing a blond wig up top and red high-heels down below.

Song couldn't figure it out.

She was no good at this kind of thing.

Fenfang called early Thursday morning, before Song was done with her first cup of coffee, and said, "We need to meet."

"What happened last night?"

"I'll tell you when we meet."

"It needs to be someplace close, my bike's bugged."

"You're kidding."

"I wish I was."

Fifteen minutes later Song headed down the street to Chang's for croissants and fruit wedges, then snuck out the back and managed to catch a bus on California just as it pulled away. Twenty minutes later she got off and walked north on Battery, turning every few steps to see if she was being followed.

She wasn't.

Still, her blood raced.

Two blocks later someone fell into step with her, appearing from nowhere.

It was Fenfang, incognito in a baseball cap, oversized sunglasses and baggy clothes. "Good thing I'm not a rattlesnake or you'd be dead right now."

Song smiled.

"So, how'd it go with Rekker?"

"Good. Very good."

They went to Gary Danko's for dinner. Fenfang—make that Rain—wore a sexy red dress and smiled the whole time.

"He got touchy," she said.

"How touchy?"

Fenfang shrugged.

"You know, like he wanted to sweep everything off the table and throw me on my back." Song must have had a look on her face because Fenfang said, "I said like he wanted to. Unfortunately for him, they had rules against that there."

"So he's definitely interested," Song said.

Fenfang nodded. "Here's the bottom line. He's going to want to get me over to his place. I'm going to let him. What I want you to do is get me something to put in his drink and knock him out. Then I'm going to have a good look around."

"You mean sleeping pills?"

"No. Something faster, almost instantaneous. Something more powerful. Something that fogged the memory. Something like roofies."

"I don't think those are legal," Song said.

Fenfang rolled her eyes.

"If they sold them at the drugstore I'd just go get them myself," she said. "That's why I'm talking to you. I don't have any connections in this country but you do."

"I don't have those kinds of connections."

"Then get them," Fenfang said.

Song chewed on it.

Then she said, "That's serious stuff. It's technically an assault."

Fenfang studied her and frowned.

"You're afraid to get dirty," she said.

"That's not true," Song said. "I just don't think it's a good plan, that's all."

Fenfang said nothing.

Delicate.

That's the word that popped into Song's head.

Delicate.

"Don't worry about it," Fenfang said. "I'll have Shaden get them."

Song exhaled, uncertain whether she should actually say what she was about to. Suddenly the words came out, almost on their own. "Just get in and unlatch a window or door or something," she said. "Somewhere he won't notice."

Fenfang looked over.

Surprised.

"Then what?"

"Then keep him occupied and I'll sneak in."

"You'll sneak in?"

Song tilted her head.

"Did I say that out loud?"

Fenfang patted her on the back.

"You're really cute when you wear your criminal face. Did anyone ever tell you that?"

66

Day 4—September 24
Thursday Morning

Thursday morning before daybreak, Teffinger's alarm radio kicked on at 4:45 to the voice of an over-hyper DJ, the point being that he'd already had his coffee and was going to flap his lips to prove it. If the guy was a dog he'd be a poodle. Teffinger muted him and closed his eyes, just for ten more seconds. The next time he opened them was an hour later, at 5:45.

That wasn't good.

He knew that but couldn't remember why.

He threw on sweats and headed out of the marina for a jog. Ten minutes into it he remembered what he was supposed to remember, namely there was a six o'clock SJK meeting this morning. If he turned back now, threw on clothes without showering and busted a few red lights, he'd only be a half hour late. He slowed the pace, deciding, then picked it back up.

Screw it.

He didn't have time.

The meeting would be noise.

It would be the equivalent of the DJ.

He needed to get all the noise out of his head.

He needed to think.

And that's exactly what he did as he pounded the pre-dawn streets of San Francisco, except the thinking wasn't about SJK like he wanted it to be, it was about Chase.

She was a woman with no boundaries.

No financial boundaries.

No intellectual boundaries.

No sexual boundaries.

No boundaries, period.

He'd never met her type before and had to admit, deep down when no one was listening, that she scared him. He had looked for his equal for a long time. Unfortunately, he still hadn't met her. He'd shot right past his equal to his superior. Until he knew her boundaries, he wouldn't be able to understand her. And until he understood her, he wouldn't be able to trust her. And until he trusted her, he wouldn't be able to love her.

Actually, that last part wasn't true.

He already loved her, although love wasn't the exact right word.

Love-lust was a better word.

Love-lust-drug might be even better.

Or love-lust-drug-adrenalin.

He had no idea where it was all headed.

He did know, however, that he'd ride the hell out of it all the way to the end.

He had no choice.

He was already strapped in.

Chase.

Chase.

Chase.

Who are you?

By the time he got back to Bad Add Vice, showered and got dressed, it was a quarter to seven. The meeting would be over by seven, meaning it was history.

His phone didn't ring.

Neva wasn't calling to get him there.

That wasn't good.

Maybe she saw something on the chief's face this morning that said the damage was done, irrevocably done, forever and hell-be-damned done.

Shit.

He walked up the wooden docks to the parking lot, hopped in Bertha and stuck the key in the ignition. "If you don't start, I'm going to push you right off the dock. I'm not kidding this time, I'm really not."

He turned the key.

Bertha coughed in protest, as if being woken rudely from a deep hangover.

Then she started.

Teffinger patted the dash, said "That's my girl," and pointed the front end toward Condor's place.

67

Day 4—September 24
Thursday Morning

Yesterday had been good which almost guaranteed that today would be hell because that's the way Jonk's life worked. The Egyptian woman actually fell for his cell phone trick and released Tag. Then the white sedan got stuck at a railroad crossing. Jonk swung left and smashed into the driver's door just as his engine overheated and conked out. The man escaped but Winter was alive.

They met up with Tag.

Then they holed up in a cheap motel on the south edge of the city to let their bodies recover.

That was yesterday, the good day.

Now it was today, the guaranteed bad one.

In hindsight, Jonk was glad the man escaped.

Otherwise, he would have killed him, meaning he'd be on the wrong end of a police hunt right now. Not being there meant he could concentrate on the treasure.

Finally, the treasure.

He stepped outside, found the hotel edgier than he remembered and headed down the street on foot for the first place that sold coffee and food.

"Screw him, screw him to hell."

That's what Tag said yesterday when Jonk told her about Typhoon Joe's directions to forget about her and stay concentrated on the mission.

Jonk cut her in for one-third of whatever they recovered if she wanted to stay involved.

She did.

Absolutely.

That meant the three of them were equal partners.

A mom-and-pop grocery store called All Natural Foods & A Few Unnatural Ones appeared up ahead. Jonk stepped in to see if they had a coffee pot, which they did. It wasn't mom or pop behind the counter, though, it was a pimply faced kid reading a comic book. Jonk bought three large coffees, bagels, cream cheese and, just for grins, low-fat donuts that probably tasted like crap but might not.

Walking back, his phone rang.

He checked the number.

Unknown ID.

He almost didn't answer but figured it might be the Egyptian guy.

It wasn't.

It was a female who spoke flawless English.

"Typhoon Joe told me to call you," she said. "I'm on the other team he told you about, the one tying up the loose end."

"Nathan Rock," Jonk said.

"Right. Nathan Rock. Typhoon Joe wants me to get together with you and bring you up to speed on a few things. He wants us to work with each other from this point on."

"Typhoon Joe fired me."

"That's not what he told me, he said you quit."

"It's all semantics," Jonk said "The net effect is that I'm off the case."

"He said you might say that," she said. "He said if you did, I was supposed to tell you you're back on."

Jonk ran his fingers through his hair.

"What's your name?"

"Tristen."

"Tristen what?"

"Just Tristen."

"Well I'll tell you what, Just Tristen. I'll think about it. Call me back in two hours."

"Two hours," she said. "Keep in mind that Typhoon Joe isn't exactly in what I would call one of his better moods."

The line went dead.

68

Day 4—September 24
Thursday Morning

It was easy for Song to talk big when she was with Fen-fang, walking down the street, not actually doing anything wrong. But after they separated and she really started to think about it, she had second thoughts about sneaking into Rekker's place. It was an illegal activity. If she got caught, she'd lose her license. Maybe it would be better to just let Fenfang drug him. At least then there'd be no breaking and entering. The more she thought about it, though, the less clean even that option seemed. It was definitely illegal to drug someone without their knowledge. Also, even if someone was invited into someone's house so that the initial entry wasn't breaking and entering, it was still a criminal trespass to go snooping into private places where no authority to go had been given.

Both ways it was a bad deal.

A bad, bad deal.

And both ways, Song and Fenfang were co-conspirators, at least in the eyes of the law. That meant that whatever one of them did, the other was equally liable for.

A bad, bad deal.

The safer course would just be for Fenfang to see what she could get out of Rekker through basic talk, if not full pillow talk then maybe second-base talk. But even then, what was the chance he'd actually say anything incriminating?

Zero.

He wasn't stupid.

There was only one choice.

Do what it takes.

Go for it.

Besides, if they found what she thought they would, nothing bad would be coming back in her direction. All the heat would be on Rekker.

She rode the bus back to Chinatown.

She thought she'd be at peace.

She wasn't.

Instead, the city felt cold.

The buildings looked hard.

And her stomach churned.

By the time she got off the bus, she knew what she needed to do, namely not become Rekker in the name of catching him, even if that meant the end of the case.

Her stomach felt better.

So did her brain.

She called Fenfang and said, "No roofies and no breaking and entering, either. You, me and Shaden need to sit down and have a talk about how to proceed."

69

Day 4—September 24
Thursday Morning

Teffinger knew in his gut how things would end with SJK. He'd follow Condor on the night in question, catch him in the act and kill him. The important thing was to not let Condor lose him. To ensure that didn't happen, he parked Bertha two blocks down from the man's house, walked to his garage and pulled on the door to see if it would open.

It did.

He walked inside like he owned the place and closed it behind him. Then he pulled out a small flashlight and studied the undercarriage of Condor's car, looking for the best place to attach a small magnetic box. Inside that box was a GPS transmitter. He was sticking it well out of sight in the bumper support when his phone rang. He answered immediately to stop the sound.

"Where are you?"

The voice was soft.

It belonged to Neva.

"Out of the office right at the moment," Teffinger said.

"I know that. We had a meeting this morning at six. I specif-
ically told you about it yesterday. Where were you?"

"I overslept."

Silence.

"The chief's looking for you. I'm about 99 percent sure he's
going to fire you."

"Thanks."

"Nick, I have to be honest, I don't know who you are anymore. In fact, the more … "

A noise came from behind the oak door that separated the
garage from the house. Teffinger closed the phone, cutting
Neva off in mid-sentence, and turned off the flashlight. A
heartbeat later the door opened.

Teffinger scurried to the passenger side of the car and
hugged the floor.

The garage door got pushed up.

Someone got in the car, cranked the engine and backed up,
almost catching Teffinger under a wheel.

He was totally exposed.

He sprang to his feet, ran to the oak door and got through,
slowing just enough to throw a quick glance at the driver.

It was Condor.

He had his head turned, looking through the rear window,
concentrating on not running over anyone. Then he got out of
the car, hand-closed the garage door and drove off.

Teffinger stood there, coffin quiet, shocked at where he was.
He listened for sounds of anyone else in the house and heard
nothing.

His phone rang.

It was the chief.

"Where are you?"

"I'm working on the SJK case."

"Doing what, exactly?"

"Nothing in particular."

"Nothing in particular?"

"Right."

"We had a meeting this morning, you weren't there."

"Yeah, I know. Sorry about that."

"You're sorry about that and right now you're working on the SJK case but doing nothing in particular."

"Right."

"I'll tell you what, when you're done doing nothing in particular, why don't you swing by my office."

Teffinger swallowed.

"Sure, no problem."

Somewhere in the house was evidence that Condor abducted London Fogg and was holding her somewhere until the date in question.

Teffinger could feel it.

He could smell it.

He could taste it.

The souvenirs of his past victims were here somewhere, too.

Condor had been wearing them, taunting the world.

Teffinger listened again for stray sounds, got none, then headed upstairs to the master bedroom. The kind of information he was looking for was personal. A bedroom was personal. They matched.

The telescope was still in place.

Teffinger took a peek through it, just for grins. It was still focused through the upper window of the bondage room but all was quiet now.

He cast his eyes around the room, then headed for the master closet.

On the way something on the dresser caught his eye.

It was a DVD in a clear plastic case.

On the front of the case was a white, stick-on label.

Handwritten on that label with a black, felt marker were the words, NICK TEFFINGER, MONDAY, SEPTEMBER 21.

70

Day 4—September 24
Thursday Morning

When Jonk got back to the hotel, Winter took her coffee and bagel in hand and said, "I'm going to take a walk. I'll be back." Jonk didn't see how anyone could have traced them to the hotel but still didn't like it. That was too bad because Winter didn't care. She didn't even slow down as she headed for the door, turning only to say, "I'll be fine, lighten up."

Then she was gone.

Tag locked the door.

"She's giving us alone time."

"Why?"

"Because I asked her to."

Then, just like that, Tag had her arms around his neck and her lips on his, at first close-mouthed, then open. Jonk pulled back and said, "You don't have to do this."

She ignored him and kissed him even deeper.

Her face was bruised from being interrogated. A cut at the corner of her right eye needed stitches and looked like it would never heal. Her lower lip was swollen on the left side where it got broken open by her tooth after being smacked. As Jonk looked into that face he realized he had never seen a more beautiful woman.

He took her slowly.

On the bed.

He'd had a lot of sex in his life.

Rock star sex.

Bang 'em hard.

Make 'em scream.

In elevators.

Bathrooms.

Back seats.

Airplanes.

He'd seen it all.

Except he hadn't.

Until now, he'd never heard a woman breathe, or seen a woman part her lips, or feel the convulsing of her thighs.

Until now, he'd only had sex.

When Winter got back, Jonk told the two women about the call this morning from Tristen, who had been tailing Nathan Rock. "Typhoon Joe's probably come to his senses," he said. "I don't want to beat my own chest, but he's going to be hard pressed to replace me, especially on short notice. If he wanted to get me back into the game, this is exactly how he'd do it."

"If that's true, then you need to renegotiate," Tag said. "Instead of 20 percent, make it 30."

Jonk chewed on it.

"That would be dangerous."

They looked at Winter, who hadn't said a thing.

She tilted her head and said, "Who the hell is Nathan Rock and how does he fit into all this?"

Good question.

Very good question.

"That's something we should probably find out," Jonk said.

71

Day 4—September 24
Thursday Morning

The logistics of arranging a face-to-face meeting with Fenfang and Shaden were difficult, especially on quick notice, but Song wanted to be sure she shaped the course of the case to keep it legal. They met at the end of the Pier T promenade. A dozen fishermen, maybe more, had lines in the water. Out in the bay, a ferry cut through the chop towards Oakland.

A large, black crane flew overhead.

A mild, salty breeze blew.

The day was nice.

Song felt good.

"The more I think about plying Rekker with roofies, or breaking into his house to snoop around, or anything else like that, the more I know we shouldn't do it," she said. "So far, we haven't done anything illegal. It's important to keep it that way."

Fenfang and Shaden looked at each other, then back at Song.

They said nothing.

Song laid out her reasons, which were several.

On a personal level, she'd taken an oath to uphold the law.

More than that, though, it might turn out that Shaden actually had killed someone. If that was the case, the last thing she needed was to be involved in any additional illegal activity. And if it turns out that she didn't kill someone, then Rekker was dirty—probably in the very ways that Shaden's boss out in New York suspected. If that was the case, the three of them might actually need to testify against him in the end. Their testimony would be diminished if they were engaging in illegal activities the whole time.

She nodded, as if to emphasize her point.

"Since Fenfang works for the law firm, I'm legally responsible for what she does," she added. "If I allow her to bend the law, it's the same as if I did it myself. We'll eventually get to where we want to be. It will take a little longer, but in the end we'll be glad we did it that way."

Fenfang and Shaden exchanged glances.

Then Shaden said, "Are you done?"

"Yes. I think so."

Shaden exhaled and shuffled her feet. "Fenfang and I talked before you got here," she said. "We knew where this was going. The bottom line is that we see it differently, how to proceed." She let the words hang, then added, "I'm sorry."

"So what are you doing, firing me?"

Shaden looked at the ground.

Then up.

"You're a straight shooter," she said. "I respect that, I really do. Right now though, at this moment in my life, I don't have the luxury of shooting straight."

Song didn't know what to say.

She looked at Fenfang.

The woman hugged her and said, "I love you like a sister but I need to help Shaden. You made a good point that as long as I'm part of the law firm, you're responsible for what I do. So I think what I need to do is quit, effective immediately. Whatever I do from this point on, you're off the hook."

On the way back to the law firm, Song could think of only one thing.

Delicate.

Delicate.

Delicate.

That's what she was.

She'd been given an opportunity to show what she had and in the end didn't have anything to show.

She'd never amount to anything.

She was destined to be small and unimportant.

Her eyes watered up.

Tears rolled out of them, more proof of what she was.

Delicate.

72

Day 4—September 24
Thursday Morning

NICK TEFFINGER, MONDAY, SEPTEMBER 21; that was the label on the DVD case. Was it indisputable proof of his illegal entry from a nanny-cam? Right now he didn't have time for it. He needed to find something that told him whether Condor kidnapped London Fogg and, if so, where she was.

He searched the house, every single room, just in case she was there, drugged, tied and quiet.

She wasn't.

He found a wall safe behind an oil painting in the master bedroom.

It was locked.

He could feel the souvenirs in there.

It was too perfect a place for them to not be.

The files on the SJK victims were in the same place and in the same condition that Teffinger found them last time, with one exception, namely there was an additional folder labeled September 26.

No name.

Nothing was inside it.

Other than that, he found nothing.

If Condor took London Fogg, he hadn't dropped any breadcrumbs, at least not here.

He better get out.

He'd already pressed his luck.

The disk in the DVD case had no writing on it, only the case itself was labeled. Teffinger found a stack of blanks, slipped one of them in the case and stuck the other one in his shirt pocket.

Then he left by the back door.

Back at Bertha, Teffinger found a handwritten note under the windshield wiper. *Not a good stalking vehicle.*

He crumpled it up and almost threw it on the ground, but tossed it into Bertha's back seat instead. No matter what else happened today, no one could accuse him of littering.

Bertha started.

Good thing, too, because he wasn't in the mood.

What he needed to do was swing by the chief's office and get officially fired.

Instead, he went to his apartment on Masonic and popped the DVD into a player.

It turned out to be a compendium of four separate cameras documenting his break-in Monday night. Most of the time, Teffinger was a mere silhouette. There were a good four or five times however when the flashlight reflected onto his face with enough clarity to show it was him. All the cameras were from the first floor. None of them were from the master bedroom.

Those same cameras would have picked him up again this morning.

He turned off the DVD player but left the disk inside.

He thought about grabbing an Anchor Steam from the fridge and swallowing the whole thing in one long gulp.

Instead, he called Neva.

73

Day 4—September 24
Thursday Afternoon

There were two Nathan Rocks in the phone book. One of them owned and operated a one-plane, skydiving business. The other was a partner in a large law firm by the name of Rapport, Wolfe & Lake, who specialized in international law. One of them was a "loose end" that Typhoon Joe was hell-bent on tying up for some reason. The lawyer was the one more likely to have some type of connection to Hong Kong, plus be involved in high-stakes games, so that's the one Jonk focused on.

The man lived in a houseboat community in Waldo Point Harbor in Sausalito.

They found a place to park near the Bayside Café on Gate 6 Road, which led into the community. Jonk put on his sunglasses, blew Tag and Winter a kiss and headed over on foot.

It wasn't good.

The boats were close together.

They were all houseboats or liveaboards of one kind or another. Activity on the dock was minimal but was there nonetheless. Everyone knew everyone in a place like that. Entry and exit was limited.

A large sign said, PRIVATE PROPERTY. NO UNAUTHORIZED EN-
TRY.

The boats weren't big compared to houses, but that was the
tradeoff for the uniqueness. Rock's particular unit was a contemporary design with round windows, strategically positioned
at the end of a long straight dock.

Jonk stepped on board as if he owned it, knocked lightly,
got no response and turned the doorknob.

It was locked.

He looked around, saw no busybody faces pointed in his
direction, walked to the back of the boat and found another
door.

This one was unlocked.

He stepped inside and closed it.

The window coverings were open.

He closed them.

Okay.

You're in.

Go.

Go.

Go.

He wasn't sure what he was looking for, other than some kind
of connection between Rock and Typhoon Joe. Five minutes
into it, he came across a leather pouch hidden at the bottom of
a dresser drawer, underneath a stack of sweaters.

He opened it.

Then he smiled.

Yeah, baby.

Oh yeah.

Oh yeah indeed.

Inside the pouch were ancient gold coins, exactly like the one Zoogie had.

They were from the treasure, no question about it.

He counted them.

Twenty.

He stuck them in his pocket and continued searching.

Nothing else of interest appeared.

He left the way he came in and headed down the dock.

Suddenly two teenage girls came out the front door of a boat, laughing and carrying on, and bumped into Jonk on the dock.

They apologized.

He said, "No problem."

74

Day 4—September 24
Thursday Afternoon

S ong had never been fired by a client, much less for lack of performance, and found the experience akin to being smacked upside the head with a dead fish. She sat by the phone, willing Shaden to call with a change of heart, but her powers of suggestion weren't strong enough.

The phone sat there.

Quiet.

Oblivious.

She walked down to her bicycle, ripped the transmitter from under the seat and threw it on the ground where she smashed it with her foot.

That made her feel better for all of two minutes before the emptiness of being a failure consumed her again. She needed motion but had nowhere to go, nowhere to be. She wandered down the street and ended up getting on a cable car. Half an hour later she got off and walked. Then she saw an empty cab, waved it down and hopped in.

"Sausalito," she said.

On the other side of the Golden Gate bridge, she gave the

cabbie instructions to Rekker's house on Harrison Avenue, had him stop a hundred meters short and got out. The fare was more than half of what she had in her wallet. She wouldn't have enough to get home. She tipped him anyway and watched briefly as he disappeared back towards San Francisco.

Why was she here?

She didn't know.

All she knew is that she was.

The place was pretty much as depicted on Google Earth. From the street it only looked like two stories. Actually, it was a three-tiered mansion carved into the hill, about halfway up on the bay side, overlooking a large marina.

Money.

That's what Rekker had.

Money, money, money.

She walked past it, to all intents and purposes just someone in the neighborhood out for a stroll. The driveway was short and had no gate. Eucalyptus trees hugged both sides of the structure and cascaded down the hill.

It looked peaceful.

Elegant.

In reality, though, a woman may have been murdered there Sunday night.

Or maybe not.

That was the question.

There was another question, too, namely why did she care about the answer any longer? After all, she was fired, off the case, on her own time.

There were no cars in the driveway.

The front door was shut.

The house looked empty.

For a split second, Song had an urge to sneak around to the back, break a window, climb inside and see if she could find bullet holes in the walls or bloodstains on the floor. If she did that, she'd be where Shaden needed her to be.

She'd be back on the team.

She'd be delicate no longer.

She actually took a step in that direction before stopping and continuing down the street.

She walked for fifteen minutes, then doubled back. This time there was a car in the driveway, an average-looking blue Honda 4-door. She already knew the cars that were registered to Rekker, namely a black Audi sedan and a white Toyota Tacoma pickup, meaning this vehicle belonged to someone else.

She memorized the license plate.

Then she had a sudden urge to knock on the front door and see who answered.

The urge was so compelling that she actually found herself walking up the driveway.

Her heart raced.

This was stupid.

Insane, even.

Still, she didn't stop.

75

Day 4—September 24
Thursday Afternoon

Teffinger watched Neva's face grow increasingly somber as she watched the DVD of him snooping around in Condor's house. When it was over, he killed the power to the TV and said, "He's got me by the short ones. What I've done in effect is give him a get-out-of-jail-free card."

Neva didn't disagree.

"So what are you going to do?"

He shrugged.

"There's only one way this can turn out the way it's supposed to," he said. "Well, I take that back, two ways actually. The first is if I catch him in the act on the night in question and he ends up dead."

"That's a long shot," she said. "Especially since he knows you have him in the crosshairs. He'll probably disappear the day before and hide out somewhere just to be absolutely sure no one's on his tail."

Teffinger nodded.

True.

"The second is if I catch him with London Fogg between

now and then," he said.

"You don't even know that he took her."

"He paid a visit to Falcon the same night Syling Wu got killed," Teffinger said, "so Falcon intersects his prior kill. London Fogg intersects Falcon in that they both worked for Passionate Interludes. They're all links in some kind of chain." He pulled his hair out of his face. "The more I think about it, maybe every new victim is connected to the prior one. Maybe he chooses his new one the same night. That way he doesn't get a gap in his lust."

"If that's the case, he sure plans ahead better than I do," Neva said. "I don't even know what I'm having for supper tonight."

Teffinger smiled.

"We know he's a planner," he said. "He dyed Syling Wu's hair. He obviously bought the dye before the night in question. He knew ahead of time who he was going to kill."

Neva wrinkled her forehead with seriousness.

"The chief's going to fire you."

"Forget about him for right now," Teffinger said. "Here's the thing. I stuck a GPS transmitter under Condor's car. The problem is, it only has a range of about two miles."

He picked up an electronic device the size of a book and handed it to her.

"That's the tracker," he said. "It bleeps the location every ten seconds and displays it with a red dot on a street map. What I need you to do is park somewhere by Condor's house, out of sight. Rent a car to do it, something that's definitely not a cop car. When he comes home you'll pick up his signal. Keep your eye on the tracker. When he starts to move, follow him and call me. I'll join in with a second car."

"Bertha?"

"No, I'll have to get something else."

She frowned.

"I could be sitting there all day."

"It'll be worth it," he said. "He's got to be checking up on London Fogg at least once a day to feed her and be sure she hasn't escaped and whatnot. If we do this right, he'll lead us right to her."

"And what are you going to be doing while I sit around all day?"

"Doing what I do best."

"Which is what?"

"Drinking coffee. I thought you knew that by now."

76

Day 4—September 24
Thursday Afternoon

The thing that interested Jonk was that the bag from Rock's floating house had exactly twenty coins—a very even number. If Rock was the one who gave Zoogie a coin to sell, that means he would have started with twenty-one—a very uneven number.

Did Rock have another bag stashed somewhere?

A bag with, say, nineteen coins?

Or, even more interesting, did he have the entire cache? Was the bag at his boat simply there as something of interest to look at now and then, or whip out to impress some woman when he got too drunk?

Interesting.

Very interesting.

Rock was the key.

He was suddenly the key to everything.

Winter knew nothing about him and had never heard Zoogie mention his name. "He never said anything about working with someone who was a lawyer, either," she added. "I think he would have mentioned that, if he was. He hates lawyers. He had one once named Trish Collins. She was a freaking bitch."

"Maybe Rock made him promise to keep his mouth shut," Jonk said.

Winter shrugged.

"Zoogie never kept his mouth shut with me."

Jonk looked at his watch. It had been five hours since he spoke to Tristen. She said she'd call back in two and, at the time, made it sound like even that was too long. Then she didn't call back at all.

What was going on?

Did the Egyptian man somehow find out about her?

Was she being interrogated?

Was the entire treasure being stolen right out from under Jonk's nose?

The coins?

The jewels?

The mask?

Back at the hotel, Jonk and the two women—Tag and Winter—logged on to the net and found out everything they could about Nathan Rock. He wasn't high-profile outside his quiet little circle of expertise. Inside it, though, he was a rock star.

World renowned, even.

Martindale-Hubble had a list of representative clients that the firm represented. One of them was Van Gogh Holdings, a Tokyo corporation registered to do business in the United States. All of the stock of Van Gogh Holdings was owned by Wild Dragon Hill, a Hong Kong corporation. All of the stock of Wild Dragon Hill was owned by Typhoon Joe.

"Rock was Typhoon Joe's lawyer," Jonk said.

"One of them," Tag said. "He's got hundreds."

Right.

One of them.

"So what did he do, pay Rock in coins for legal services?"

Jonk shrugged.

He didn't know.

"I need to talk to the woman, Tristen, and pick her brain," Jonk said.

Suddenly the phone rang.

It was the call he'd been waiting for.

Tristen.

"Are you up for the meeting or not?"

"You were supposed to call back in two hours," Jonk said.

"I know," she said. "Typhoon Joe called and said he didn't want you back on the team after all. Then he called me again five minutes ago and said he did."

"So which is it?"

"Right now you're in," she said. "We'll meet tonight, you and me, alone. Get a pencil, I'm going to give you instructions."

77

Day 4—September 24
Thursday Afternoon

Song was ten steps away from Rekker's front door when a vision popped into her head—a vision that the Honda in the driveway belonged to the man who'd been following her, the man with the blue bandana. She pictured him answering the door, making a strange face—like What the hell are you doing here?—then grabbing her neck with an iron hand and yanking her inside.

The vision pounded her heart.

It was too real.

Too compelling.

It made her turn and walk away.

Before she got to the street she hated herself.

Delicate.

She was too delicate.

It would never change.

Ever.

That's why she'd never amount to anything.

She walked down the hill to Bridgeway where the shops and

marina were, flagged down a passing cab outside Taste of Rome and took it as far as it would go with the money she had left, less a little for the cable car. Then she walked for a half hour, got to a trolley line and took it to Chinatown. She had two dimes left in her purse when she unlocked the door to her office and stepped inside.

Shaden had told her to forget about the $10,000 that got stolen.

She wasn't prepared to do that, however.

She calculated the hours she worked before she got fired.

It didn't come even close to $10,000.

She was still in the hole.

At her desk, she took her glasses off and laid her head down on her arms, just to rest her eyes for a few minutes. At some point later which could have been thirty seconds or two hours, the ringing of a phone pulled her out of a fitful sleep.

She picked it up, put her glasses on and said, "Hello?"

"Is this Song Lee, the attorney?"

The voice belonged to a woman; someone she didn't know.

"Yes," she said. "Who's this?"

"That's not important," the woman said. "The reason I'm calling is to warn you that someone's going to kill you. It's going to happen tonight. Do you understand what I just said?"

Song's hand shook.

She knew she should answer.

She couldn't.

"This isn't a joke," the woman added.

The line went dead.

The phone dropped out of Song's hand and shattered into two pieces when it hit the desk.

78

Day 4—September 24
Thursday Afternoon

After Neva left, Teffinger got in Bertha and stuck
the key in the ignition. He patted the dash and said,
"Don't be a bitch," then turned the key.

Silence.

No starter noise.

No engine noise.

No nothing noise.

He popped the hood, jiggled the battery cables and tried
again. This time Bertha responded, but she also had a new
groaning sound, something he'd never heard before, in addition to her usual coughing and blue smoke.

His phone rang.

He didn't want to answer, partly because it might be the
chief who was still expecting Teffinger to swing by his office,
but mostly because Bertha was busy filling the garage with car-
bon monoxide.

He answered the call, said "Hold on," then closed Bertha's
hood and pulled her out of the garage. "Okay," he said. "It's
me."

"Where are you?"

The voice belonged to Chase.

He told her.

"Want me to come over?"

He did but said, "I'm in the middle of this SJK thing. How about tonight?"

"Maybe you should use me as bait," she said

Teffinger shook his head.

"You never say what I expect you to," he said. "Why is that?"

"I don't know, but I'm serious," she said. "I'm blond. He likes 'em blond. Seems like a match made in heaven. Plus, no one's ever given me a yellow rose. I'm due for one."

Teffinger wasn't amused.

"Don't even joke about it."

Driving down Haight Street he spotted a mom-and-pop florist, which was strange because he'd passed by hundreds of times and never noticed it. On the spur of the moment, he swung in and bought a dozen yellow roses plus a vase.

He'd give them to Chase tonight.

He wedged the vase between the seat and the passenger door and made a mental note that it would fall out if someone opened the door.

Then he did something else unexpected.

He drove over to Condor's and put one of the roses on his doorstep.

He wasn't sure why.

Maybe it was a message he was going to kill him.

He was two doors down when a Lexus sped up the street and jerked to a stop in Condor's driveway. Teffinger ducked behind a UPS truck and watched as a man got out. He had the build and bushy blond hair of a surfer. Teffinger expected him to ring the bell when he got to the top of the stairs. Instead, he picked up the rose and studied it with a puzzled face.

Then he stuck a key in the doorknob and disappeared inside.

Strange.

Who did Condor know well enough to give a key to?

Teffinger didn't see anyone looking out the windows so he walked past and looked at the vehicle's license plate just long enough to memorize it.

Two minutes later the man came out carrying a black briefcase.

He got in the car and disappeared down the street.

79

Day 4—September 24
Thursday Night

Thursday night after dark, a mean thunderstorm swept in from the Pacific and engulfed San Francisco in chaos. The wipers of Winter's car—a Camry rental—swept back and forth at full speed and still couldn't keep up with the slop. Winter concentrated on the road as she drove, barely talking. Jonk sat in the passenger seat, staring out the windshield with his one good eye. They wound over to Lincoln Boulevard and then cut off to the right onto the service road that dead-ended in a large public lot for Baker Beach. They circled through it and saw only one car. A couple of teenagers poked their heads up from the back seat as they passed. Winter parked back-end-in at the far northeast corner, where Jonk's meeting with Tristen was supposed to take place, and killed the engine.

Rain hammered the roof.

"Get in the back on the floor," Jonk said.

"Why?"

"Just a precaution."

She did it.

Jonk got out of the car and sat on the front fender. Lightning arced around him. He didn't care. Five minutes later headlights punched through the weather down the access road. They slowed to a crawl when they got into the parking lot then stopped thirty meters away and went out.

A woman got out and came towards him.

Her walk was strong and purposeful.

Her hands were empty.

Right now she was nothing more than a black silhouette in a black night. It wasn't until she got right up to him that Jonk could make out her features. She was attractive, late twenties or early thirties, and wore a dark, long-sleeve shirt that hung down over jeans, not tucked in. Her hair was already flat from the weather.

"I love the rain," she said.

"Good to know," Jonk said. "You're Tristen, I assume."

"I am. Let's walk on the beach. Do you mind?"

"No. Lead on."

They headed that way through an eerie blacker-than-black nightscape, concentrating on where they put their feet and not stopping until they got to the water's edge. The waves were large, furious and deadly. The whitecaps were so pronounced that they were visible even through the storm.

"Typhoon Joe's glad to have you back on board," Tristen said. "Your cut's still 20 percent even though we'll be working together, so don't worry about being diluted."

Good.

"Tell me about Nathan Rock."

"Nathan Rock's a lawyer," she said. "He's been doing legal work for Typhoon Joe for over ten years. They're friends. Typhoon Joe told him about the Egyptian treasure he bought.

Later it got stolen. After that, one of the coins came on the market here in San Francisco, which is where Rock lives. Naturally, Typhoon Joe began to wonder whether Rock was behind the theft."

"Why didn't he tell me?"

"He wanted you to focus on things from the other end, namely the coin that came onto the market," she said. "Then he'd feed you any information he got on Rock if something actually turned up."

"Did something actually turn up?"

Suddenly lightning arced.

The world lit up.

Just a flash.

Here and gone.

Diluted by the rain.

But it was enough for Jonk to see that the woman was pulling a pistol out from under her shirt. There was murder on her face. She got it all the way out and began to raise it to his chest.

He swung a fist at her face.

80

Day 4—September 24
Thursday Night

Across the alley from Song's apartment was a wall of connected buildings between two and three stories high. One of them had an exterior fire escape. Thursday night after dark, Song climbed that fire escape to the roof with a pair of binoculars in hand and watched her apartment to see if someone actually showed up to kill her.

A heavy rain set in.

It got thicker, colder and heavier.

Then lightning came.

Lots of it.

She took shelter against an air conditioning unit, unable to see her apartment from that angle but getting up every three or four minutes to check. She left all the window coverings open and the lights out. If someone walked around in there with a flashlight, she'd see it.

So far everything was status quo.

If no one came, that meant that the threat was nothing more than a scare tactic initiated by Rekker which, in turn, meant he was dirty beyond the dirtiest dirt.

She had no idea what Fenfang and Shaden were up to at the moment, not having talked to either of them since the fatal meeting this morning. If she had to guess, though, Fenfang was screwing Rekker's brains out in his bedroom right now while Shaden snooped around. Either that or Rekker was passed out with a bad case of the roofies while the two women worked their way into his private places.

They'd get results.

In the end, that's what the world was all about.

Getting results.

The world wasn't about playing by the rules.

She was a rule-player.

Other people were doers.

That was the difference.

The weather didn't just beat down, it took over Song's body to the point of demanding her full concentration. She couldn't think, she could only feel the slamming of the water on her head and ears.

She needed to get up.

It was time to check on her apartment again.

Her body didn't move, though.

It just stayed where it was.

Suddenly she had a weird thought, namely that she never left her window coverings open at night. What if the guy knew that? What if he figured out they were open right now so she could see inside? What if he was in the shadows somewhere, not watching her apartment but instead trying to find out where she was watching from. What if he was silently sneaking up the fire escape this very moment?

If that happened, she was trapped.

She got to her feet but didn't go to the alley edge to look at her apartment. Instead, she went to the other side of the roof to see if there was a way out.

There wasn't.

It was a four-story drop to the street. The only possible escape would be to jump to the roof of the adjacent building which was at least fifteen feet lower.

Get out!

Get out!

Get out!

That's what her brain screamed.

She turned.

Lightning flashed.

It lit up the black silhouette of a man standing on the roof by the fire escape.

Her heart pounded.

The man stepped towards her.

She dropped the binoculars and jumped over the roof's edge.

81

Day 4—September 24
Thursday Night

As a kid in San Francisco Teffinger peddled his bike over to the historic ships on the Hyde Street Dock whenever he could. The sea wood, the engineering and sheer size of the vessels were pure magic. What fascinated him the most, however, were the ghosts of the sailors. It took a certain amount of intestinal fortitude to get on something made of wood and take it over a stormy horizon into the unknown. The star of the dock was an 1886 three-mast trading vessel named Balclutha. A year ago a teenager was found dead on the dock. Teffinger drew the assignment and got to know the security people on the pier.

Now they gave after-hours access to the ship whenever he wanted.

Thursday night after dark the wind kicked up.

A storm was coming in.

Teffinger got a guard to let him and Chase inside.

Ten seconds later the rain started.

Armed with flashlights, he showed her the cargo hold, the crew's quarters, the galley, the rudder mechanics and all the rest. They ended up in the captain's cabin, which was fully restored to its original condition, including a bed.

"Pretty impressive," Chase said. "So how many women have you brought here, all told? Ten? Twenty? A hundred?"

Teffinger made an inquisitive face, adding it up.

"Including you or not including you?"

"Including me."

"Including you," he said. "So I'll need to add one more ... okay, hold on, math's not my strong point."

"Just give me a ballpark," Chase said.

"I can give you an exact number, just give me a minute," he said.

He counted the fingers on his left hand and then his right. Then nodded his head with each additional count.

"Okay, I have it," he said. "You don't want names, right? Just the number?"

Right, just the number.

"Are you sure you want to know?"

"Yes."

"Okay, but remember, you're the one who asked the question."

"Come on, quit stalling."

"You're not going to get mad at me, are you?"

"Probably not."

"Probably?"

"Okay, I won't."

"Are you sure?"

She punched him on the arm. "No, I'm not sure. So tell me."

"All right," he said. "The total, including you, is . . . Wait a minute, it was right on the tip of my brain . . . Okay, it's back, the total including you is one."

Chase shined her flashlight in his face.

"Liar."

She sat down on the bed.

"So if we fool around right here on this bed, that will be the first time you've ever christened this ship."

"*Christened,*" he said. "Good word."

She pulled her shirt over her head and dropped it to the floor.

Her bra followed.

She stood up, put her arms around Teffinger's neck and said, "Show me who you are."

82

Day 4—September 24
Thursday Night

The gun in Tristen's hand went off at the same time Jonk's fist connected with her, not on her head though, more on her shoulder. It was a glancing blow, not hard on, but was enough to make her stumble back and trip to the ground. Jonk dived at her with one thought and one thought only, namely to get the gun away before she fired again. He got a hand on her arm but she continued twisting the weapon towards his face and pulled the trigger for the second time.

Orange flames shot out of the barrel.

The bullet flew so close to his head that he actually felt the vacuum.

His ears rang from the explosion.

He wrestled the gun away then flipped the woman onto her back and straddled her chest. He raised the weapon to smash it down on her head, smash it down so hard and furious that her skull would shatter into a hundred pieces.

Then something snapped inside his head.

And, just like that, he lowered his hand.

The woman didn't move.

She didn't say a word.

She didn't do anything to push him over the edge.

Jonk stayed where he was, letting the thunder inside his veins die down to the point where he could think. Suddenly a pain came from the left side of his body. He put his right hand under his shirt and found a blood-filled wound. The first shot must have hit him.

How bad?

How bad was it?

He stood up.

He was losing blood.

He needed to get out of there.

Now.

This second.

"Tell Typhoon Joe he just made the biggest mistake of his life," he said. "Do you understand?"

Silence.

The woman said nothing.

He shouted, "*Do you understand?*"

"Yes."

"Good."

He almost kicked her to make his point but didn't.

Then he turned and staggered towards the parking lot as the wind whipped the storm into his face.

Five steps later he abruptly turned with the gun in hand to see if she was charging for another attack, maybe with a knife.

She wasn't.

She was still on the ground.

Lucky for her.

The bitch.

He got to the parking lot but was so disoriented that he had no idea where the car was. He couldn't see a thing. Everything was blacker than black and consumed with the storm.

He headed to the right.

Winter was parked somewhere on the edge of the lot.

If he followed the edge he'd eventually find her.

His blood ran slower.

His breathing got more normal.

His brain started to function again.

He now realized that the whole thing had been a setup from the first time Tristen called. Typhoon Joe had already decided to kill Jonk. The problem was that he had no idea where Jonk was. So, what he needed to do was draw him out. That's why Tristen pretended to be part of the other team investigating Rock and set up the meeting. Either that or she actually was part of that team and also didn't mind killing someone for a little extra money. Either way, the whole thing was a setup from the start.

One thing was for sure.

Typhoon Joe had fucked with the wrong man.

He'd learn that sooner or later.

For starters, Typhoon Joe wouldn't see a drop of the treasure.

Not one solitary drop.

Jonk would find it and keep it all.

Then he'd send Typhoon Joe an email letting him know, just to rub his face in it. Sure, Typhoon Joe would hunt him to the ends of the earth.

Who cares?

Screw Typhoon Joe and the horse he rode in on.

Jonk thought he heard something behind him that wasn't the storm.

He turned.

83

Day 4—September 24
Thursday Night

When Song jumped over the edge, all she could do was stare in horror at the adjacent rooftop as she hurled towards it. Pain was coming and there was nothing she could do to stop it.

Brace!

Brace!

Brace!

Then, *wham!*

She hit before she was ready.

Her body contorted.

Pain exploded from somewhere in her legs.

Then her head slammed into something and everything went black.

84

Day 4—September 24
Thursday Night

C hase was a tidal wave rolling through Teffinger's veins. There in the captain's cabin they made sweet, wild, un- inhibited love as the rain beat down on the deck above their heads.

Exhausted.

That's what he was when they were done.

Exhausted from letting her squeeze so much life into his body and brain and being. It was as if she had stuck a valve stem on his body and pumped him full of her life blood.

They were dressed and just about to head topside when his phone rang.

He answered and the voice of Brandi Summers from the office came through. "Got some job security for you."

"Now? It's raining."

She laughed.

"Yeah, the nerve of some people," she said. "The victim's a woman. She has lots of tats."

"Tats?"

"Tattoos," she said. "Get with it, will you."

The word flashed him back to Monday night. As if he was still there, he saw the tattooed little beauty strung up in a standing spread-eagle position being choked to death by Chase, the very woman he just made love to.

"How'd she die?" he asked.

Brandi didn't know.

"The word is that the rain washed her down onto Bayshore Boulevard, down near the San Bruno Mountain State Park." Teffinger knew exactly where she was talking about. The road cut through a number of areas with steep, unimproved terrain. A gulley washer could bring a body down with no problem.

So, this was it.

This was the call he hoped to never get.

This was the body of the woman Chase killed.

"I'm on my way," he said.

Chase studied him with a serious face and said, "What's wrong?"

"Body," he said. "I have to go."

"A murder?"

"Don't know yet."

"Take me with you," she said.

"Can't," he said. "It's off limits."

"No it's not," she said. "Not if I'm with you. I'll stand wherever you say and do whatever you say. I won't be a bother, I promise."

"Why?"

"I want to see you in action."

He exhaled.

"Trust me, it's not that exciting."

"Come on," she said. "Be a sport."

Teffinger chewed on the irony of bringing a killer to the

crime scene of the victim. It couldn't be more wrong on every level. On the other hand, he'd be able to see the expression on her face. He'd be able to look into her soul.

He brushed the hair out of his face and said, "Sure, why not. Let's go."

"Really?"

"Yeah. Really."

The body was all the way across town, which gave the rain plenty of chances to leak through Bertha's top into Teffinger's lap. Ordinarily, he'd be cussing and shifting.

Tonight he didn't care.

He was too busy willing the heavens to make the victim someone other than the woman from the dungeon.

The storm got even worse.

The wipers swished.

The city lights went by as washed-out blurs.

Then they were there.

He pulled up behind a black-and-white and killed the engine.

The sound of the rain intensified.

He turned to Chase.

This might be his last look at her not being a killer.

He kissed her on the lips and said, "Stay here for a moment," then stepped out into the storm without an umbrella and headed for the body.

85

Day 4—September 24
Thursday Night

J onk kept hearing noises behind him in the storm as he
edged around the outskirts of the parking lot but every
time he turned he saw only the same thick wall of blackness that surrounded him in every direction. Something wasn't
right though, he could feel it.

His side was on fire.

His blood was cold.

Movement became more difficult with each passing step.
The gun got heavier and heavier in his hand. His index finger
came out of the trigger and wrapped around the handle.

How much farther?

He shouted out, "Winter!"

He stopped and listened.

She didn't answer.

He called again and listened harder.

He still heard nothing other than the raging of the storm.

Damn it.

He kept walking, taking the small, safe steps of a blind man.
Every few steps he called Winter's name but got no response.

The storm was too thick.

Then he saw something ahead, something blacker than the storm, something the size of a car.

"Winter!"

No answer.

He went that way, faster now, at half a trot. A noise came from somewhere out in the blackness, not from behind this time, from the side. He turned just in time to see the dark silhouette of a figure lunging at him through the air. Before he could react, the impact came.

He fell.

The body that hit him was heavy and muscular.

A man.

Not Winter.

Not Tristen.

He swung at the face and connected, but with only a graze. Suddenly the figure was on top of him raising a knife into the air. He grabbed the man's arm and held it at bay.

The attacker put his weight on his arm.

The knife inched closer and closer to Jonk's face.

Shit!

He was going to die.

Do something!

Now.

Now.

Now.

He kneed the man in the groin.

When the pressure came off, he twisted to the left, got the gun out of his belt and fired.

The yellow explosion from the barrel was so bright that it lit the man with a flash as the bullet entered his body. The recoil was fierce and deadly. Blood splattered, indicating a hollow point. The man didn't make a sound, not even a gurgle. He rolled to his side and stayed motionless. Rain splattered off his face.

Jonk got to his feet and headed for the car.

"Winter!"

No response came.

Ten seconds later he got to it and jerked the door open. The dome light came on. Winter's limp body fell out and landed with a dull thump on the ground. Her head and face were bloody from multiple punches.

Jonk shook her and got no response.

He didn't know if she was dead or not.

She seemed dead.

Then something overpowered him, something that made him scream at the top of his lungs and kick the side of the car.

Hard.

Viciously.

Then again.

And again.

As if it was the enemy.

Bam!

Bam!

Bam!

The metal crushed in.

Terrible pain shot up his leg and drove straight into his brain.

He didn't care.

Screw it.

Screw everything.

He slumped to the ground, took Winter in his arms and

pressed his forehead to hers.

Then he rocked her.

She didn't respond.

She was limp.

Her body was cold.

Colder than his.

86

Day 4—September 24
Thursday Night

Every crime scene before this one had been work, important work with high stakes and justice in the balance, but work nonetheless. This one, by contrast, was surreal. Teffinger walked past a black-and-white parked perpendicular in the road, blocking one lane of traffic from the north.

The light bar bounced blue and red flashes off the hillside. Eerie.

Teffinger never got used to the lights.

He didn't like them.

Another black-and-white sat across the road fifty yards to the south, equally ghost-like. Midway between the vehicles, in the closed lane adjacent to the hill, three portable light stands were on the asphalt, pointed towards the body which was ten steps off the shoulder in a crevice, face up, half submerged under a wash of storm water.

The victim was naked.

There was ink on her.

Tattoos.

Teffinger checked in with the scribe, got a flashlight from the crime unit and shined it on the ground as he walked towards the body, being careful to not disturb any obvious evidence.

His heart raced.

Finally he got to the body, bent down and shined the light directly on it.

He recognized the tattoos.

This was the woman from the dungeon.

There was no question about it.

Damn it.

Damn it to hell.

There were no readily apparent signs of trauma. He couldn't find any gunshot wounds or knife stabs or indications she was hit with a blunt instrument. Her skull was intact and there was no blood in her hair. There were marks on her throat, consistent with strangulation. Judging by the odor and by the stiffness of the body, she'd been dead days.

Meaning Monday night.

He shut the flashlight off and turned his face toward the sky. The storm beat down.

Hard.

Hurtful.

He didn't move.

He didn't flinch.

He didn't care.

He needed it.

The water washed his brain.

From the road someone shouted, "Teffinger, you okay?" He brought his face down, opened his eyes and turned the flashlight back on.

"Yeah, I'm fine."

He headed that way.

Paul Wu, one of the better crime unit guys, grabbed Teffinger's shirt as he walked by and said, "Hey, what's the deal?"

Teffinger stared at him.

Blue and red lights reflected on his face.

Eerie.

Surreal.

"Go ahead and process it," Teffinger said. "Tell the coroner to leave the body in place until I give the go ahead."

"Will do." A pause. "Are you sure you're okay?"

He nodded.

Then he headed for Bertha.

87

Day 4—September 24
Thursday Night

J onk put Winter in the back seat and took off. With his one eye it was dangerous to drive, especially at night in a storm, but it was even more dangerous to stay there. He didn't know if Winter was dead.

He wiped his prints off the gun as he drove.

Then he threw it out the window as he passed a grove of trees down Lincoln Boulevard.

As soon as he did, he regretted it.

He wasn't far enough away from the scene.

Some stupid Samaritan would find it sooner or later and turn it in.

He might have missed a print.

Or his blood might be on it.

Shit.

That was stupid.

Too late, though.

He couldn't go back now.

It would take him an hour to find it.

Tag was in Sausalito with binoculars, learning what she

could about Nathan Rock. Jonk dialed her up and told her what happened.

"Feel Winter for a pulse," she said.

"I'll have to pull over."

"Then pull over."

"I have no idea where I am."

"Just pull over and do it."

The traffic was thicker than he wanted but he pulled over and did it.

"I think I got one," he said.

"We need to get her to a hospital."

"How? I don't know the roads. I have no idea where I am. I can barely see to drive."

Silence.

Then Tag said, "Drive to the first intersection you can find and stop the car there somewhere safe. Then tell me what the two roads are."

He did.

"Okay," she said. "I'm going to call 911 and tell them to get an ambulance there ASAP. Wipe your prints off everything in the car as good as you can and get out of there before they arrive. Do you understand?"

Yes.

He did.

Fully.

He did as instructed, kissed Winter on the cheek as the flashing lights and sirens came up the road and then disappeared into the night.

88

Day 4—September 24
Thursday Night

After the crime unit processed the scene, Teffinger walked Chase over to the body through the storm and shined a flashlight on the victim's face. Chase had some type of reaction but before Teffinger could turn his head to look directly at her she was expressionless. He ran the light down the victim's body over the tattoos and then up to her neck.

"Welcome to my world," he said.

"How long has she been dead?"

"I'm guessing since Monday night. She's too young to be lying there," he said. "Don't you think?"

"Maybe."

He tilted his head.

"Maybe?"

Chase closed her eyes and turned her face up to the storm.

Then she looked at Teffinger and said, "Life isn't about length. It's about intensity."

He wiggled the light on the victim's face.

"I'll bet she'd disagree with you if she could."

A beat.

Chase said, "I like her tattoos," then turned and walked back towards Bertha.

DAY
FIVE

September 25
Friday

89

Day 5—September 25
Friday Morning

S ong woke up in a bed that was too soft to be hers. Someone was next to her—Fenfang—still sleeping. She had
to relieve herself, badly, this second, and headed for the
bathroom. There, she remembered the events of last night,
namely jumping down to the adjacent roof during the storm,
hitting her head on something that made her brain turn black
with disorientation for a few heartbeats, then getting to her
feet and into the interior stairway. At street level she ran and
ran and ran until her lungs gave out. Then she made her way
to Fenfang's place.

Her clothes were on the shower rod, still wet.

She slid them to the end and took a long, hot, heaven-sent
shower.

Dry clothes were on the sink when she got out.

Two minutes later she walked into the kitchen, towel drying
her hair. Fenfang handed her a cup of hot coffee and said,
"The guy last night—did he have a gun?"

"I don't know. It was too dark."

"It would be interesting to get back onto that roof you

jumped on and see if there are any bullet holes in it."

Later that morning she checked the roof but didn't really know what a bullet hole looked like. There were scars on the roof and dents on the rooftop units that could have come from bullets or could not have.

Her apartment was as she had left it.

So was her office.

No one had broken in.

Right now, midmorning with the sun shining, she felt safe.

Tonight would be a different story.

Her phone rang half a dozen times—all clients.

Then she got a call from a voice she didn't recognize. "Is this Song Lee, the lawyer?"

"Yes. Who's this?"

"My name's Haley Key," she said. "The word on the street is that you've been trying to locate me."

Haley Key.

Haley Key was Detective Finger's girlfriend, the person who testified during Kyle Greyson's trial to the effect that Finger planted evidence to frame the defendant.

They met an hour later at Chef Hung's Restaurant, down the alley a short ways from Song's office. The woman was petite, average looking, and had a nervous tic every so often on the left side of her face.

Song said, "Before I ask you what I'm going to ask you, rest assured that whatever you say is going to stay with me. It's not going to come back to bite you in any way, shape or form. Do you understand?"

"Okay."

"I mean it," Song said. "This isn't about you. It's about Dirk

Rekker, the attorney."

"Okay."

"Here's the thing," Song said. "You testified at trial that your then-boyfriend, Detective Frank Finger, planted evidence."

Right.

That was true.

"My question is this—and please don't take it personally—but what I want to know is whether Rekker somehow got you to say that."

The woman tilted her head.

"What do you mean?"

Song squirmed.

"What I'm trying to figure out is whether Rekker black-mailed you or threatened you or did something to somehow get you to testify the way you did."

"Wow, that's quite a question."

Right.

It was.

"So what's the answer?" Song said.

90

Day 5—September 25
Friday Morning

Teffinger dug his head even farther into the pillow when the first rays of light seeped into the starboard window of Bad Add Vice. He had stayed up until one in the morning last night, drinking Anchor Steams and wondering what to do about Chase. The clock by his head said 5:30. If he got up and scrambled, he'd be late for the six o'clock meeting but not by much.

He rolled onto his back and gauged his ability to get vertical.

He could do it but it would be painful.

Screw it.

If he got up now he'd be useless all day.

He rolled back over to his side.

At some point later his phone rang and pulled him out of a deep sleep with all the subtleness of a cattle prod. The clock said 7:54. The incoming number was the chief.

Teffinger sat up but didn't answer.

Instead he got the coffee pot going and took a shower.

A message was waiting for him when he got out.

It was from the chief.

"You were supposed to swing by my office yesterday," he said. "You didn't do it. You were supposed to be at the meeting this morning. You weren't there. The better way to phrase it would be, You weren't there, again. I don't know what's going on with you, Teffinger, but I've got too much on my plate to figure it out. You forced my hand on this. I'm sorry you did, but you did. I'm going to have to suspend you pending an investigation. Swing by the office by the end of the day and turn in your gun and badge. I'm sorry it's come to this, I really am. I had high hopes for you. I'm sorry we had to do this by phone."

Teffinger sank to the mattress and put his head in his hands.

Then he deleted the message.

The storm of last night had moved on. A few early morning clouds still hung in the air but it looked like it would be a decent day. He locked up the sailboat walked down the dock to Bertha.

He stuck the key in and turned.

Bertha started.

Before he shifted into park, his phone rang.

It wasn't the chief.

It was Brandi.

"Got another body for you," she said.

He started to tell her he was suspended, but the words were too hard to say.

"What kind of body?"

"A guy named Troy Trent."

Troy Trent.

Teffinger knew the name but couldn't place it. Then he remembered. Trent was the surfer-looking-guy who went into Condor's house yesterday with a key and came out a few minutes later with a briefcase.

"Where's he at?"

Brandi told him.

"I'm on my way."

Trent, it turned out, had been stabbed in the back three times with a large knife. It happened in his own driveway, between his car and the front door. Keys were clutched in his hand, ready to open the door he never got to. Between three and four in the morning, that's when it happened.

Mere hours ago.

Condor did it.

Teffinger could feel it.

It had something to do with that entry yesterday.

That briefcase.

Maybe this is how Teffinger would reel Condor in; not with the SJK killings, but with the murder of Troy Trent.

91

Day 5—September 25
Friday Morning

I t was clear that the lawyer, Rock, was behind the initial theft of the treasure from Typhoon Joe. Where did he stash it? That was the question. Jonk and Tag got up early Friday morning and drove to the man's floating house in Sausalito, not knowing exactly what they were going to do yet but knowing they were going to do something.

Jonk's side hurt just as much now as it did last night.

More in fact.

Tristen's bullet had cut deeper than he needed.

Tag's needle and thread stitch job of last night was good enough to close the wound and stop the bleeding, but in hindsight the stitches were too far apart. She should have put in double what she did. That couldn't be corrected now. The area was so red and tender that he could barely touch it, much less get pierced with a needle ten more times. There was no visible infection, though.

That was good.

They pulled to the side of the road a hundred yards short of the marina as the sun broke over the horizon.

In the parking lot were three or four police cars with the lights flashing, plus an ambulance.

What the hell?

Jonk and Tag approached on foot.

He wore a sweatshirt with the hood up.

She wore a baseball cap.

They both wore sunglasses.

There was traffic up and down the street, but no pedestrians.

Jonk had a sinking feeling that the presence of the cops had something to do with Rock. It didn't take long to confirm his suspicion. The cops were at Rock's slip.

"Do you think someone killed him?" Tag asked.

Jonk nodded.

"It might have been Tristen," he said. "She knew about him. It could have been our Egyptian friends, too. Maybe they got wind of him somehow."

"Now what?"

Jonk picked up a rock and threw it into the bay.

"Whoever killed him probably interrogated him first," he said. "My suspicion is that Rock told them where he hid everything. That's why he's dead now. They had no use for him after that."

"That's not good," Tag said.

Jonk agreed.

Not good.

Not good at all.

"The more I think about it, I don't think it was Tristen," he said. "It was the Egyptian guy and his little girlfriend. We need to find them and we need to do it now, this second."

"How?"

He spotted a pop can on the ground, picked it up and tossed

it into a trash container.

"Let's go to that warehouse area where they kept you," he said.

Tag wasn't impressed.

"They'd never go back there," she said.

"I agree," he said. "That's why we're going."

92

Day 5—September 25
Friday Morning

Haley Key ate shrimp stir-fried with veggies and swore up and down as she chewed that her testimony at Kyle Greyson's trial was accurate and truthful and not the product of any blackmail or coercion by Dirk Rekker.

She was lying.

Song could feel it.

She could see it in the woman's tic.

Lying or not, she was a dead end. She wasn't going to give up Rekker, that was clear.

Nothing.

Nothing.

Nothing.

That's all Song ever got.

She headed back to the office under a nice San Francisco sun, wondering whether to report yesterday's death threat to the police. Passing her bike in the alley, she reached under the seat to see if another transmitter had been planted.

It was clean.

In her office, she kicked her shoes off, walked across the

carpet in her bare feet and made a fresh pot of coffee. When she turned, a man was standing behind her, not more than three steps away. He wasn't the blue-bandana man but was just as rough looking if not more so. He had long black hair and reminded her a little of Nicholas Cage from the movie Bangkok Dangerous. She must have looked like she was about to scream because the man held up his hands in surrender, took a step back and said, "Whoa, lady, calm down."

"Who are you?"

"My name's Condor," he said. "Jackson Condor. Are you Song Lee, the lawyer?"

"Yes."

"Do you have time to meet with me about a legal matter?"

She sensed trouble.

She didn't like him.

There was something about him that was off.

"What kind of legal matter?"

"If we talk, whatever I tell you is privileged, right?"

She nodded.

"Correct."

"Does it stay privileged even if you decide not to represent me?"

"It does."

He tilted his head.

"Are you the kind of lawyer who actually keeps your client's secrets a secret?"

She studied him.

"What's your issue, Mr. Condor?"

93

Day 5—September 25
Friday Morning

The dead man, Troy Trent, had a nice house on Irving, one block south of Golden Gate Park. He was a man of taste. A half-dozen original Edgar Payne landscapes hung on the walls. Teffinger found the mysterious briefcase in the den—empty.

He looked around the interior.

Condor was guilty and the evidence was here somewhere.

Where to start?

He called Neva and said, "Did Condor's car leave his place last night?"

"No."

"No?"

"No."

"Are you sure?"

"I'm glad you asked," she said. "Because you owe me big time. I actually slept in my car last night, two blocks down from his place, on the chance he'd take off in the middle of the night and head for London Fogg. It wasn't pretty. Cars aren't designed for sleep."

"Bertha is," Teffinger said.

"I'm talking about cars that aren't their own zip codes," she said. "Condor never left. The GPS stayed locked on his garage all night."

"Maybe he found the transmitter and left it sitting in there," Teffinger said. "Then he took off."

"Could be," she said. "If that happened, I wouldn't know. I was just going by the signal."

Right.

Understood.

"Are you still down the street from him?"

She was.

Four blocks down.

In a coffee shop.

It didn't take long for Teffinger to discover something interesting about the victim, Troy Trent, namely that he was into porn.

S&M porn, to be exact.

He particularly favored the movies of an outfit called Concrete Cactus. Two whole drawers in his bedroom dresser were filled with their movies.

Baby's First Bondage.

Dungeon Girls.

Sluts in Ropes.

Tied and Tamed.

It was a full hour later before Teffinger found out the next thing of interest, which happened while he was going through the man's financial records. Trent, it turned out, received a string of big checks from Concrete Cactus.

No wonder he had a lot of their movies.

He was financially connected to them.

In fact, maybe he *was* them.

An investor or part owner or something.

The next thing of interest came from his cell phone records, which showed a lot of calls both to and from Jackson Condor.

Teffinger called Neva.

"As long as you're sort of hanging around with time on your hands, you can do me a favor," he said. "Get into the Secretary of State records and find out what you can about a company named Concrete Cactus. I have information to suggest that our newest job security, Troy Trent, might be a shareholder or partner in that group. They make S&M films by the way. What I'm interested in finding out is whether Jackson Condor is also involved in that group. Somehow Trent and Condor are connected. Concrete Cactus might be the link."

She grunted.

"What are you going to do while I'm doing all the work? Emphasis on the all."

"I'll be thinking of more things for you to do."

Two minutes after he hung up his phone rang. It was Detective Richardson, from the office. "We got a name for last night's tattoo victim."

"What is it?"

"Amanda Wayfield."

"Dig up everything you can on her."

A pause.

Teffinger sensed a problem.

"Will do it but it'll have to wait until after this SJK thing unless you want to override Northstone and the chief."

"Override them but don't let them know."

"That can get me fired."

"That's why you can't let them know."

94

Day 5—September 25
Friday Morning

The industrial warehouse where Tag had been held captive and interrogated by the Egyptian man and his girlfriend was vacant, abandoned and cold.

"Now what?" Tag asked.

Good question.

"All we can hope is that Rock didn't give up the location," Jonk said. "My feeling though is that he did. Someone's gathering it up right now and planning their escape from the city."

They passed a small diner, swung in and ordered pancakes and coffee.

Girlfriend.

Girlfriend.

Girlfriend.

The word kept bouncing around in Jonk's brain, but he didn't know why. The woman with the Egyptian man was his girlfriend. That became abundantly clear to Tag during her captivity.

Then it came to him.

He nudged Tag's leg lightly under the table.

She looked at him.

"I just figured something out," he said. "I always thought the Egyptian guy was someone hired by the Egyptian government, a mercenary. But I was wrong."

"How so?"

"When I met with Typhoon Joe, he told me how he bought the treasure from a man named Amaury, who had been part of the official search team. During the search Amaury figured out where the treasure was but didn't tell anyone. Later, he and his girlfriend went back and uncovered part of it. He's got to be the one running around San Francisco."

Tag wasn't impressed.

"You said before that Typhoon Joe wanted to hire him instead of you but he couldn't do it because he was already in the middle of heading back to dig up more of the treasure."

Jonk took a sip of coffee, undaunted.

"He was lying to Typhoon Joe. The best part of the treasure is the mask. He's after it, while it's loose. The rest of the treasure can sit under the dirt and wait. It isn't going anywhere. That's what I'd do if I was him. Go after the mask now while the going was good."

Tag squeezed his hand.

"If he was part of the official search team, there must be pictures."

"You'd think."

Tag took out her handheld and logged on to the net. Within five minutes, she had a picture of the search team. She turned the display to Jonk and tapped her finger on a face. "Second from the left."

Jonk nodded.

Now they had a name.

Amaury Bustani.

And a photo.

Whether it would help them was another matter.

95

Day 5—September 25
Friday Morning

Song heard shocking news midmorning. Nathan Rock— an international lawyer with the firm of Rapport, Wolfe & Lake—was murdered last night in a Sausalito marina where he lived. Song pulled up the image of Rock getting out of a silver BMW Wednesday night and walking into Danny Dan's for a clandestine meeting with Rayla White, a law clerk from the firm's criminal division.

Somehow that meeting was related to his murder.

It had to be.

She paced.

Should she tell the cops about what she saw?

Technically, she got the information while working on a case for a client, Shaden. That happened before she was fired. She wasn't positive about how the rules of professional conduct worked, but was fairly certain that information obtained by an attorney while working on behalf of a client couldn't be disclosed to a third party without the client's permission. That made sense, too. The cops would want to know why she was following Rayla White. That question would lead directly into all the confidential information that Shaden had given her, including the fact that Shaden may or may not have killed a woman Sunday night.

Should she ask Shaden whether she could speak to the cops?

The more she thought about it, the more wrong it seemed.

There was no upside to Shaden.

It was Shaden, not Rock or the cops, who Song was hired to help.

It was bad enough that she really hadn't helped Shaden in the end. What kind of lawyer would she be if she set out on a course of conduct that actually ended up hurting her client?

No.

Leave it alone.

The cops would get to Rayla White sooner or later on their own accord in any event.

On her desk was an envelope with $20,000 cash inside—a retainer given to her by Jackson Condor. Song twisted it in her fingers for a few moments and almost picked up the phone to tell him that she had second thoughts.

She wasn't the right lawyer for him.

He should get someone else.

Instead, she put the envelope in a backpack, peddled her Fugi down to the bank and deposited the money in a trust account, getting yet another raised eyebrow from the teller.

Then she headed back to her office to work Condor's case.

And work it fast.

96

Day 5—September 25
Friday Morning

Teffinger sat down on Troy Trent's couch and put his feet up on the coffee table. The crime unit was gone, the body was gone, the black-and-whites were gone, the news cameras were gone and the lookey-loos were gone. The motion and noise and buzz and activity and shouting and jockeying for position had all been replaced by a vacuum. Teffinger sat in the middle of that vacuum, waiting for something brilliant to fall out of the sky and land in his brain.

So far, it wasn't happening.

He got up and wandered around, taking his time, casting his eyes here and there, searching for whatever it was he missed the first time.

He felt empty.

Condor was the one who killed Trent; Teffinger was sure of it but there was no proof.

Not an iota.

Teffinger's hope of averting the next SJK murder by getting Condor off the streets was gone.

Maybe he should go over to Condor's place and question

him about Trent.

Shake the tree.

See if anything fell out.

Maybe he could make Condor believe he had evidence he didn't.

Maybe he could scare him enough to drive him out of town.

His phone rang and the voice of Neva came through. "Remember how you already owe me big time," she said. "Well now it's even bigger time."

"Good, put it on the list."

"I already have."

"Just out of curiosity, how big is that list?"

"Huge."

"How huge?"

"Huge enough that I had to build a separate room to keep it in," she said. "Anyway, according to the Secretary of State's records, Concrete Cactus is a California corporation wholly owned by two other companies called D-Drop Ltd. and DAG, Inc. Those companies, in turn, are owned by others. It goes on and on like that. It's a huge spider's web. In the end, there are two shareholders at the top, namely Jackson Connor and Troy Trent."

Teffinger looked out the window.

A couple of teens were going down the hill on skateboards.

"Thanks," he said. "I'll get back to you."

Teffinger had heard the name D-Drop, Ltd. before but couldn't place it. He opened the dresser drawer and flipped through the DVDs again, then stuck one called Dirty Blond Bimbo in the player to see what they were like.

The women were drop-dead gorgeous.

Forced sensual pleasures were interposed with rough S&M, rocking the victim between the two extremes.

Teffinger fast-forwarded through it.

To his surprise, it ended with one of the women being murdered while bound.

It was an actual murder.

There was no question about it.

What the hell?

He played it back at normal speed, three times, then at slow speed. It wasn't until the last playback that he was able to tell that the murder wasn't real after all.

It was a fake.

The best fake in the world, but a fake.

Curious, he popped in another one.

Lust Slaves.

Something about it seemed familiar. He was a full five minutes into it before he focused on the background and the apparatus rather than the women. Then he realized it was shot in the same room where he had seen Chase strangle Amanda Wayfield through the telescope in Condor's bedroom.

Then he remembered where he heard the name D-Drop before.

That's who owned the building where the dungeon was located.

He fast-forwarded through.

It also ended in a murder, although not as realistic as the other one.

He popped in a third.

It ended in a murder.

Incredibly convincing.

But not real.

97

Day 5—September 25
Friday Morning

R ock was behind the initial theft of the treasure from Typhoon Joe. But how? He had to have had help. It was too big a job for one person to figure out how to get the treasure out of Typhoon Joe's possession to begin with, much less sneak it out of Hong Kong undetected and then all the way to San Francisco. It would be nice to know when Rock last went to Hong Kong and who accompanied him, the theory being that the other person was a co-conspirator.

That person would be as valuable as Rock.

In fact, maybe Amaury wasn't the one who killed Rock.

Maybe it was Rock's co-conspirator.

Greed.

Greed.

Greed.

Never underestimate it.

Tag tapped her PI resources and found out something interesting—Rock hadn't been to Hong Kong, or anywhere else in Asia for that matter, in over a year—long before the treasure was even purchased by Typhoon Joe, much less stolen.

Jonk scratched his head.

"How could Rock be behind the theft if he never even went there?"

"He must have just set it all in motion after Typhoon Joe confided to him about it," Tag said. "Someone from Hong Kong had to be the front man. We need Rock's phone records—the incoming and outgoing numbers—to see who he was talking to."

"Can you get them?"

She frowned.

Then she said, "Probably not but let me see."

An hour later they entered the opulent lobby of the Mark Hopkins InterContinental Hotel on California Street and took the elevator to the Top of the Mark, a vista bar on the nineteenth floor. Through the glass, San Francisco stretched in all directions with particularly stunning views of Alcatraz, Fisherman's Wharf and the Golden Gate Bridge.

An older gentleman with a white beard waved at them from a table.

Three martinis sat before him.

He slid one across to each of them and said, "They have a hundred martinis on the menu here. They only need one, this one. It's called the French 75. I took the liberty of ordering it for you."

Jonk said "Thanks," and took a sip.

Martini's weren't his thing, but it actually wasn't bad.

"Why are we meeting here?" Tag asked.

"Because life is short," he said. "At my age it's even shorter."

They chatted until their drinks were done.

Then they slipped the man an envelope under the table.

He showed his appreciation by slipping them a flash drive.

As they parted the man said, "The owner of these records got himself murdered last night. But I suppose you already know that."

Right.

They did.

"We didn't do it," Jonk said. "Just for your information."

"I wouldn't care even if you did," the man said. "Just for your information."

Back at the car, Tag fired up the flash drive in her computer and wasn't disappointed. The phone records were clearly Rock's and were clearly authentic. They showed myriad calls to and from a Hong Kong number starting approximately a month before Typhoon Joe's treasure got stolen.

It took hardly any effort to find who owned that number.

He was a man named Park Ching.

98

Day 5—September 25
Friday Morning

S ong wondered if Rayla White was the one who called yesterday to warn her that she was on someone's murder list. It made sense in a way. Rekker was after her and Rayla worked in his department. She might have overheard him making plans. On the other hand, maybe she was working in cahoots with him to throw a scare Song's way.

Friend or foe.

Which was she?

Either way she was definitely in the middle of things.

She was with Shaden the night they broke into Rekker's house. She met with Rock at a dive bar on Wednesday. Last night, Rock was murdered.

Right now, Song didn't have time to think about it.

She needed to work on Condor's case.

She pushed up her glasses and got busy.

An hour later the door opened and two people walked in, Fenfang and Shaden.

Their faces were grim.

Fenfang slumped into the seat in front of Song's desk and said, "I think Rekker's wise to the fact that my case is fake. He keeps asking me about the details."

"That's what lawyers do," Song said.

Fenfang shook her head.

"This is different. He's trying to trip me up. He's trying to get proof that his suspicions are right."

Shaden nodded in agreement.

"The fake case was your creation," she said. "We need you back on the team. We need to get the details flushed out before Fenfang says something she shouldn't."

Song leaned back.

"I'm hired, I'm fired, I'm hired, I'm fired," she said. "Believe it or not, that takes a toll."

Shaden came around the desk and hugged her. "I'm sorry," she said. "I haven't handled this well. I've been the client from hell. It's just that I'm scared to death. I need to find out if I killed someone. I'll never have a day of peace until I know one way or the other, not to mention that I have to figure out whether to drop my life and head to Mexico. Forgive me?"

Yes, she did.

She looked at Fenfang and said, "What are you getting out of Rekker so far? Anything?"

"I'm getting his hands on my ass," she said. "That's about it. I haven't let him all the way in, though. He's still lust-drunk. He's still in play."

"Will he talk, eventually?"

"I don't know," she said. "All I know is that he hasn't yet. Worse, for some reason, I can't get him to invite me over to his house, so we haven't had a chance to do the roofies thing. He wants to screw in the car for some reason. Maybe it goes back to his teenage years, I don't know—it's strange. I'm getting more and more nervous. He's an extreme man under the surface. I don't think he'll do anything negative to me as long as my case might be real. If he stumbles onto something that shows him it's not, though, I don't know what will happen. I really don't."

"In that case, my advice is to abandon the whole thing," Song said. "We'll figure out something else."

Fenfang shook her head.

So did Shaden.

"We're too close," Fenfang said. "We need to push forward."

A strange thought came to Song. She must have gotten lost in it because Shaden nudged her and said, "Hey, what's going on in there?"

She focused.

"Under the fake case, a killer's supposed to be after Fenfang. That's the whole damsel in distress thing we were going for since day-one."

Right.

True.

"Maybe instead of better details, what we need is for that guy to show up."

Fenfang and Shaden exchanged glances.

Impressed.

"You mean hire someone to make an attempt on Fenfang's life?" Shaden asked.

Yes.

That's exactly what she meant.

"A fake attempt, obviously, not a real attempt," Song said. "We'll do it when she's with Rekker. In fact, we'll do it when they're in a car making out."

99

Day 5—September 25
Friday Afternoon

Three DVDs caught Teffinger's eye. They were in the second drawer of Trent's dresser, at the far right end. Whereas all the others had color packaging and snapshots of scenes on the back, these were in clear plastic cases, as if they hadn't been packaged for release yet.

He popped one in the player.

It was the same MO as the others.

Hot women.

Bondage.

Pleasure mixed with pain.

In hindsight, that's why Condor had the telescope in his bedroom. He'd watch his own videos being produced. Why from there, though, instead of from the scene?

Teffinger fast-forwarded to the signature ending and saw something that made his face sweat. The woman was tied in the exact same way the SJK killer bound his victims, namely on her stomach with her hands behind her back, her legs bent at the knees, her ankles tied together and a rope strung from her feet to her neck. Unlike the other murder scenes that generally lasted less than five minutes, this one stretched on for a long, long time. The woman's legs eventually pulled straighter and straighter in spite of her frantic efforts and she choked to death while the camera zoomed in on her face.

Was it real?

Teffinger watched the final moments again, in slow motion.

It looked real.

He watched it again.

If it was fake, he couldn't tell.

He played the second clear-case DVD which, again, ended in a murder so visually compelling that it might be real, although it wasn't a SJK replica.

He put in the third DVD and recognized it within the first few seconds. It was Chase in the dungeon Monday night, working over Amanda Wayfield, whose body washed out of the San Bruno Mountains last night.

His phone rang just as the victim took her final breath.

He answered and the voice of Donald Westlake, the coroner, came through. "Teffinger," he said. "I just wanted to let you know I've conclusively determined the woman from last night, Amanda Wayfield, was choked to death. You definitely have a homicide on your hands."

Teffinger swallowed.

Then he stood up and paced.

"When did it happen?"

"Monday night, best guess."

"Thanks."

"You okay?"

"Yeah, sure."

"You sound strange."

"I'm okay," Teffinger said.

"Yeah, well, for the record, you sound strange."

"Duly noted."

Teffinger popped the DVD out of the player and stuck it back in the plastic case.

He stuck that case in his shirt pocket.

The other two DVDs went back into the drawer where he found them.

Then he headed for Bertha.

100

Day 5—September 25
Friday Afternoon

Jonk might be a foreigner in San Francisco but back in Hong Kong he had no shortage of connections. He called one of them, a PI named Quon, and gave him the assignment to find out everything he could about Park Ching—Rock's co-conspirator—as soon as he could. An hour later, Quon phoned back.

"Park Ching is an arranger," Quon said. "By that, I mean he arranges stuff for whoever needs stuff arranged."

"What kind of stuff?"

"Any kind of stuff," Quon said. "He hires people to get jobs done. He's basically a middleman. He doesn't do much of the actual work himself. His gift is being able to find people he can call, no matter what the job is."

"Are you talking about hitmen?"

"That would be an example but only one of many," Quon said. "He's a lot more diverse than that. Whatever someone wants, Ching can make it happen." A beat, then, "He's run into a little problem, though."

"Like what?"

"Like he got himself killed."

"Someone killed him?"

"Deader than dead," Quon said.

"When?"

"Just recently," he said. "Wednesday night."

Jonk paced.

"I need to get his phone records," he said.

Quon laughed.

"Yeah, right."

"I'm serious."

"Guys like Park Ching don't leave electronic footprints," he said. "That's how they get business and that's how they stay in business."

"Yeah, well, he's dead, so he must have left something somewhere," Jonk said. "Dig into it. I want to know who he's been talking to over the last two months."

"Impossible."

"At least try."

"I don't want to waste your money."

"Look, I appreciate it's a long shot," Jonk said. "Dig into it, though. You'll get paid even if you come up short. In fact, if it will make you feel better, I'll wire a retainer to your account as soon as we hang up."

A pause.

Then, "We go back, so that's not necessary. Don't expect much though. That's all I'm saying. The only thing I can promise is that you'll get my best efforts."

"Understood," Jonk said. "Let me give you a little more background. Ching used somebody—probably a team—to steal some ancient Egyptian treasure from Typhoon Joe."

"Typhoon Joe?"

"Right."

"Damn, no wonder he's dead."

"I want to know who he hired," Jonk said.

"You don't go up against Typhoon Joe and live," Quon said. "Not in a million years."

101

Day 5—September 25
Friday Afternoon

Song had no clue who to call to arrange a fake attempt on Fenfang's life. She didn't travel in those circles and left the project for Fenfang and Shaden to figure out. They hadn't talked about it, but it appeared that Fenfang was back on the payroll as part of the law firm, which meant that Song was legally and professionally responsible for whatever she did. That wasn't good but, quite frankly, she was too tired to keep fighting it. Whatever was destined to happen was going to happen. It wasn't worth it to keep worrying about it.

When the women left, she refocused on Condor's case.

She suddenly had a thought and called Fenfang. "When you hire somebody, be absolutely sure he or she understands it's a fake, not real."

Fenfang laughed.

"You worry too much."

"The other thing is to be sure it gets set up so it doesn't result in a fight or confrontation between that person and Rekker," she added. "We don't want Rekker to end up killing someone or vice versa."

Right.

Good thought.

"We won't do anything without running it by you first," Fenfang said.

"Promise?"

"Yes, promise."

An hour later she was facing her monitor on the credenza against the wall when she heard a noise behind her as if someone had entered the room. Before she could turn, something swung through the air and struck her on the head.

Her glasses flew.

Pain exploded in her skull.

Everything turned confusing and dark.

Her body fell towards the floor.

She braced for the impact.

Halfway down everything went black.

102

Day 5—September 25
Friday Afternoon

Bertha didn't start until Teffinger popped the hood
and jiggled the battery wires. When she fired up, he
slammed the hood, kicked the bumper and called
Chase. "We need to meet right now." He expected her to say,
Why? What's going on? But there must have been a tone in his
voice because she said, "Okay."

"The boat."

"Fine, the boat," she repeated. "I'm on my way."

Teffinger almost clipped a car as he pulled into thick traffic.
The other driver honked and gave him the finger. Teffinger
stuck his arm out the window and gave him the finger back.
The other driver shook his fist and then rammed Teffinger's
back bumper.

He slammed on his brakes.

Bertha slid sideways to a stop.

The other car came to a stop behind him.

Teffinger gripped the steering wheel with all his might,
keeping himself locked into position because if he got out he'd
beat the guy to death with his fists.

A second passed.

Then another.

And another.

Without looking back, he jammed the transmission into drive and took off.

He hadn't gotten two blocks when his phone rang. He answered without checking the incoming number and was immediately sorry he did.

It was the chief.

"Someone said you're still working cases," the man said.

"That's true."

"Well stop it, you've been suspended."

"I don't care."

He hung up.

When he got to the boat, Chase wasn't there yet. He pulled an Anchor Steam from the fridge and swallowed it in three long gulps. Then he got another. When Chase showed up, he took her into the cabin, sat her on the bed and said, "I have something I want you to see."

He hit play.

Chase jumped onto the screen of a flat-panel TV, wearing the mask, but they both knew it was her. Teffinger let her watch herself work over Amanda Wayfield for a minute and then fast-forwarded to the end.

"I found this in a dead man's house," he said.

"Whose?"

"Troy Trent." A beat, then, "You killed Amanda Wayfield."

She exhaled.

Then she looked at him briefly before diverting her eyes.

"I know," she said.

She balled up on the bed.

Then she cried.

103

Day 5—September 25
Friday Afternoon

Tag called in every favor she had in town to no avail. Then out of the blue one of her contacts who knew nothing a half hour ago called her back and said, "Marriott Marquis on Fourth Street."

"Are you sure?"

"Positive," he said. "He's under the name Landon Lee. You owe me a blowjob."

She laughed.

"I'm half tempted to give it to you."

"Well, call me when you get the other half in place."

"You're too much."

She hung up and slapped Jonk's ass. "Our little Egyptian friend Amaury is staying at the Marriott Marquis under a different name; Landon Lee. Let's go."

104

Day 5—September 25
Friday Afternoon

Song regained consciousness to find her eyes blindfolded and her hands tied behind her back. Karaoke vibrated up through the floorboards into her ear. With her legs not tied, she was able to press against the wall and struggle up into a standing position. Then she scraped her face against the corner of the desk until the edge snagged the blindfold and pulled it up. What she saw she could hardly believe.

The place was trashed.

Everything that had been in a drawer was on the floor.

Everything.

In that mess was a pair of scissors.

She managed to get them into her hands and then cut the materials that bound her wrists, which turned out to be strips of cloth ripped from her own T-shirt.

She felt her head.

There was blood but it was dry and matted.

The office had no mirror so she walked up to her apartment.

The door was shut but not locked.

Inside, everything was as trashed as the office.

She didn't care.

She was alive.

Everything else was just stuff.

No one had hit her or beaten her up after she passed out.

Her face was untouched.

So was her body.

She warmed up the shower, stepped inside with her clothes still on and stuck her head under the spray. The water at her feet turned red. She stayed as she was until the water cleared up, then took off her clothes, tossed them over the top and gently massaged her head with soap.

Who did it?

That was the question.

Who did it and why?'

What the hell were they looking for?

She had nothing of interest to anyone.

Maybe it had something to do with Condor.

But what?

He'd only been a client for half a day.

On the other hand, maybe it was related to Rekker. Maybe he had the place under surveillance and spotted Fenfang and Shaden when they made their visit. Maybe he figured out Fenfang wasn't a sweet little innocent client. Maybe he was trying to find out what they had on him, if anything.

Then again, maybe it was even related to Rayla White. Maybe the woman looked out the window of Danny Dan's when Song wasn't paying attention and spotted her.

It might even relate to Nathan Rock, for that matter.

How?

She didn't know.

But it could.

Something was going on with him.

Something powerful enough to get him killed.

There was too much going on.

Somehow it was all connected.

Somehow she was in the middle of it.

She considered reporting the assault to the police but then thought, Screw it. They didn't do anything the last time they were here.

They weren't going to get her out of this mess.

Only she could.

105

Day 5—September 25
Friday Afternoon

Teffinger went topside and slammed down an Anchor Steam while Chase cried in the cabin. Then he went down, took her in his arms and rocked her on the bed.

"I'm not going to turn you in," he said.

She trembled.

"You have to."

"Actually I don't," he said. "I got suspended this morning. Technically I'm not even on the case. I'm a civilian. I'm going to have to return the DVD to the scene but it will probably just end up rotting in the drawer. Even if someone finds it, they won't connect it to Amanda Wayfield and even if they do they won't recognize you because of the mask. The only reason I knew it was you is because of the tattoo and because I know your movements. So you're safe."

She laid her head on his chest.

"Can I tell you what happened?"

"I saw what happened."

"It's not that simple," she said. "I have a younger sister, Jacqueline St. John. She's twenty-two. Last year she disappeared.

That's how this whole thing got started."

"What do you mean, got started?" Teffinger said.

"Jacqueline was wild from birth," she said. "She left the house when she was fifteen and went to New York. She never graduated from high school even though she's smarter than me times two any day of the week. She had a face and body that let her get her way and ended up bouncing from guy to guy. Last year she dropped off the face of the earth."

"What happened?"

Chase shook her head.

"I don't know," she said. "In spite of our differences, we kept in touch. I was her rock and strangely, in a way, she was mine. One day when I called her, her phone didn't work, and that was it. I've never heard from her since. That was more than a year ago."

"I could look into it, if you want," he said.

She squeezed him.

"I hired a private investigator," she said. "What he found out is that according to Jacqueline's boyfriend at the time—a guy named Sean Strappen—Jacqueline had been talking about getting into porn, just for kicks. He said he'd leave her if she did because it was no different than cheating. She promised that if she did it, it would only be with women. He still didn't want her to do it and she dropped it—at least, that's what she told him. Her phone records, however, showed several calls to and from a phone number here in San Francisco. That number turned out to belong to someone named Troy Trent."

Teffinger raised an eyebrow.

"Troy Trent?"

Right.

Troy Trent.

As in the dead man.

"The PI dug deeper and found out that Trent was affiliated with a company called Concrete Cactus, which in turn produced S&M movies. He watched a bunch of them and discovered they always ended in a snuff—that was their MO. They tried to make the murders look as authentic as possible. All the movies were filmed in one of three different settings. The PI traced the dungeons, for lack of a better word, to New York, Denver and San Francisco. Are you with me?"

Teffinger nodded.

He was.

He was indeed.

"The PI came up with a theory that Jacqueline had set up a filming in New York, behind her boyfriend's back," Chase said. "It was his belief that she was the submissive and when it came to the part where they killed her, things got out of control and she actually ended up dying. To support that theory, the PI tried to find out if Troy Trent was in New York during the time when Jacqueline disappeared."

"Don't tell me," Teffinger said, "he was."

Chase nodded.

He was.

He was indeed.

"After that, the PI tracked every DVD produced by Concrete Cactus," she said. "Jacqueline didn't show up in any of them. He thinks that's further proof of what happened. It's his theory that the DVD was never released because there had been an actual murder."

Teffinger swept hair out of his face.

He pulled up a visual of the two clear-case DVDs from Trent's dresser.

Was one of them Chase's sister?

"Makes sense," he said.

"Unfortunately, he was at the end of his rope at that point," Chase said. "There was nothing more he could do. That's when I decided to infiltrate Concrete Cactus."

106

Day 5—September 25
Friday Afternoon

The Marriott Marquis—where the Egyptian, Amaury, was staying under the alias Landon Lee—was a stunning, 39-story contemporary structure at the corner of 4th and Mission in the financial district. Tag and Jonk parked on P-2, took the elevator to the lobby and walked into the lobby bar, an enclave called Bin 55. Part of the Friday Afternoon Club was already there getting a buzz on.

They sat at a table with a view into the lobby and ordered white wine.

Then they waited.

Less than thirty minutes later, Amaury and his girlfriend strolled across the lobby with no suitcases in hand and disappeared out the front door. They waited for five minutes and then walked over to the reception desk.

An elderly woman smiled and asked if she could help them.

"We're here to see Landon Lee," Tag said. "Could you call his room and tell him Carol and Bob are waiting for him in the lobby."

Sure.

No problem.

The woman pressed 2203 on the phone.

Jonk memorized it.

2203.

2203.

2203.

Then the receptionist frowned and said, "He's not answering."

Tag looked at her watch.

"We're a half hour early," she said. "We'll just come back. Thank you so much."

They headed outside and strolled down the block. Five minutes later they came back, walked nonchalantly to the elevators and got out on twenty-two.

A maid's cart was halfway down the hall.

They walked over to 2203 where Jonk pulled out his wallet, searched inside and then swore. They walked down to where the cart was and found the maid inside a room making a bed.

Jonk flashed his driver's license at the woman and said, "I'm Landon Lee, Room 2203. I did something stupid and left without taking my keycard with me."

The woman studied him.

"The front desk can give you a new one," she said.

Jonk pulled out a twenty and held it out.

"I'm really in a hurry," he said. "If you could let us in, that would be great."

She looked at the money

Then at him.

"I'm really not supposed to do that," she said.

Jonk nodded.

"I understand," he said. "Thanks anyway."

As he turned, the woman said, "I guess I could make an exception this one time, since you're in a hurry."

Jonk handed her the bill.

She took it.

"Thanks," he said. "I really appreciate it."

The room had one large bed and a bank of windows along the wall with nice city views. The lines were contemporary and clean. A long desk sat in front of the windows. On that desk was a laptop and a small spiral notebook.

They checked the closet.

Inside were four large suitcases.

Jonk picked one up.

It was heavy.

He threw it on the bed and opened it.

Eight nylon bags were inside, filling it almost to capacity.

He unzipped one.

It was filled with gold coins.

Ancient gold coins.

He zipped it up and put it back in the suitcase. There was a little room left, so he stuck the laptop and the spiral notebook in there as well.

With a beating heart, he picked up two of the suitcases.

Tag grabbed the other two.

Then they walked out of the room, kicking the door closed as they headed down the hall.

107

Day 5—September 25
Friday Afternoon

Song called Fenfang and Shaden to let them know that she'd been attacked and warn them that whatever was going on might spread to them. They were potentially in danger and needed to take precautions. Neither woman answered, so she left messages. Then she locked the office door and got busy again on the Condor case.

The going was slow.

It was hard to concentrate.

108

Day 5—September 25
Friday Afternoon

Chase infiltrated the Concrete Cactus. Her first filming was Monday night in a building here in San Francisco. She insisted on wearing a mask, not wanting her law career destroyed. "Troy Trent was in the room directing. I was supposed to keep choking Amanda until he told me to cut." She diverted her eyes, then looked up. "I could feel the life going out of her but kept pressing my fingers into her throat and waiting for Trent's cue. I was counting on him to know what her limits were. I should have stopped when my gut told me to but I was too afraid to blow it."

Teffinger studied her.

So, that question was answered once and for all. Chase actually was a murderer.

Now another question surfaced—Did Chase kill Troy Trent?

The evidence fit.

She thought he killed her sister. Then he got her into a position where she killed someone else. Last night, she had to confront Amanda Wayfield's dead body. That sparked the realization that she might be on her way to getting caught. So she killed Trent out of revenge while she still had a chance.

He almost asked her, point blank, Did you kill Troy Trent? But he didn't.

He didn't want to know the answer.

He could understand how she killed Amanda Wayfield.

He could still love her, even knowing that was part of her past. Troy Trent was different, though. His murder was intentional. It was in cold blood. He was stabbed repeatedly in the back.

She nudged him.

"What's wrong?"

"Nothing."

"I know nothing when I see it," she said. "That's not nothing."

He pulled two beers out of the fridge and handed her one.

Suddenly she got serious.

"Teffinger, I still need to know about Jacqueline," she said. "I need to get into Trent's house. This is my chance. I'm not talking about you letting me in or anything like that. I'm talking about me breaking in on my own."

"That's not smart."

She leaned against the cabin wall.

"The more I think about Monday night, the more I think Trent knew Amanda was dying. I think he knew when to call it off but didn't."

"Why would he do that? That would ruin the whole shot because he wouldn't dare release the film. He'd have to scrap it."

"My guess? He did it because he got off on it," she said. "It was a personal snuff show directed and produced by him for an audience of one—also him."

Teffinger chewed on it.

That could actually be true

If Trent was as sick as Condor, it could definitely be true.

"If that's what happened to Amanda, maybe it was the same exact thing that happened to Jacqueline," she said. "Maybe she didn't die as a result of a fake murder getting out of control. Maybe she was killed with full intent, just so Trent could get his rocks off."

"Maybe."

"That's something I need to find out," she said. "I also need to know how deep Condor was involved in all of this. I need to know if he knew what was happening. I need to know if he watched the films afterwards and jacked off to them."

"What are you going to do if you find out he did?"

She looked directly into his eyes and didn't hesitate.

"I'm going to put this world out of his misery."

109

Day 5—September 25
Friday Afternoon

J onk and Tag managed to muscle the suitcases all the way
to the car without incident and then drove down 4th
Street, not caring where they were going so long as it
was away. They couldn't stop smiling. Tag punched the radio
buttons, landed on an old 50 Cent song, "In Da Club," and
cranked it up. When it was over, Jonk lowered the volume and
said, "So where do we stash this stuff?"

Tag scrunched her face.

Her place would be too dangerous.

Same for a hotel.

"Zoogie's sailboat?"

Jonk chewed on it. Amaury knew about it—that's where he
intercepted Winter—but he'd undoubtedly searched it by now.
The chance of him going back was low. Still, low was more
than zero.

"No," he said. "It needs to be someplace fresh."

"How about one of those U-Haul storage places?"

Maybe.

But Jonk didn't like the idea of being away from it at night.

"We need a house," he said.

That turned out to be a good idea in theory but a bad one in execution. Rentals required references, credit checks and the like, meaning Tag would have to use her real name. In the end as a temporary solution, they rented a room in a two-story, zero-star hotel called The Blue Toucan, paying cash and using a fake name. They got the suitcases into the room. Jonk guarded them while Tag stashed the car on a side street two blocks away and hoofed back on foot.

When she got back, Jonk already had all four suitcases on the bed, opened.

"Well?" she asked.

"Good news and bad news," he said. "They're all filled with gold coins. None of them are duds. But the mask isn't here. Either are the jewels."

They counted the coins.

The number turned out to be approximately one-fourth of the inventory list.

"This is good, but most of the treasure is still out there somewhere," Jonk said. "The mask is what I want. That's the one thing that's priceless."

He leafed through the spiral notebook taken from Amaury's desk, which turned out to be filled with Egyptian handwriting. The last few pages, however, had some English words that related to San Francisco.

The last entry on the last page was interesting.

Song Lee.

Tag Googled it and found that the name belonged to a San Francisco attorney with an office in Chinatown.

"She's an attorney and so was Rock," Tag said. "Maybe they were working together."

Jonk walked to the window, pulled the covering back and looked outside.

Everything was normal.

Then he turned to Tag and said, "Let's find out."

DAY SIX

September 26
Saturday

110

Day 6—September 26
Saturday Morning

Teffinger woke before daybreak in the cabin of his boat with no Chase scrunched up next to him. His head hurt mildly but not wildly from too many Anchor Steams last night. Chase was supposed to come over at nine and spend the night but didn't show. Maybe she was busy breaking into Troy Trent's. Maybe she needed quiet time. Teffinger didn't know. All he knew is that he drank beer and closed his eyes to rest them for a moment.

Now it was morning.

He was on top of the covers, still dressed in yesterday's clothes.

No messages were on his phone.

Strange.

He called her, got her voicemail and left her a message.

Then he threw on sweats and headed out for a jog.

This was it.

The big day.

September 26th.

SJK day.

Unless Teffinger got lucky, Condor would take his next victim by midnight.

Probably London Fogg.

They'd find her body tomorrow or in a month. With Condor, you never knew.

Teffinger picked up the pace, stretching his legs and pumping his arms. Nothing felt as good as cool morning air in his lungs. The oxygen made him an animal. That's when he was the most alive.

He did a five-mile circle and slowed to a walk at the marina's edge, letting his metabolism wind down.

The sky was beginning to wake up but not by much. The sun still hadn't punched over the edge.

There were no messages on his phone.

He got the coffee pot going and took a shower.

When he got out, it was 6:30.

He didn't know quite what to do.

Northstone and the chief were holding their final team meeting right now.

He ate two bananas and a large bowl of cereal, then filled a thermos with coffee and walked down the dock to Bertha, who was still sound asleep.

He slapped her on the ass as he walked up and said, "Morning, Glory."

She actually started.

No problem.

Sipping coffee, he swung by Condor's place.

The lights were off.

The windows were dark.

Then he had a wild thought.

He parked down the street, walked back on foot and snuck

into Condor's garage to see if the GPS transmitter was still in place.

Condor's car wasn't there.

The transmitter was hanging from a string in the middle of the vacant space.

Shit.

He left, walked back to Bertha and called Chase.

She didn't answer.

It was 7:30.

She was usually up by now.

He called Rapport, Wolfe & Lake to see if she was at work. A receptionist answered, even this early in the morning, but didn't get an answer when she buzzed Chase's office.

"Sorry," she said.

He drove into the financial district, found a place to park Bertha for an amount that was almost as much as she was worth, then wandered over to the lobby of the Transamerica Pyramid.

Chase didn't walk past, not any time in the next half hour.

He called her.

She didn't answer.

He called the receptionist.

Chase hadn't shown up to work yet.

Damn it.

What the hell was going on?

He swung by Troy Trent's place to see if her car was there.

It wasn't.

Then he headed across the Golden Gate to her house.

Her car was in the driveway.

She didn't answer the door, not for the bell and not for the pounding. He walked around to the back and found the sliding glass doors of the lower level wide open.

"Chase, it's me."

No answer.

He stuck his head in the dungeon as long as he was right there, found it empty and headed upstairs.

The woman's purse was on the granite countertop.

Her keys were in the purse.

So was her cell phone.

So was her wallet.

She, however, was nowhere.

Not inside.

Not outside.

Not anywhere.

He punched the wall. He punched it so hard that his fist went all the way through the plaster.

Then he ran outside and hopped into Bertha.

She didn't start.

He punched the windshield.

His fist didn't go through but the glass shattered into a spider web.

His knuckles bled.

He didn't care.

111

Day 6—September 26
Saturday Afternoon

Song was at her desk all morning and through lunch, frantically working on the Condor case. Today was the deadline. She needed to be done by five at the latest.

Midafternoon, someone turned the knob. When the door didn't open, they pounded on it.

"Song! Are you in there? Let me in!"

The voice was Fenfang's.

She sounded panicked.

Song opened the door to find the woman in tears.

"They have Shaden!" she said.

"Who?"

"I don't know," she said "They called me and told me they have her. I didn't believe them but they let me talk to her. She sounded terrible. She was scared to death. They told me to stay calm. They're going to call me later and tell me what to do to get her back."

"We need to go to the police," Song said.

Fenfang grabbed her by the shoulders and shook her.

"No!"

"But—"

"They warned me not to do that," she said. "They said if I did, Shaden was dead. Then you and me would be next. They meant it. They said to just stay calm. They're going to tell me what to do. As long as I do it, they're going to let Shaden go. Everything will be fine."

"What are they going to tell you to do?"

"I don't know," she said. "I don't have a goddamn clue. All I know is that whatever it is, I'm going to do it."

112

Day 6—September 26
Saturday Afternoon

Teffinger got back into San Francisco to find the city smothered under a low bank of windy clouds. He parked Bertha on a side street three blocks from Condor's house and headed over on foot. His walk was brisk. His eyes were intense. His thoughts were dark.

Condor's garage was empty and the interior door was locked.

Teffinger headed around the side to the back.

That door was locked.

So were the windows.

He muscled up to the deck off the man's bedroom. The sliding door was locked. Screw it, enough was enough. He kicked it. It cracked but didn't break. He kicked it again, and again, and again.

Then he was inside.

He searched, non-destructively at first, then more aggressively as his frustration increased. After an exhaustive hour he still had nothing.

No SJK souvenirs.

No evidence of Chase.

No evidence of Troy Trent.

No evidence of London Fogg.

No nothing.

The SJK files he found before in the credenza were now missing.

He made a sandwich and waited.

Condor didn't show up.

Not for an hour.

Teffinger called Neva and said, "I need a BOLO out for Condor's car."

"On what charge?"

"Hit and run," he said.

"What?"

"He hit Bertha while I was driving, then he took off."

Silence.

Neva knew he was lying.

"Teffinger, don't take yourself down," she said. "It's not worth it."

"Just get the BOLO out, please and thank you."

He got a beer from Condor's fridge and drank it by the front window as he watched the street.

An hour went by.

Then another.

Then another.

Teffinger's watch said 5:07.

Then the man came home.

Teffinger was sitting on the granite countertop when Condor walked into the kitchen.

Condor saw him, froze, and then said, "This is actually a

good thing. Let me make a quick phone call, then we'll talk."
He pulled out a phone, dialed and said, "Song, it's me. How are
you coming on my project?" A beat. "Good, listen, I know this
is short notice but can you jump in a cab and come over to my
place right now? Bring the whole file. Teffinger's here waiting
to meet with us and he doesn't have much time."

The man hung up, pulled two Bud Lights from the fridge,
handed one to Teffinger and looked around.

"You made quite a mess," he said.

Teffinger popped the tab and drank the whole can in one
long swallow. Then he crushed it in his hand and tossed it into
the sink.

"Where's Chase?"

"Who?"

"I'm about two heartbeats away from beating you to death
with my fists," Teffinger said.

"I'm not SJK," Condor said. "I know you think I am but
you're wrong."

"Bullshit."

Condor reached into a cabinet, pulled out a pot, filled it
with water, set it on a burner and fired up a flame under it. "Do
you like spaghetti?" he said.

Fifteen minutes later a timid Asian woman with glasses rang
the doorbell. Condor introduced her as Song Lee, a lawyer.
Then he said, "Since you've been so obsessed with thinking
I'm Condor, to the point of breaking into my house at least
twice not to mention sticking a GPS transmitter under my car,
I thought it would be wise to show you that you're wrong.
What I've done is go back through the SJK newspaper clippings to get the exact dates and details of all the killings. I have
solid alibi's for four of them. In fact, for three of them, I was

actually out of town."

"You're not fooling anyone," Teffinger said.

"I knew you'd react like that," Condor said. "What I've done is given all my information to this pretty little lady right here and asked her to verify that it's all true."

Teffinger looked at Song.

She nodded and said, "What he's saying is the truth. I've verified his whereabouts. I've checked credit card receipts, airline tickets, and personally talked to a large number of people like hotel receptionists, taxi drivers and the like." She opened a briefcase and pulled a thick stack of folders out. "All the information is right here. We can go over it line by line if you want."

113

Day 6—September 26
Saturday Night

Twilight changed to night and the last rays of light squeezed out of the San Francisco sky. The wind and clouds morphed into a mean storm that dropped black rain with a heavy hand.

Whoever had Shaden still hadn't called.

Song and Fenfang sat on a couch in the dark, hardly talking, while the weather beat on the windows.

Then Fenfang's phone rang.

She listened, walked to the window and looked out, then said, "Yes, I see it." She kept the phone to her ear for ten more seconds.

Then she headed for the door and said, "I have to go."

Song fell into step.

"Not without me."

"We already talked about it."

"That doesn't mean we resolved it," Song said. "I'm coming and that's that."

Fenfang gave her an evil look and then said, "Your funeral."

They headed outside without umbrellas and got into a white

van at the end of the alley.

No one was inside.

The keys were in the ignition just like the caller said they'd be. Fenfang cranked over the engine and took off as if she knew where she was headed.

"Where are we going?" Song asked.

Fenfang powered the wipers from medium up to full speed and said, "I'm going to tell you a few things. You're going to hate me and I deserve it, so don't feel guilty about it when it happens."

Song wrinkled her brow in confusion.

"I was a high-priced escort in Hong Kong," Fenfang said. "One day a man I knew by the name of Park Ching approached me about a job. He wanted me to arrange an accidental meeting between me and a man named Typhoon Joe, who's one of the wealthiest men in Asia, in case you've never heard of him."

No.

Song hadn't.

"Typhoon Joe had recently purchased a cache of Egyptian treasure on the black market, worth a lot of money," Fenfang said. "My job was to cozy up to him and figure out a way to steal it. If I could do that, I'd get a 10 percent cut. It took a full month and a lot of planning, but I eventually pulled it off. I was supposed to give it to Ching and he was supposed to have it smuggled into San Francisco where it would be delivered."

"To who?"

"To the people who hired Ching."

"And who's that?"

"I don't know, he wouldn't tell me," Fenfang said. "I didn't want to part with it before being paid, so I told Ching I needed to accompany it to San Francisco. He had no problem with that. By the time we got here, I felt like 10 percent wasn't enough. Typhoon Joe knew I was the one who took it and I began to fully realize just how far and long he'd hunt me. We came into San Francisco by boat. The shipment was offloaded into a black van. Neither the boat guys nor the van driver had any idea what the cargo was. I talked the driver into pulling into one of those all night convenience stores and going inside to get me a cup of coffee. He left the engine running and I took off. The next morning I rented a self-serve storage unit, the kind that you drive up to. I unloaded half the boxes into there and left the other half in the van which I parked in a Metro parking lot."

"Wow," Song said.

Yeah.

Right.

Wow.

"I called Ching and told him I'd changed my mind and that my cut was now 50 percent. I told him where to find the van with the other half inside." A pause, then, "That's when I got scared. I was in a noodle shop the next morning wondering what to do, when you and I met. You were nice. I felt comfortable with you. I pictured myself staying at your place, off the radar screen, just for a day or two until I could get my bearings. On the spur of the moment I made up a story about being on the run from an abusive relationship. You believed me and took me in."

"All that was a lie?"

Fenfang nodded.

"It was. By the way, the guy in the blue bandana whose been following you, he's someone I hired to look after you, just in case someone figured out where I was." She turned the defroster on. "The call I just got relates to the treasure. Somehow someone tracked me to you and Shaden. That's why they took Shaden, to force me to give them the treasure. That's the ultimatum. That's where we're headed right now, to the storage unit."

"You're actually going to give it to them?"

"Yes."

The wipers swished back and forth.

"We're almost there," Fenfang said. "What I'm supposed to do is load the van, park it in behind a bar called Tipsy's down on Mission Street, lock it and walk away."

"Then what?"

"Then they'll free Shaden after they verify that everything's there."

"Do you really believe that?"

"Do I have a choice?" She looked in the rearview mirror and said, "See that car with the bluish tint to the headlights? It's been behind us for awhile."

114

Day 6—September 26
Saturday Night

The lights in Song's apartment were off but the woman was home, her and someone else. Every once in a while they pulled the window covering to the side and peeked out. What the hell was going on? Jonk didn't know. All he knew is that his body was getting beaten to death from a storm that showed no signs of giving up. He called Tag, who was sitting in the car at the end of the alley, and said, "I'm almost ready to give up."

"Fine, come on back."

"Two more minutes," he said. "I'll give it two more minutes."

One minute later the women emerged from the building, got into a white van at the other end of the alley and took off. Jonk ran back to Tag and bounded in the passenger door.

Go.

Go.

Go.

They got caught at a light as the van disappeared down Jackson. It could have been fatal but the next few lights were more forgiving. They got to within a comfortable gap and then maintained position.

"Where are they going?" Tag asked.

"That's what we're going to find out."

A block passed.

Then another.

Tag said, "Look in your mirror and check out the car behind us."

Jonk checked.

His pulse pounded.

"It's Amaury," he said.

"That's what I thought," she said. "How'd he find us?"

"He didn't. He found Song."

"What are you saying, that he was staking her out, just like us?"

"That's my guess."

"God, nothing's easy."

The van pulled them over to I-101 and headed south. A heartbeat after they passed Cesar Chavez Street, Amaury sped up until he got alongside. His passenger window powered down. He looked directly at them and raised a gun.

Tag jerked the wheel and rammed him just as flames shot out of the barrel.

115

Day 6—September 26
Saturday Night

The proof Song gave regarding Condor's alibis for four of the SJK murders was definitive and indisputable. All this time, Teffinger had been wrong. Not only that, he'd been so blinded by his myopic vision that he let himself stray from the principles that had shaped him. He'd illegally broken and entered into an innocent man's home, several times. He'd dropped out when everyone needed him. He'd forced the chief to suspend him.

Worst of all, he had used up all his time.

He went to the boat, sat in the cabin and drank Anchor Steams in a slow but constant chain.

Hours passed.

Evening came.

Then evening went and night came.

A storm moved in.

It pounded the boat and tried to pull it from the slip but each time dock lines snagged it and bounced it back into position.

His watch said 9:13.

SJK had probably already struck by now.

Teffinger still had no clue where Chase was but her remarks about setting herswelf up as bait for SJK keep reverberating in his skull. Had she actually figured out a way to do that?

Shit.

It was over.

Everything was over.

Catching SJK was over.

His job was over.

His reputation was over.

The love of his life was a killer, and now gone on top of that.

Suddenly someone pounded on the hatch. He set the beer down and opened up, more tipsy than he realized. A woman was there, someone he didn't know and had never seen before, in her late twenties, wearing jeans, a T and tennis shoes. Her clothes and hair were drenched. She stayed where she was and made no motion to come in.

"You're Nick Teffinger, the detective in charge of the SJK hunt. We have to go!"

She looked panicked.

"Where?"

She grabbed his hand and pulled him out.

"Now!" she said. "I'll explain on the way."

"How do you know where I live?"

"Just hurry!"

They ran down the dock and hopped in her car. She had the engine cranked over and her foot on the accelerator before Teffinger even got his door closed.

"If we're too late it's my fault!" she said.

"Too late for what?"

"Too late to stop SJK."

The wipers swung at full speed.

"My name's Rayla White," she said. "I'm a law clerk at Rapport, Wolfe & Lake in the criminal division. I work in Dirk Rekker's department and have access to the files. I stumbled onto something that tells who the SJK killer is."

"Who?"

"There are two of them actually," she said. "One's Kyle Greyson and the other one is Troy Trent."

"Two?"

"Yes."

"Kyle Greyson killed the first victim, Paris Zephyr," she said. "During the trial, he hired a man named Troy Trent to commit a similar murder to make the jury believe that the killer was still on the loose. Trent killed Jamie van de Haven."

Teffinger shook his head.

No.

No.

No.

"That can't be right," he said. "The jury never even got information about Jamie van de Haven. Her body wasn't even found until the next week."

"Her body would have been found before the end of the trial except everything was cut short when it turned out that the detective, Frank Finger, planted evidence. In the end that's why Greyson got acquitted, but he didn't know that was coming. It was just something really lucky that came around after he had already hired Trent."

Teffinger pushed hair out of his face.

It could be true.

"After that they basically took turns, although the order got jumbled sometimes. It's all in Rekker's files."

"Why are you waiting until now to tell somebody?"

"I didn't find out about it until recently," she said. "It all falls under attorney-client confidentiality. I knew Rekker would never breach that confidentiality so I arranged a meeting off-site at a bar with one of the other top lawyers in the firm, a man named Nathan Rock, and told him what I'd found. The next thing I knew, he was dead. I don't know if he had a confrontation with Rekker and then Rekker killed him, or what."

"Look out!" Teffinger said.

She slammed on the brakes seconds before smashing into the back end of a pickup.

"I started to follow both Greyson and Trent around," she said. "Greyson's been making trips to a dock area."

Teffinger pictured Chase there.

"Go!" he said.

"I am!"

116

Day 6—September 26
Saturday Night

With the treasure in the back, Fenfang parked the van behind Tipsy's as directed, locked the door and disappeared on foot into the storm. Song hid in the back with the boxes. Two minutes later a key entered the door lock. A man got in, started the engine and took off.

No one was in the passenger seat.

The man was alone.

The radio came on, got punched to a heavy metal station and then the volume cranked up.

Good.

Song could breathe without being detected. She needed to clear her throat but didn't. The more she concentrated on not doing it the more she wanted to.

The man jerked his head up and down to the beat and sang when an evil chorus came up. His voice was rough and mean and filled with hate.

He might be on drugs.

They drove a long ways.

Forty-five minutes or an hour passed.

They kept going.

Song had to relieve herself and would have, right there in her own pants, except for the fear he'd smell her.

Then the van stopped.

The radio died.

The squeaking of an overhead door rising came from ahead. The man pulled forward into an enclosure. The rain stopped hammering the roof. The overhead door squeaked down behind them. He drove for a ways—too far to be in a simple garage, then stopped and killed the engine.

He got out and pissed on the ground.

Then he slammed the door shut and walked around to the back.

Song scampered into the front and curled up on the passenger side floor.

If he walked over, she was dead.

It was that simple.

He briefly inspected the boxes and then walked off.

Song stuck her head up and looked around. The van was inside a large empty metal building with a dirt floor. Only a few overhead lights were on. The man was walking to the corner which had a separate enclosure with a door.

"Lucy, I'm home," he shouted.

Song waited until he disappeared through the door and then headed over.

Shaden was in there.

She could feel it.

Her foot twisted on something half buried in the dirt. She looked down and saw the end of an old, rusty tire iron punching through the surface. A few kicks got it loose enough to pull out. It was rough and rusty to the touch.

She gripped it with a tight fist and then walked briskly towards the door.

She got to it, took a deep breath, then pushed it open slowly. Shaden was bound tightly to an old steel chair, gagged, with fear etched on her face and water in her eyes. The man stood over her, holding a knife with the blade pointed at her eye, not more than an inch away. He wore an unbuttoned flannel shirt. His hair was long and greasy.

His back was to the door.

He moved his face close to Shaden's, twisted the knife in his fingers and said, "This is actually one of the most humane ways to do it, through the eye. That's because there's no skull behind the eye. The blade goes straight into the brain without hitting something and slowing down. Once it's in, I twist it to the right. The whole thing takes less than a second."

Shaden pulled against her bonds, frantic.

Muffled screams came from behind her gag.

Suddenly the man turned.

Song went to swing the tire iron but froze.

Her hands shook.

Her whole body shook.

The man's mouth broke into a grin.

"Looks like we have a party," he said.

Song closed her eyes and swung.

117

Day 6—September 26
Saturday Night

The man's skull cracked with a terrible sound. He collapsed to the floor where he gurgled and twitched for a few seconds. Then he got coffin quiet and his eyes stayed open. Song got Shaden loose. They ran to the van and got the hell out of there with Shaden behind the wheel.

Black rain pounded against the windshield.

They hardly talked.

Song called Fenfang, found out where she was and had Shaden swing over to get her.

"Now what?" Song asked.

"We need to get the treasure into a different vehicle and then Fenfang needs to get out of town with it," Shaden said. Then to Fenfang, "The man after you is a New York lawyer named Lloyd Taylor. He's the one who attacked you in your office yesterday."

Silence.

"How do you know that?"

Shaden sighed.

"Let me back up," she said. "You have the right to know

some things. Some bad things. You were hired by a man named Park Ching to cozy up to Typhoon Joe and steal his treasure. What you don't know is who hired Ching. Correct?"

"That's right."

"Typhoon Joe confided to one of his lawyers, Nathan Rock, about the treasure," Shaden said. "Rock's a partner in Rapport, Wolfe & Lake here in San Francisco. Rock is tight with another lawyer in the New York branch of the firm, a man named Lloyd Taylor. Rock and Taylor together came up with the idea to hire Park Ching."

"How do you know?"

"Hold on, I'm getting there," Shaden said. "When you got to San Francisco with the treasure, that's who it was supposed to be delivered to—the two lawyers. You kept half, though."

"Right," Fenfang said. "I deserved it."

"No argument," Shaden said. "It was half in volume, but your half had the mask and the jewels. You actually kept 80 to 90 percent of the overall value. Rock and Taylor split up what you gave them, then set out to get the rest. Eventually they tracked you to Song's place. Rock broke in to the office and the apartment, looking for the treasure or evidence as to where it was. He didn't find anything."

"Wow."

To Song, "Sorry about that."

Back to Fenfang, "To their credit, they weren't violent men, at least at that point in time. They came up with a plan. That's when I got involved. Until then, I had no idea that any of this was going on."

"What plan?"

"Their plan was for me to cozy up to you—get on the inside, if you will—and find out where you had the treasure stashed. They came up with a case that would give me an opportunity to hire Song and then, by extension, get to you. They knew you were living with Song and that her apartment was right above her office. They knew that if I became a client I'd get an opportunity to meet you in a trusted way and get on the inside. So they came up with a fake case and flew me out here to San Francisco to play my part."

"Fake case?" Song asked.

Shaden looked at her and sighed.

"I'm sorry, I really am," she said. "You were going to be paid well."

"Are you telling me that the whole story about you coming to San Francisco to investigate Rekker and ended up shooting a woman—all that was fake?"

Shaden nodded.

"It was," she said.

Song shook her head in disbelief.

"Why Rekker?"

"I don't know why they chose Rekker," Shaden said. "Obviously, they needed to name someone high-up in the firm. The feeling I got was that Rock didn't like Rekker for whatever reason. Anyway, that's not the point. The point is that everything got messed up when Rock got killed. It was apparent at that point that someone else was after the treasure, probably Typhoon Joe or one of his drones. Now only me and Taylor were left and we needed to act fast. That's when we came up with the next plan."

"What was that?" Fenfang asked.

"The plan was to pretend that I'd been abducted and would be killed unless you did what they told you to," Shaden said. "Lloyd Taylor hired a man named Bart Sinclair to pretend to be the abductor. He's the one who called you on the phone. When they let you speak to me to verify I'd been taken, I was sitting in a chair next to him, perfectly fine. I was just pretending."

Fenfang's eyes narrowed.

She said nothing.

"You did what they told you to," Shaden said. "Before Sinclair took off to pick up the van behind the bar, he assaulted me and tied me to the chair. I'd been double-crossed. If it wasn't for Song, I'd be dead right now and Sinclair would be hooking up with Taylor somewhere to hand off the treasure." She paused. "I'm not asking either of you to forgive me."

Song said nothing.

Fenfang said nothing.

Then Shaden said to Fenfang, "You need to get out of town with the treasure. I'm going to take care of Lloyd Taylor."

"How?"

"He tried to kill me," she said. "What's fair is fair. It may take me some time to do it, but it's going to happen, you can count on it."

They drove in silence.

Then Fenfang exhaled and said, "Even if you kill Taylor, I still have Typhoon Joe to worry about. He'll hunt me forever. I was okay with that at the beginning but to be honest it's taking a toll. I've come to a decision."

Really?

What?

"I'm going to give Typhoon Joe back what I took from him," she said. "I'll tell him about Lloyd Taylor. He'll take care of the man. You won't have to kill him. After he's dead, you can go back to your law job as if nothing ever happened."

"Why would you do that for me?"

"I don't know." She smiled and added, "Don't make me think too hard about it. I might change my mind."

Shaden reached over and held Song's hand.

"I'm sorry for what I did."

Silence.

Then Song squeezed and said, "I'm glad you told me in the end."

"You're a hell of a lawyer," Shaden said.

Song grunted.

"Right," she said. "Delicate is more like it."

"You're the only lawyer I know who actually saved her client's life," Shaden said. "I'd hardly call that delicate."

118

Day 6—September 26
Saturday Night

Rayla White raced down Hunter's Point Boulevard, closer and closer to the bay, and hydroplaned to a stop when she got to the Indian Basin docks. "That boat, there," she said, pointing. "That's where Greyson's been going."

Teffinger opened the door.

The storm immediately pounded the interior.

"Stay here! Call 911 for backup."

"I don't have a phone."

Teffinger reached into his pocket.

It was empty.

Shit.

"Just stay here."

He ran towards the boat without shutting the door. It was a large steel vessel in an obvious state of decommission. No lights came from it.

The gangplank was up.

The deck was too high and far.

He jumped for the stern line, dangled over the water as he

almost lost his grip, then walked his hands overhead until he got close enough to swing onto the boat.

He opened a steel door and went inside.

He heard nothing.

He saw nothing.

It was blacker than black.

He was halfway back out when a light flickered inside, twenty steps away. It was coming up a stairway from somewhere down in the guts of the boat. It got lighter and lighter as he made his way towards it. At the stairs he slowed and went down quietly.

He didn't have a gun.

He looked around for a weapon but the space was clean.

Suddenly he heard the muffled sound of a woman's voice.

Below, he could hardly believe what he saw. There were two tables in the middle of a room. On each one was a naked woman, hogtied and gagged in the SJK position, struggling to keep their legs bent and not choke to death.

One was Chase.

The other was a black woman.

There were two men sitting in chairs, drinking beer and watching the show.

Teffinger let out a war cry and charged with every ounce of strength in his body.

ONE
MONTH
LATER

Late October

119

One Month Later

Late October

The Egyptian air was hot, even at this time of year and even as the sun went down. Jonk brought the Jeep to a stop and killed the engine. He wiped sweat from his forehead, took a long swallow from a canteen and passed it to Tag, who took a long noisy slurp and then passed it to Winter. A lot had happened since that fateful night a month ago on I-101 when Tag jerked the wheel into Amaury's car as he fired at them.

Amaury crashed and died.

That was a good thing.

Jonk and Tag lost sight of the van.

That was a bad thing.

An hour later they had a realistic chat over coffee and decided to cut their losses and get out of town with what they had, namely one-fourth of the gold coins.

A week later Jonk spotted numbers written on the inside flap of Amaury's spiral notebook. They didn't mean anything for a day and another and another. Then, while he wasn't even thinking about it, it popped into his brain that they might be GPS coordinates. When he checked to see where they would be if in fact they were coordinates, he discovered something interesting.

They fell in Egypt.

Even more interesting, they fell in the exact area where the expedition had initially searched for the treasure.

"More?" Winter asked, offering the canteen.

Jonk shook his head.

Tag said, "I'll take a little more."

She took a swallow then screwed the cap on.

Jonk checked the GPS one more time and said, "If this thing's working right, we're right on top of it."

ONE MONTH LATER

Late November
Saturday

120

Two Months Later
Late November
Saturday Evening

Teffinger popped Bertha's hood, opened his toolbox and started disconnecting the old ignition wires. New ones sat on the ground, still in the packaging, ready to go in.

No more jiggling.

At least that was the plan.

If Bertha wanted to torment him, she'd need to find a new way to do it.

His mind wandered as he worked.

It was a good thing Rayla White was such a fast driver. If Teffinger had gotten to the ship two minutes later, the result might have been different. As it happened, he was able to get both women loose before either died.

One of them was Chase.

The other one—the black woman—was London Fogg.

Teffinger beat Kyle Greyson to death with his bare fists. That was ruled justifiable and no charges were brought. The other man escaped while Teffinger was fighting Greyson. He turned out to be Dirk Rekker, Greyson's attorney. What he was doing there was still a mystery. What wasn't a mystery is that he stabbed Rayla White and made off in her car.

Luckily the knife missed her heart by an inch.

She didn't die.

The day after that fateful night in the ship, the chief showed up unexpectedly at Teffinger's boat and said, "Let me buy you a beer."

Teffinger pushed hair out of his face.

"Okay."

They went to a dive bar and drank Anchor Steams until the bartender turned the lights off and put them in a cab.

The next morning, Teffinger showed up to work.

At 6:00 a.m.

The beer that had gone down so smoothly last night now pounded inside his skull with little hammers.

He didn't care.

He was back where he belonged.

Neva spotted him first and walked over.

"Are you really back?"

"I think so."

She sniffed the air, said "You smell like beer," and handed him a mint. "Better not let the chief find out."

He nodded.

"Right."

Condor was arrested for the murder of Chase's sister, Jacqueline St. John, whose last moments of life were memorialized in one of the three clear-case DVDs found in Troy Trent's dresser.

She was the one killed in SJK style.

Teffinger's phone rang just as he got the positive cable disconnected. It was Chase.

"Are we still on for tonight?" she asked.

"Who is this?"

She laughed and said, "Not funny. I'm going to wear a short white dress and a black thong."

"Sounds reasonable."

Ten minutes later his phone rang again and a man's voice came through, one he didn't recognize. It sounded far away.

"Do you know who this is?" the man asked.

"No."

"This is your good friend, Dirk Rekker."

Teffinger's heart raced.

"You have a lot of nerve calling me," he said. "Half the world's hunting you right now."

"Yeah, I know."

"So, where are you?"

"Mexico."

"Really?"

"Don't get your panties all bunched up," Rekker said. "You'll never find me."

"We have an extradition treaty with Mexico," Teffinger said. "Did you know that?"

"I'm a lawyer. What do you think?"

"Were a lawyer," Teffinger said. "Past tense."

Rekker chuckled.

"Were," he said. "Good catch. Enough chitchat, here's a few things you'll be interested to know. First off, all my lawyer files that point to Kyle Greyson and Troy Trent being the SJK killers, they're partly true but not completely true. Part of them I fabricated."

"You're playing games."

"Hear me out," Rekker said. "I wanted to win Greyson's trial. He came up with the idea of having a second murder take place during his trial. He knew a man who would do it, Troy Trent. He wanted me to set it up and had five million dollars transferred to an offshore account in my name. I paid Trent a million and kept four."

"So you have enough money to stay hidden? Is that what you're telling me."

"No," Rekker said. "Trent got hung up and couldn't do the job when he was supposed to. I stepped in and did it. I killed Jamie van de Haven, not Trent. Then I doctored my files to make it look like Trent, just in case."

"Bullshit."

"Why would I lie?" Rekker said. "Trent killed the third victim, though, Pamela Zoom. Me and Greyson wanted him to do it so he'd be fully vested. We had him do it when we were both in London with iron-clad alibis." He laughed. "All this time you've been thinking there were two SJK killers. There were really three."

Teffinger paced.

"This last one was going to be a double," Rekker said. "Greyson took London Fogg and I took Chase."

"Why Chase?"

"Why Chase?" Rekker repeated. "Because she's a bitch."

"I'm going to get you," Teffinger said. "You know that, I hope."

Rekker exhaled.

"Chase is a bitch but you're actually not a bad guy, Teffinger," he said. "So I'm going to tell you one more thing. Chase wasn't the one who killed Amanda Wayfield. I'm the one who killed her."

Teffinger shook his head.

"Bullshit."

"I did the number six SJK murder, which was Syling Hu," he said. "She wasn't a blond. Did that ever strike you as strange?"

"You're the one who's strange."

"I had a reason to choose her," Rekker said. "Dig into my past and you'll figure it out. Getting back to the issue, though, I killed her early in the evening before Kyle Greyson was supposed to go out and establish an alibi. Then I doctored my legal files to make it look like Greyson had once again confided in his lawyer and admitted killing another SJK victim. Later, I found out that he was with Amanda Wayfield at the time I was killing Syling Hu. She was an alibi for him, one I didn't plan on. I don't like loose ends so I arranged to meet her one night, which was a Monday. She told me that earlier in the evening she did an S&M scene for big money. She showed me choke marks on her throat. She was proud of them. I figured, what better way to kill her? So that's how I did it. Then I dumped her body on the side of a hill off Bayshore Boulevard."

Teffinger flicked hair out of his face.

It was true.

It made sense.

He couldn't wait to see the expression on Chase's face when he told her.

"There's one more thing I want to say before I go," Rekker said.

"What's that?"

"You still have job security, compliments of me."

"What's that supposed to mean?"

"What it means is that the SJK saga is going to continue," he said. "I'll be back in the early summer, June 5th to be precise. I'll see you then. I might even see Chase, too. You never know."

About the Author

Formerly a longstanding trial attorney before taking the big leap and devoting his fulltime attention to writing, RJ Jagger (that's a penname, by the way) is the author of over twenty hard-edged mystery and suspense thrillers. In addition to his own books, Jagger also ghostwrites for well-known, bestselling authors. He has been a member of the International Thriller Writers since 2006.

RJJagger.com